PANDORA'S ORACLE

'If a superior alien civilization sent us a text message saying, 'We'll arrive in a few decades,' would we just reply, 'OK, call us when you get here — we'll leave the lights on'? Probably not, but this is more or less what is happening with AI. Although we are facing potentially the best or worst thing ever to happen to humanity, little serious research is devoted to these issues . . . All of us — not only scientists, industrialists and generals — should ask ourselves what can we do now to improve the chances of reaping the benefits and avoiding the risks.'
Stephen Hawking, April 2014

PANDORA'S ORACLE

CALUM CHACE

THE SEQUEL TO
PANDORA'S BRAIN

THREE CS PUBLISHING

For Julia and Alex

PANDORA'S ORACLE

A Three Cs book.

ISBN 978-1-8383668-0-3

First Published in 2021 by Three Cs.

Copyright © Calum Chace 2021

Calum Chace is a best-selling author of fiction and non-fiction books, focusing on the subject of artificial intelligence. He is a global keynote speaker on artificial intelligence and related technologies, and runs a blog on the subject at www.pandoras-brain.com.

Before becoming a full-time writer, Calum had a 30-year career in journalism and business, in which he was a marketer, a strategy consultant and a CEO.

A long time ago, Calum studied philosophy at Oxford University, where he discovered that the science fiction he had been reading since boyhood is actually philosophy in fancy dress.

SELECTED REVIEWS FOR "PANDORA'S BRAIN", THE PREQUEL TO THIS BOOK

"I love the concepts in this book!" **Peter James, author of the best-selling *Roy Grace* series**

"Pandora's Brain is a captivating tale of developments in artificial intelligence that could, conceivably, be just around the corner. The imminent possibility of these breakthroughs cause characters in the book to re-evaluate many of their cherished beliefs, and will lead most readers to several "OMG" realisations about their own philosophies of life. Apple carts that are upended in the processes are unlikely ever to be righted again. Once the ideas have escaped from the pages of this Pandora's box of a book, there's no going back to a state of innocence.

Mainly set in the present day, the plot unfolds in

an environment that seems reassuringly familiar, but which is overshadowed by a combination of both menace and promise. Carefully crafted, and absorbing from its very start, the book held my rapt attention throughout a series of surprise twists, as various personalities react in different ways to a growing awareness of that menace and promise." **David Wood, Chairman of the London Futurist Group**

"Awesome! Count me as a fan." **Brad Feld, co-founder of the Foundry Group and Techstars**

"It's hard not to write in clichés about Calum Chace's debut novel: "a page-turner," "a hi-tech thriller," "action-packed," and "thought-provoking" all come to mind. But in a world where most people aren't thinking past their next text message and what they're having for lunch, Chace has crafted a novel that provides a credible look at where the human race could be tomorrow - and the next day. It's the future of sci-fi: a totally realistic, totally readable book that challenges you as it entertains. So, if you like to read and if you like to think, I have one piece of advice—open Pandora's Brain." **Jeff Pinsker, CEO at Amigo Games**

"Pandora's Brain is a tour de force that neatly explains the key concepts behind the likely future of artificial intelligence in the context of a thriller novel. Ambitious and well executed, it will appeal to a broad range of readers.

In the same way that Suarez's Daemon and Naam's Nexus leaped onto the scene, redefining what it meant to write about technology, Pandora's Brain will do the same for artificial intelligence.

Mind uploading? Check. Human equivalent AI? Check. Hard takeoff singularity? Check. Strap in, this is one heck of a ride." **William Hertling, author of the** *"Avogadro"* **series of novels**

"I was eagerly anticipating a fiction adventure book on precisely this topic! Very well done, Calum Chace. A timely, suspenseful, and balanced portrayal of AI and the most important decisions humanity will make in the near future." **Hank Pellissier, producer of the Transhuman Visions conferences**

CHAPTER 1

"Don't wait up for me, honey. You know how these meetings can drag on."

The bodyguard was standing by the open door of the shiny black car. "Morning, Hiro," the scientist greeted him, climbing into the back seat. The bodyguard bowed slightly and said nothing as he closed the door and walked round to the driver's side.

During the drive to the airport, the scientist watched the roofscape slide past. Reading in cars made him sick, and if he had no urgent calls to make he liked to let his mind wander, a rare indulgence which he told himself encouraged creativity. On this occasion his thoughts snagged on the problem of his marriage: it seemed to be declining in inverse proportion to the rise in his fortunes. He needed to solve this problem, and soon. That was OK: he was good at solving problems.

He was roused from this reverie as the car arrived at Seoul Air Base. Located in Seongnam, a satellite of Seoul and home to about a million people, the airfield was used by senior government officials, as well as being home to a wing of South Korea's air force and a helicopter-borne battalion of the US Army.

Hiro drove right up to the small VIP lounge building in the south-west corner of the airfield, separate from the military buildings which populated the rest of the site. The scientist presented his papers to an ostentatiously respectful member of the jet charter company staff, who directed him immediately to his aircraft, which she said was already serviced and fuelled and waiting for him.

As he followed Hiro towards the jet, the scientist glanced up at the cockpit window and noticed that the pilot was a Westerner. This was unusual but not unprecedented, and he wondered briefly whether the pilot was a moonlighting member of the US battalion. Even at a brief glimpse, he looked military: broad-shouldered and powerful. The scientist wrenched his attention back to the forthcoming meeting: the other people attending, and their various agendas. The pretty face of the flight attendant hardly registered as he climbed the steps into the aircraft and took his usual seat, towards the rear of the cabin.

Ten minutes into the flight the scientist was making some last-minute changes to the slides he would present at the meeting, and it took him a moment to register the fact that the pilot had left the cockpit and come through to the cabin. The flight attendant turned towards the pilot with an enquiring smile, but it was Hiro - faithful, reliable Hiro - whose instincts hit the mark. He was rising quickly to his feet, hand moving to his holster, aware that something was wrong.

Hiro's instincts were his undoing, although in truth they only brought his death forward by a few minutes. The bullet that ended his life was expertly aimed, tapping a neat hole in his forehead.

Hiro's head jerked back under the impact of the bullet, and his eyes rolled upwards to the cabin ceiling, looking for an answer to a question his brain had not had the time to frame. His legs buckled, his body folding to the floor.

The pilot watched the scientist and the flight attendant dispassionately, assessing their reactions. Confident in his own marksmanship, he already knew that Hiro posed no threat. Satisfied with the scientist's stunned immobility, he turned his attention to the flight attendant.

"I don't like shooting women," he declared matter-of-factly, watching intently for her reaction. Finding comprehension in her features, he continued. "You speak English - good. I hoped you would." Pointing his gun steadily at the attendant with his right hand, he opened an overhead locker with his left hand and pulled out a parachute pack. "Here, put this on," he ordered, throwing the pack at her with a force that made her stagger backward a couple of steps.

The scientist was returning to full consciousness, and had turned his face to the pilot. What he saw terrified him. The pilot was a big man. His uniform was too small for him, which exaggerated a physical presence that commanded attention - and fear. He looked like a special forces soldier, with a very powerful physique, short haircut, broken nose and cauliflower ears. He looked like he could snap a normal person in two with his bare hands, and wouldn't particularly mind doing it. He made the scientist want to sit very still, and if possible, to shrink back and disappear into his seat.

"Put it on," the pilot told the flight attendant again. "Quickly!"

She hastened to do as he commanded, fumbling with the straps and buckles as fear and confusion interfered with muscle memory. "Please, sir ... please..." she began.

"Don't!" His voice was slightly louder than before, but its authority came from his evident experience of command in violent situations. He lowered his tone again, not reassuring, but matter-of-fact. "There's no need for you to say anything. You're going to exit the aircraft unharmed. I told you, I don't like shooting women."

The pilot glanced at the scientist to ensure that his attention was focused on the weapon.

The attendant was making progress with the parachute, but it was painfully slow. "Make sure it is on correctly," the pilot said. "We are over water, and your pack has a buoyancy aid and an automatic distress signaller. Once I have de-pressurised the cabin, we can open the door and exit the aircraft safely."

"De-pressurised...?" the attendant began.

"Yes. Sit down and buckle up," the pilot replied. Addressing the scientist as well, he added, "Make sure there are no loose items near you. Put any papers and litter into the seat pocket."

The attendant sat down awkwardly, and lengthened

the belt until it accommodated the pack as well as herself. The pilot waited until her belt was securely fastened, then he walked over to Hiro's dead body. He removed the pistol from the bodyguard's holster and frisked the corpse for additional weapons, finding none. He removed a belt from a locker and wrapped it round the body, fastening it tight with three separate buckles. Then he walked up and down the aisle, inspecting the cabin carefully, and putting any unsecured items into overhead lockers.

He returned to face his captives. "Cover you ears," he ordered, before taking a seat in front of them. He fastened his own belt, and then fired the gun at the window the other side of the plane two rows in front of him.

The three living human occupants of the plane were pulled hard against their belts as air rushed out of the now-empty window frame. A couple of loose objects which the pilot had missed whooshed past them as they were sucked violently into the void. Hiro's weighted body was dragged towards the open window, but the force of the exiting air was not enough to raise it from the floor.

Once the pressure was equalised, the pilot stood, and gestured to the attendant to do the same. He pointed toward the exit, and the attendant made her way in that direction. She looked over at the scientist, mutely expressing her regret and looking for absolution, not expecting to find it. Looking back at the pilot to make sure he still wanted her to go ahead, she lifted a lever and pressed a button underneath it. The door hissed open, and swung slowly into the cabin. The attendant stood in the doorway, waiting for the final instruction, feeling the pull cord in her right hand as she steadied herself against the door frame with her left. Stray locks of her jet black hair jerked randomly, licking and slapping her terrified face.

The pilot nodded, saying nothing, his dark eyes expressionless.

The attendant stepped through the doorway into the void, and fell. She looked back up at the plane and felt a rush of relief at escaping that dreadful scene. This was followed by a pang of remorse and guilt at having left the scientist to the mercy of that terrifying man. Suddenly realising that she had forgotten to count to five, she pulled the cord, bracing herself for the familiar mid-air arrest as the parachute opened and slowed her descent.

It didn't happen. She pulled the cord again, and again nothing happened. A terrible sense of dread chilled her heart. She punched the bulge in the front of the pack to open the reserve 'chute. Again nothing happened. The chill in her heart deepened as she realised that the pilot had murdered her - killed her as surely as if he had put a bullet in her head. She would land in water but she would not survive the impact. He had sent her out of the plane with a faulty parachute pack. Her mind shrieked in desperation, terror and rage, and her lungs responded with an extended scream that no-one could hear. She died of heart failure before she hit the water, and the weights placed in the pack by the pilot made sure that her lifeless body sank straight to the bottom of the sea, never to be seen again.

Inside the plane, the pilot turned to the scientist, pointed to Hiro's body, and spoke in a soft voice freighted with menace. "Move him to the door, and wait there till I get back." He opened the door to the cockpit, stepped inside, and shut the door again behind him.

The scientist's mind was racing. He was almost rigid with fear, but his analytical brain refused to stop trying to solve problems. The pilot had allowed the attendant to live, so maybe there was hope that he would also survive. He walked over to Hiro's dead body and looked down at its face frozen in an expression of surprise. Poor Hiro. He didn't deserve such a sudden and brutal end. He had been a reliable and faithful servant. The scientist stepped round to stand above Hiro's head and bent down to the shoulders to lift the corpse by the armpits and start dragging it towards the exit. Hiro was a big man, and with the belt of weights added, it took a lot of effort to drag the body along the cabin floor.

Why did the pilot want the body thrown out of the plane? Why did he allow the attendant to leave? Was he going to fly the plane - and the scientist - to a foreign country? Was this a kidnapping? For sure, what the scientist knew was worth a great deal of money in certain quarters.

His thoughts were disturbed by a loud crash in the cockpit. The pilot was destroying something. The scientist wondered if he was destroying the black box, but he had read somewhere that they are located in the tail of an aircraft, and are pretty hard to destroy. Then he realised the plane was starting to descend.

He started to cast about for something - anything - he could do which would disrupt the pilot's plans. There were no weapons available, and he wouldn't know what to do with a gun if he had one. The weights on Hiro's body. The pilot had been fastidious about fastening them, so they were important. On instinct, the scientist set about trying to unclasp them. He had made some progress when he heard the cockpit door open, and the pilot stepped back into the cabin. The scientist froze as he noticed the pilot was now wearing a parachute pack.

"Get a move on. We haven't got all day," the pilot growled at him. The scientist strained to pull the body towards the exit, and when he had achieved this he looked up at the pilot for further instructions. Why was the pilot going to jump? Was he going to give the scientist a parachute as well? Why abandon the plane?

"What are you waiting for? Throw him out."

In a turmoil of fear and revulsion, the scientist did as he was told. He steadied himself against the frame of the door as he pushed and pulled, pushed and turned Hiro's body until it was more outside the plane than inside, and then it toppled out of the exit and tumbled away into empty space. The weights belt was still attached, but the scientist hoped that it would come undone when the body hit the sea, so that at least some part of the pilot's plans would come unstuck. He began to wonder again what lay in store for him, and the answer was quick in coming.

"Go back to your seat and buckle up. It's going to be a bumpy landing."

So he was staying in the plane after the pilot had jumped. The scientist gave an involuntary shudder. What did that mean? How could the plane land safely without a pilot? Why go to all the trouble of hi-jacking the plane, only to crash it into the sea?

The pilot watched the scientist return to his seat, and checked that his seat belt was fastened. He walked to the doorway. The scientist saw the pilot's lips move, but did not hear the words as he stepped through the doorway.

The nose of the plane dipped further, and the scientist's head was pressed against the seat in front. Fear blocked out any further speculation about his fate, or the pilot's scheme. The scientist screamed the whole time that it took for the plane to reach the sea.

The impact was an explosion of noise as the aircraft's metal surfaces writhed and tore apart. The scientist's neck broke, and several of his internal organs ruptured as they were thrown against his ribs and the seat restraints. Amazingly, he retained a level of consciousness, and layered on top of the pain and the fear were two final agonising thoughts: he wasn't dead, but he soon would be - by drowning. And there would be no time later to solve the problem of his marriage.

CHAPTER 2

"Sorry to interrupt, Boss, but you asked for a heads-up at the earliest."

As Lester Parnell opened the door to his boss's office, and leaned into the room to announce his presence, eight people turned to look at him. Parnell ignored all of them except his boss, senior NSA Agent John Michaels.

Michaels excused himself from the meeting and joined Parnell in the corridor. He smiled at Parnell.

"You look like the cat that got the cream. So the mission was a success." It was a statement, not a question.

"Unreservedly," Parnell confirmed. Both men grinned at Parnell's use of a word which belonged in Michaels' semi-academic world of documents and meetings, and not in Parnell's world of physicality and danger.

"Outstanding!" Michaels mirrored the good-natured idiom reversal. "So your unconventional choice of asset for the job paid off?"

"Couldn't have pulled it off more cleanly myself, sir," Parnell replied, reverting to the serious and respectful tone he normally employed with Michaels – and with very few other people.

Michaels put a hand on Parnell's shoulder and tilted his head downwards slightly to look Parnell more directly in the eye. "That is high praise indeed. I look forward to reading the report. You know the drill. Level five clearance, and my eyes only within this department."

"Copy that. I've transferred funds to him from the contingency budget, as per instruction, and I'll include a request to re-allocate the expenditure as an appendix to the report."

"Good," Michaels replied. "The asset is pleased with his new relationship with us? Standing by for further engagements?"

"I'm not sure that 'pleased' is a state of mind he is familiar with, sir. There are definitely a couple of continents missing from his mental map of the world. But he knows we understand and appreciate his skill set, and I'm sure that he will be ready and willing when we need him again."

Michaels nodded. "And you're still confident that he has no idea who we are, and that there's no possibility of anyone else tracing his activity back to us?"

"Affirmative. Arm's length protocol."

"Does he have any other new clients yet? I doubt we are the only people who have noticed that he is now a free agent. What else does he do with his time?"

Parnell frowned. "Speaking frankly, sir, I hope

that neither of us ever finds out what he does in his spare time. In his case, the longer the arm's length, the better."

"Fair enough." Michaels smiled grimly. "I'm afraid we may have another mission for him sooner rather than later."

"Understood, sir. Not a problem. Speaking of missions, isn't that new Mexican battle simulation due for delivery soon?"

Michaels nodded. "I'm expecting a call in the next couple of days. I'll let you know."

Parnell nodded stiffly: it was hard to escape the habit of saluting someone he viewed as a superior officer. Michaels turned to go back into his office, and Parnell directed a contemptuous glance back at the bureaucrats whose time he had just stolen.

****

As soon as Michaels could excuse himself from the meeting, he put in a call to China.

"Good morning, Chan. How are you?"

"I am very well, Agent Michaels. Good afternoon to you. How are things in the Old Line State?"

Michaels smiled at Chan's delight in displaying his knowledge of obscure facts about America and her people. And the way Chan managed to combine near-perfect pronunciation of American words with his heavy Chinese accent.

"All good here, my old friend. Is the line secure your end?"

"Always, when you call, Agent Michaels," Chan replied. Michaels pictured the gold tooth appearing in Chan's mouth as he smiled.

"Good. I'm calling to let you know that the assignment we discussed has been completed. The potential disruption from your friends across the Yellow Sea has been averted."

"Yes," Chan said slowly. "A tidy job. Although... we were surprised by your choice of asset."

Michaels was taken aback. He took the receiver away from his ear and looked at it for a moment. "Congratulations! Your sources on the ground must be very thorough."

"You would expect otherwise?" Chan retorted with a chuckle. Michaels could tell that the golden tooth was fully on display. He made a quick recovery.

"Our asset is very good at what he does. And while his provenance may be dubious, we judged that would be actually be helpful on this occasion."

"You mean by providing what you call ... plausible deniability in the event of things going south? And also ... eminent expendability."

It was Michaels' turn to chuckle. "Exactly that, Chan. Exactly that." He paused. "Does it ever worry you, Chan? The amount that we know about each other? I mean, our countries, but also the two of us? Do you ever wonder how much we do know about each other?"

"No. It is the way things must be. It is safer." Chan's tone was darker. Not unfriendly, but harder to read. "And no, I never wonder how much you know about us - about me. I do not want to know."

But Michaels was sure that Chan had a very good idea of how much Michaels knew about him. And right now, he was sure that Chan was thinking that Michaels probably knew about his lover. He was also pretty sure that this was something they would never discuss. It was a shame in a way. Life had dealt Chan some difficult cards, and Michaels would have liked to help. But there were limits to their friendship. That too was the way things must be.

Chan interrupted his thoughts. "Do your people still believe that we do not need to take any further actions? With any other potential sources of disruption, I mean."

"Not at the moment," Michaels replied. "Our assessment is that no-one else is a present threat. But we should discuss the candidates when we meet."

"Yes. And we concur, although we are keeping a close eye on one possible combination."

"I think I can guess who you mean," Michaels nodded grimly. "Let's compare notes in person soon. In fact that is the other reason why I called. I'm expecting delivery soon of the Mayan battle simulation we have discussed, and I am hoping you will be able to join me to review it."

****

Early that evening, Parnell walked into in a hotel bedroom, placed his holdall on the bed and unzipped it. He took out a device the size of a paperback, switched it on and toured the room, pointing the device at windows, phone sockets, pictures, furniture. After a thorough inspection he switched the device off and returned it to the bag. He took out a bottle of scotch and a mobile phone and made a call.

"It's clean, Walker. You can come up."

He walked to the counter and opened the bottle, pouring two drinks, adding ice from the refrigerator. Two minutes later there was a light knock on the door. He opened it, offering the drink.

"Your usual."

A big man with a military haircut grinned as he entered the room and accepted the drink. The two men sat in neighbouring armchairs and savoured their whiskies.

"You're looking pleased with yourself," Walker said. "Life among the paper-pushers still agreeing with you?"

Parnell gave a wolfish grin. "Let's just say that every now and then I have to exert a little discipline among the ungodly, which relieves the tedium." He turned serious. "How is the recruitment going?"

"Couple of setbacks, but it's coming together," Walker replied. "Reynolds is staying put - thinks he's up for promotion shortly. Can't say I share his confidence, although he does deserve it, after all the shit he went through on their behalf."

"Want me to destabilise that situation a little? I could talk to a couple of people and suggest they postpone that decision for a while?"

Walker shook his head. "No need. Reynolds is a

good man, but we're not running out of candidates. He has his heart set on this and we don't need to foul it up for him to achieve what we need."

"Fair enough. Your call," Parnell said. "Who else?"

"Scott and Younger are in, as you know. It's going to take a couple of weeks longer than I expected to extricate Scott from his contract, but that's no problem. Looks as though Cuadrelio and Bergsson will join too. I'm particularly pleased about Cuadrelio: he has great skills."

"That is good news," Parnell agreed. "I didn't think Cuadrelio would go for it."

"Turns out he's been looking for a new gig after getting passed over for promotion a year ago. Passed over in favour of some youngster who was at college with the boss's son."

"Ha!" Parnell exclaimed. "Nepotism pops up everywhere, doesn't it. And it always fucks you in the ass sooner or later. What about the Chinese guys? We must have three good guys with fluent Cantonese and Shanghainese."

"Don't worry," Walker reassured him. "I've got seven excellent candidates. They all have the specified skills, the experience, and the motivation. There'll be no problem selecting three from that group. I'll get you their profiles in the next couple of days."

"Excellent. Sounds like you're on target. I want us to be in a position to deploy the first two guys next month."

"Roger that. So the funding's in place for the next stage? And you still have the political support?"

Parnell frowned. "You let me worry about that. But since you ask, yes, we're covered. All the people who need to approve are either fully on-board, or so deeply compromised they have no room for manoeuvre. As far as Fort Meade is concerned, we're good to go."

The two men contemplated their drinks for a few moments, before Parnell spoke again. "You didn't mention Jackson. He's not coming on board?"

Walker looked down and shook his head. "Didn't make it back from a recent assignment. Sounds like there was a clusterfuck by the paper-pushers and he was leading a team where it should never have been sent. They're covering up like crazy, which is why you haven't heard about it."

"Damn!" Parnell breathed. "He was a good man." He held up his glass and initiated a ritualistic exchange from the Rangers creed. "Knowing the hazards of my chosen profession…"

"Rangers Lead The Way!"

"Rangers Lead The Way!"

CHAPTER 3

John Michaels always felt disoriented after speaking with Chan Lu. He was sure that Lu shared his sense that they were kindred spirits, and down the years, Michaels had come to trust Lu a good deal more than he trusted many people within his own organisation. But the simple facts of their respective positions, combined with decades of experience and training to ensure that he kept his guard up when they spoke. Before he made his next call, he needed to stretch his legs for a moment, so he headed to the bathroom.

Once Michaels had satisfied himself that he was alone in the washroom, he went straight to the sink without visiting the urinals or the stalls. He placed his hands either side of the basin and rested the weight of his upper body on his straightened arms. He stared at his reflection. As always, he was slightly disoriented as he looked at a face which he knew beyond doubt to be his own, but which did not entirely coincide with his own self-image. For the millionth time, he wondered whether other people had the same feeling when they looked in a mirror.

The face that looked back at him was in pretty good shape considering its 61 years. It was clean shaven, with regular features and a strong jaw. The lines suggested smiles as well as stress, and he still had a good head of salt-and-pepper hair. Michaels knew that in certain lights he could be described as ruggedly handsome, although few people had ever considered him exceptionally attractive. His wife Mary was one of those few; she said he was like a mature character actor playing a senator, or a successful financier. And she should know, as the senior echelons of Wall Street was her domain. She also said he had the sort of face that movie-goers would think they recognised but could not give a name.

He smiled as he thought of Mary. They had been married for 27 years, and she was still his best friend as well as his lover, his confidante and his counsel. Neither of them was sure whether this was because of or despite the fact that their respective jobs meant they were often in different cities - even different countries. Tonight, for instance, she would be in their duplex apartment overlooking Central Park, while he would be in their house on the north-eastern outskirts of Washington DC. They tried to spend weekends together, and they exchanged numerous emails each day, and usually a phone call in the evening.

He stepped back from the sink to take a wider view. His tailored clothes were expensive, but not at all ostentatious. His stomach was flat, thanks to daily visits to the gyms at work and at home. He pressed his lips together in a mirthless smile, and nodded to himself. He'd do.

Michaels' next call was more straightforward. Simon Winchester was a supplier based in the UK, America's closest ally as well as its oldest enemy. He was the founder and owner of a video game development company in Brighton, on the south coast of England. He was under the impression that Michaels worked for the Department of Defense rather than the NSA, and their contract was structured accordingly. It was a common pretence: many contractors and service providers were more comfortable working for the military than for the intelligence services, and it tended to raise fewer questions. And in this instance, it was more plausible for the DoD to be Winchester's client than for the NSA.

"So how's the weather over there, Simon?"

Winchester laughed. There was a slight time lag between his facial expression on the screen and his voice. "You know, it's not really true that all conversations with an Englishman have to start with a discussion about the weather. But since you're kind enough to ask, it's bloody wet. It's been raining since I can't remember how long, and we're all worried about drowning."

"Perhaps you'd better move away from the coast, then?" Michaels said.

"I have! I live up on the South Downs - the hills behind Brighton here. If the water gets as high as that it really will be the end of days. How is it over there? Still enduring the great freeze?"

"Yeah, it's cold alright," Michaels replied. "Kids are loving the frozen water everywhere. Me, I've had enough. If I didn't have a lot on at work I'd be in the south of France, thawing out."

"Well you certainly are a busy guy," Winchester said, steering the conversation towards their business together. "It always takes a while to get hold of you, and I'm surprised how rarely we have spoken during the course of this project. I'm not complaining, mind, but it's unusual. To be honest, it made me nervous at the outset that we would mis-understand your requirements. As it turned out you are very good at providing clear and rich specifications, so it has been fine."

"Yes, I'm sorry about that." Michaels' hands were raised in mock surrender. "I'm rarely the master of my own diary. As you've probably gathered, the dirty little secret around here is that I work for my assistant rather than the other way around."

"Ha!" Winchester grinned. "Well, it's been a pleasure to work on this assignment, and I hope we'll have the opportunity to do so again. If you do any more projects like this, that is."

"I think that is likely, depending how this one works out with our guys. We've got high expectations for this simulation."

"I don't think you'll be disappointed," Winchester nodded. "A combat simulator based in a Mayan city was an inspired idea. Bloodthirsty bastards, those Maya, and our guys really enjoyed getting down and dirty with the close-quarters scenes. But what I wanted to talk to you about is the user interface. You have been very clear all along that you didn't want us to build in the usual drivers for keyboard, mouse and joystick. We assumed you are planning to use an advanced virtual reality interface, and I wanted to let you know that we've just finalised a strategic acquisition that gives us the capability to offer that."

"Yes, I saw that announcement," Michaels said. "A good move, I suspect."

"Thanks. We're excited about it. The guys who are coming on board are the best in their field, in my humble opinion. So with this new capability combined with our intimate knowledge of the runtime engine and the scenarios in your simulation, I think we can offer an unbeatable package."

Michaels smiled indulgently. "Nice try. Unfortunately the reason we split out that part of the project is also compelling. You've done a good job and you've been very patient, so I'm going to let you into a badly kept secret. And this is strictly off the record, OK?" He waited for Winchester to signal agreement before continuing.

"Ever since Edward Snowden threw all the chips in the air, the Pentagon has been paranoid about contractors. We still have to use them all the time, because that is how we access the best talent, but we are under a lot of pressure to divide projects up so that no one firm has complete visibility over them."

Winchester looked puzzled. "But Snowden was NSA, wasn't he? Not military."

Michaels nodded. "Well, strictly speaking he was

employed by Booz Allen, the consultancy, but yes, he was seconded to the NSA. But their paranoia has leached into the Pentagon."

Winchester nodded cautiously. "I see. Sounds like it could lead to some ... ah ... inefficiencies."

"You bet!" Michaels agreed, with a rueful smile. "But low-price procurement has never exactly been the military's core competence, as you business people say."

Seeing that Winchester was struggling to work out how best to respond to this, Michaels followed up with a question of his own. "Am I right in thinking that Matt Metcalfe worked at your firm for a brief period when he left school? I was reading a profile of him the other day and I was intrigued to see your name pop up."

Michaels knew very well that Matt had spent half his gap year between school and university working for Winchester. He was pretty sure he knew much more about that period of Matt's life than Winchester did - or any other period of Matt's life, for that matter. In a world full of people who were hungry for every detail of information about Matt Metcalfe, Michaels was confident that he was a leading expert.

"Yes. We get asked that a lot." Winchester was obviously wary. "Did that have anything to do with your decision…"

Michaels interrupted him. "Not at all. Like I say, I only found out the other day," he lied. "But I am curious - what was he like as a person?"

"I didn't get to know him very well," Winchester

said. "We're not a big firm, but he was young - only an intern - and I didn't spend much time with him. Which of course I regret, with the benefit of hindsight."

"I can imagine!" Michaels sympathised. "But he did good work, right? Otherwise you wouldn't have hired him. Did he get on well with the rest of the team?"

"He was a smart kid, that's for sure," Winchester said, relaxing again. "We hired him on the strength of some code he wrote while he was at school, and sent to us on a speculative basis. He was fairly quiet when he was with us - more of a watcher than a joiner, if you know what I mean. He did get on well with another temporary guy we had at the time, an American called Sam. Matt went to stay with Sam in New York for a while after he left us."

"Yes," Michaels nodded, "I read about that. "New York made a big impression on him, apparently."

"It does tend to do that," Winchester smiled. "I well remember my first visit to Manhattan. A city for giants, it seemed to me at the time." Michaels watched as Winchester paused to savour the memory and then hauled his mind back to Michaels' question. "Matt was a bright kid, and a nice kid. A good all-rounder who did everything he was asked quickly and efficiently. Terrible shame what happened to him; still right at the beginning of his life."

"Yes, terrible," Michaels agreed. "Amazing adventure, but terrible." He snapped back to professional mode. "Anyway, back to business. I understand we will be able to run the simulation early next week?"

"Yes, we're on track for that. We're just doing the

25

final checks now."

"That's great. I'm really looking forward to it. And in the meantime you'll be pleased to know that I've signed off your latest stage payment."

As Michaels closed the browser he smiled in satisfaction at the confirmation that Winchester knew nothing about Matt's interest in the Maya. It wouldn't have made any practical difference if he had, but it sealed off a possible source of awkward questions.

CHAPTER 4

After dinner, Michaels opened the French windows, and took Chan on a tour of the garden. It was a mild evening, and the floodlit garden was beautiful, with dashes of colour declaring that the plant kingdom was recovering from winter. The parterre was rectangular, occupying the width of the house, and leading twice that distance away from it. It was laid out formally with square blocks of lawn separated by sandy-coloured gravel paths, and borders planted with early spring flowers.

"Your house is very beautiful," Chan said with genuine enthusiasm as they embarked on a clockwise tour. "And this is a charming garden. Would it be described as the English style?"

Michaels smiled. "Thank you. So Mary tells me. This is her domain, not mine. I couldn't tell you the names of any of these flowers, I'm afraid. She does tell me, but I forget them again immediately."

"Is that a policy?"

"No, it's just that I have a great memory for some

things, and a lousy memory for others. I used to get frustrated by it, but I don't let it bother me any more. I avoid wasting time on the things I have no aptitude for."

"Aptitude?"

"Sorry. Natural ability."

"No no. I always learn new words when I speak with you. That is a good thing."

There was a pause in the conversation as they took in the colour and the faint fragrance of the flowers. Chan broke the silence. "I am honoured that Mary was able to join us for dinner. She is a very busy woman."

"That she is, but she was determined to join us," Michaels replied. "She knows how important our working relationship is."

Chan bowed his head and steered the conversation back to business. "How many scenarios like the one we will see tomorrow do you have for Matt to work through?"

"Only a dozen at the moment, but if these all work well we can easily commission some more. Wouldn't want him getting bored repeating the same old scenes."

"No, of course. And how accurate are they, historically speaking?" Chan asked.

"A lot of the specific events and people are mixed up or made up, but the important little things are mostly right: the buildings, clothes, weapons, rituals. Matt never studied the Maya in a formal sense, but he had read a few books about them. We aimed to make it accurate enough to avoid a jarring clash between his surroundings and his prior knowledge. But at the same time we didn't want to limit the developers' creativity. Tikal's great rival in the southern Maya lowlands was Calakmul rather than Palenque, but Palenque is better known, and its most successful leader, Lord Pakal, is probably the most famous Mayan ruler. If we were being accurate, we would have located the battle at Dos Pilas, a client city of Tikal's, which, unlike Tikal, is actually on the Rio Pasion."

"It was a curious choice that Matt made - to come back as a Mayan warrior," Chan said. "It sounds like a hard life."

"Yes, I agree," Michaels nodded. "I think it was a romantic choice, based on a whim rather than careful consideration. He was in a rather stressful situation when he was told to choose a time and place in history to come back to. And he had to decide quickly, so he can be forgiven for not thinking it through properly."

"That is a big understatement!" Chan laughed. "He thought his uploaded mind had been plucked out of the internet by an alien civilisation – a civilisation which had simulated his universe to test some socio-logical hypotheses. 'Rather stressful' is a very mild way of putting it." He turned serious again. "What period would you have chosen to have come back to, if you were placed in his situation?"

"I don't know. I have asked myself that question many times. Who would I want to be if I had to go back to a point in history at least a hundred years before I was born? It's a tricky one because the world has changed so dramatically since then. Life expectancy, medicine, transport, information and scientific understanding, social organisation - everything has transformed, improved enormously. Matt could choose to be from a wealthy background, which would save him from a lot of the indignities and discomfort of life before the twentieth century, but still…"

"Since he was coming back as an adult, his life expectancy wouldn't be much reduced by coming back in an earlier period," Chan contributed. "The huge improvement in life expectancy last century was largely due to the reduction in child deaths."

"That's true. You probably wouldn't choose to come back exactly a hundred years before Matt was born, or you would find yourself fighting in the trenches in the First World War. I think maybe I'd have chosen to return as an English gentleman in the mid eighteenth century. The Enlightenment was in full swing and people were breaking down the old dogmas of church and monarchy; the scientific method was starting to yield fascinating insights into how the world works and there were brilliant thinkers everywhere. It was probably the last time in history when you could keep pretty much up-to-date with the latest thinking in most fields of human knowledge." He paused. "How about you?"

"Probably the first few decades of the Qing dynasty, in what you call the seventeenth century. It was a time of peace and prosperity in China, with good government by the Manchu rulers. What I would not have chosen is to come back as a Maya warrior."

Michaels nodded, and the two men fell silent. Michaels cast his mind back to when he heard the astonishing news that an American firm called Von Neumann Industries had succeeded in uploading a human mind into a computer. And not just any mind, but the one belonging to Matt Metcalfe, a young man whose fame was sealed when he was murdered in broad daylight by a religious extremist.

VNI had cut Metcalfe's brain into very thin slices, and scanned the precise locations and connections of every neuron. They had modelled that structure inside a silicon computer, and found a way to run the model so that it performed the exact same "braining" process as the original brain had done - generating a human mind.

It was a breathtaking achievement. The global community of neuroscientists and artificial intelligence researchers had been stunned by its brilliance and its audacity. The great majority of them had assumed that such a development was still decades away, and most lay people had not even begun to contemplate the possibility.

VNI and Matt's parents had hoped that their achievement would be accepted – perhaps even applauded - because of the rush of sympathy for Matt and his family. But the news about Matt's uploading was leaked before they were ready, and the public debate quickly spiralled out of control. Despite the genuine widespread affection for Matt, there were huge concerns about what he had become, and what sort of danger he represented. Religious commentators complained that uploading Matt was a presumptuous attempt to usurp the role of their deities, and denied that Matt could be accorded the status of human, or even a conscious entity. That argument was demolished for most people by a televised interview between Matt and a respected BBC journalist: it was clear that Matt was a living, thinking creature, with profound emotional responses, and a wry and engaging sense of humour.

But the concern about the danger he posed was less easily dismissed. Scientists, pundits and politicians all noted that Matt's cognitive abilities were expanding rapidly, and predicted that he was about to make what they called a "hard take-off" towards super-intelligence. There was an escalating chorus of strongly-expressed concerns that this was a threat to the rest of humanity. Matt was hosted inside a supercomputer in London, with no access to the internet, and no way to affect the material world. For the time being he was contained, but if he achieved super-intelligence, he would become thousands of times smarter than any human - perhaps millions of times smarter - and he would eventually find a way to escape. Sharing our planet with a creature many times more intelligent than ourselves was a perilous prospect. After considerable soul-searching, and with real regret, the decision was taken to shut Matt down.

The official story of what happened next - the story told by VNI and Matt's parents - was that Matt realised what was going to happen and shut his own processing down suddenly and without warning. Even though the people involved stuck rigidly to this account, it seemed so implausible that a thousand conspiracy stories grew up round the events. Some claimed that the US government had taken control of the supercomputer that hosted Matt, and was using him to develop a race of super-soldiers. Others argued that Matt was not the sort of person to commit suicide, so he must have escaped. Perhaps he was lurking in some dark corner of the internet, drawing up plans for revenge on a species which had killed him not once, but twice.

Michaels and Chan were two of the few people in the world who knew what had really happened – because they had made it happen. John Michaels ran the USA's Oracle programme, a venture within the NSA to develop a superintelligence, and contain it so that it could represent no threat to its creators. Chan Lu was in charge of the equivalent Chinese initiative. They already knew each other well, and had collaborated secretly for several years to avoid a damaging rivalry between their countries' cutting-edge AI programmes.

When they heard about Matt's uploading, they agreed to join forces to capture him. As Matt was streaming his sub-minds into various digital storage facilities he had prepared around the world, they intercepted and quarantined his controlling sub-mind. They told him that he was the "guest" of an advanced species which had created – simulated – him, his family and friends, and the whole world that he had just left. They knew that this was an explanation for how our world was created that Matt already suspected to be true, and they were greatly relieved that he fairly quickly accepted his bizarre new situation.

In the absence of a fully worked out long-term plan

for his future, they wanted to keep his mind running, so they invited him to choose a time and place in humanity's history where he could be re-born. To their surprise, he had chosen to be a Mayan warrior, and they had set about creating new simulations for him to inhabit until they could devise a more permanent arrangement.

Chan broke the silence. "I assume there is still no progress in tracing Matt's other sub-minds?"

"No," Michaels replied. "In addition to all the searches we have discussed and developed with you and your team, we have recently run sophisticated new diagnostics on patterns of information flow around the web, looking for the signature patterns we see in Matt's sub-mind. There doesn't seem to be anything out there, although we can't be sure. Our people still think the sub-mind we have played an organisation role for all of Matt's sub-minds, and that when it was intercepted, they had no way of communicating with each other. They may have evaporated, or they may be latent in various networks, and capable of being revived if Matt were ever to be let loose on the net again." Michaels glanced at Chan and hastily added, "Which of course is not going to happen."

"No, of course," Chan agreed. "Do you still think he could re-create his whole mind from the sub-mind you are hosting?"

"We don't see why not. Or at least, we assume that he could create another mind of similar scale and potential. As you know, our interviews with Vic Dami-ano and Matt's father David confirmed that his mind was expanding at a remarkable rate before he fled the Von Neumann Industries supercomputers. There's no reason to believe that he couldn't do the same thing again. If we let him."

Chan looked at Michaels sharply. "I sense you are feeling regret, Agent Michaels. Perhaps even guilt?" When Michaels did not react, Chan continued. "You should not. He was an innocent young man, and from what we can tell he was a good person. But we do not know what he would have become in the days and years to come. The Chilean diplomat who made that critical speech at the UN…"

"Riquelme," Michaels suggested.

"Yes, Signor Riquelme. He was correct. Matt was - how did he put it? - an existential threat to humanity. We did the right thing in intercepting him and containing him. And after all, we have not killed him. I can assure you there are many people who would have killed him without hesitation if they stood in our shoes."

"Yes, we have kept him alive," Michaels admitted. "But for our own purposes, not for the good of Matt Metcalfe. For our own secret purposes – which we haven't even determined yet. Look, I'm not arguing against our decision. I would make the same choices again today. It's just a shame, that's all."

"You are sentimental, Agent Michaels. Yes, our treatment of Matt Metcalfe is perhaps ungracious. But it is also inevitable."

"You're right, of course." Michaels hugged himself, rubbing his hands up and down his arms. "I'm getting cold - shall we go inside?"

As they went back into the house, Chan's phone rang. He excused himself, and Michaels caught a worried frown; he wondered whether his old friend was in danger. Political battles within the NSA could be fierce, but in the PLA the stakes could be far higher. Michaels had known senior officers who were rising stars one minute, and were executed for corruption the next. His concern was professional as well as personal. His comment about their collaboration was heartfelt. When China and the USA found out how close they both were to achieving the goal of creating conscious machines the results could have been disastrous. Michaels had no time for alternative histories - real history was confusing enough - but if the people in charge of the two countries' artificial general intelligence programmes had been anyone but Chan and himself, it might have proved impossible to bridge the gap and prevent serious conflict.

He cast his mind back to when he first met Chan. It was 1979, and he was a fresh-faced young CIA agent in his mid-twenties, revelling in his first foreign assignment. Pro-Soviet communists had seized power in Afghanistan the year before, and the CIA set up a covert operation to help China defend itself against possible Soviet-Afghan attack.

As ever, the Agency's motivations were complicated. Relations between China and Russia had begun to sour in 1956 when Khrushchev denounced Stalin, and in 1961 China formally denounced Russia as revisionist traitors. There were some minor military skirmishes

along the border, and China responded to the growing Soviet influence in Afghanistan by supporting
the Afghan Mujahidin, and ramping up their military
presence near Afghanistan in Xinjiang, an enormous
province in western China. In 1971 relations between
China and the US began to thaw, and the CIA seized
the opportunity to put pressure on their Soviet enemy,
and to deepen relations with a powerful new ally. John
Michaels was part of the team assigned to exploit that
opportunity.

Michaels had spent just three years with the CIA
at Langley by then, having graduated top of his class
at Stanford, majoring in international relations, and
speaking passable Mandarin. He was a quick learner,
and highly regarded. On the assignment in Xinjiang
he was impressed by the intelligence and diligence of
his Chinese counterparts, and particularly by a young
PLA officer called Chan Lu. Chan was four years older
than him, and his opposite in many ways: lacking in
formal education where Michaels had received the finest education money could buy; unsophisticated and
rough in manner where Michaels had travelled the
world and already talked like a seasoned diplomat. But
the two of them recognised in each other the ability to
solve problems and get things done with the minimum
of fuss. They took advantage of the occasional opportunities to talk in private, and forged a bond which had
lasted ever since.

The next time they met was a decade later, during
a refit of monitoring stations at Qita and Korla, again
in Xinjiang province. The sites were being upgraded to

help China monitor Soviet missile and space activity, and - again covertly - CIA's signals intelligence personnel provided specialised equipment. Michaels and Chan were both more senior now, and could arrange to spend more time together than the previous occasion. Their friendship was consolidated, and after that they were able to arrange to meet from time to time at conferences and during country visits.

When they first met, Michaels' Mandarin was better than Chan's English. By 1989 Chan had overtaken him, and was on his way to becoming fluent. Michaels knew this was risky for Chan. It meant he could gain exposure to American technology and know-how, as well as the material benefits that could flow from dealing with the richer country. But it also meant he could fall under suspicion whenever the political wind blowing westwards turned chilly. Chan managed to navigate these currents, and Michaels often wondered what that involved.

In 2011, an NSA analyst wrote a report about a new group within the Third Department, the branch of the PLA responsible for monitoring foreign data communications. She noted that a number of the PLA's best programming staff had been recruited to this group, which had also procured an unusual amount of hardware, as well as external software services. From the evidence she compiled, she concluded that the group was working on an advanced form of artificial intelligence, probably in connection with drone warfare and robotics. The officer in charge of the group was identified as Chan Lu.

Michaels, who had moved across from the CIA to the NSA a couple of years before, was asked to see what he could find out. He flew to Beijing, ostensibly for a week of meetings with various US personnel, and he arranged to meet Chan Lu on two occasions during the trip. During the first meeting Chan was friendly but unforthcoming. During the second, he told Michaels that the PLA was aware that the NSA was experimenting with artificial intelligence systems using algorithms created on the back of the massive amounts of data the Agency was acquiring from diverse sources. PLA experts had concluded that the Agency was heading towards a decisive lead in AI technology, and had tasked him with closing the gap.

It was clear to the two men that this was a serious potential flashpoint between their two countries, given the decisive military advantage that could be conferred by a major breakthrough in AI technology. They decided to seek permission to establish a permanent back-channel to allow them to share information, build trust, and keep each other informed of any such breakthrough. They argued that the only safe future lay in their two countries maintaining an approximate parity in the space.

There were heated discussions at the highest levels within the hierarchies on both sides. The most hawkish people on both sides argued strenuously that their counterparts were not to be trusted. They hated the idea of abandoning the pursuit of a decisive superiority.

Eventually the more diplomatic approach won out. Their proposal was accepted, and to facilitate it,

Michaels was placed in charge of the NSA's AI research activity.

CHAPTER 5

Mat-B'alam and his battalion of Jaguar warriors tied their canoes to trees at the edge of the river, and waited. The canoes were big – some of them carrying as many as fifty men. The Jaguars were from the city of Palenque, and over the course of the next few hours, they were joined by fighters from Bonampak, Piedras Negras and Yaxchilan - cities linked by the Usumacinta River and its tributaries. This was the biggest fighting force deployed in the Maya rainforest for generations.

The air was heavy and humid as they waited for the drums which would let them know that their other allies from the cities of Calakmul and Caracol had completed their long march to the battlefield. Mighty Pakal, the ruler of Palenque, had spent years negotiating this alliance with the other chiefs, and today was the day when the alliance would be tested - and sealed in blood.

The city of Palenque was rising. Its elaborately decorated temples and palaces were now among the most impressive stone buildings in the whole of the

Maya highlands. Its warriors were powerful: superbly trained, and experienced in battle. If they were successful today, the swaggering pre-eminence of Tikal would be smashed. If they failed, the consequences would be hard to bear. Other cities had risen to challenge Tikal, and so far they had all been crushed by Tikal's elite Hawk warrior squad.

But no city had previously had the advantage of Palenque's great leader, Lord Pakal. Pakal was a phenomenon, combining great physical strength with outstanding skills in strategy and negotiation. Very few cities' negotiators left Palenque without agreeing to Lord Pakal's proposals. His people, and most importantly his warrior clan, considered him infallible. His elite fighting group, the Jaguars, were building a reputation to rival that of Tikal's Hawks.

Mat-B'alam was neither the strongest nor the fiercest of the Jaguars, but he was very fast, and he was intelligent, creative, and resourceful. He was named after the god of travelers, merchants, and mischief. He had earned the respect and loyalty of his men by discerning danger before it overwhelmed them, and for his ability to turn the tables on his enemies. Many of the Jaguars owed their lives to Mat-B'alam's quick intelligence and inventiveness: the path towards Lord Pakal's grand alliance against Tikal had involved battles with several of the cities which now proclaimed allegiance to Palenque's cause.

The warriors squatted, and checked their equipment while they waited. Most of them wore short cotton protective jackets packed with rock salt, and tight bindings of leather or cloth on their forearms and legs. A few pulled on elbow, wrist, and knee protectors made of various alloys of copper, worked to fit comfortably and to glance off sword and knife blows.

They daubed blue paint on their faces. They checked that the sharp blades of their weapons had not been nicked or blunted during the two-day river journey. Their primary weapons were macuahuitl clubs - hefty wooden truncheons embedded with vicious slivers of sharp obsidian. They also carried swords or short stabbing spears, or wooden axes, hardened with fire and edged with flint or obsidian blades. Many of them carried projectile weapons too: spears, sometimes set in atlatl spear-throwers. Most of them had shields - either long and flexible, made of hide, or smaller, rigid, and round.

The warriors were ready. They waited only for the sound of the drums of Calakmul. They were quiet, but far from restful. Every man wondered whether he would see the end of that day, and return home to his family. Some were impatient; others were more scared than excited. All were tense.

When the sound of the drums finally came it was leaden, sluggish, as if wearied by its journey through the humid air. But it stirred the spirits of the crouching warriors: the wait was over and the drama was about to begin.

An advance party of three hundred Jaguars set off toward the city. They were a formidable force by the standard of normal Mayan warfare, but today they were a small minority of the massive forces assembled for the attack on Tikal. Their job was to draw the Hawks out of the city and start the process of wearing down Tikal's defences.

The narrow path from the river broadened into a sacbe, a raised "white road" made of rubble and stone and topped with limestone stucco. Gigantic kapok trees were dotted either side of the sacbe, and beyond them stood isolated tropical cedars and mahogany trees. Otherwise, the smothering rainforest had been cleared to a distance of a full minute's sprint from the road, a sign that the city was close. It also meant there was nowhere for Hawk warriors to stage an ambush.

They marched towards the city. Every now and then Mat-B'alam and his lieutenant, Jaguar Claw, exchanged remarks in low voices. Most of the other fighters were quiet, harbouring their own private thoughts.

As they approached the city, they were able to make out the shape of giant earthworks, which did double service as defensive fortification and canal system, carrying precious water into the densely populated heart of Tikal. At its lowest they were the height of a man, and in parts they rose to the height of two men.

Drawing closer, they were rewarded with their first sight of the enemy. One by one, a force of Tikal's Hawk warriors appeared at the top of the earthworks and looked down at the advancing Jaguars. More and more appeared, until there were around 200 glaring down at the invaders.

Mat-B'alam led his men onward until he judged they were a little beyond the reach of Hawk spear throwers. He raised his hand to signal a halt, and waited. His men drew up alongside and behind him, three ranks deep, a hundred across.

"Lost your appetite, you scum? Thought you came for a fight?" The challenge came from the chief of the Hawks - a brute of a man in resplendent headgear, with a voice that rumbled.

Mat-B'alam made no reply but turned to Jaguar Claw and said calmly, "He's mine." Jaguar Claw nodded, and looked at each of the nearest men in turn, checking that they also understood. Mat-B'alam turned back to the Hawks, but made no reply.

"Well what are you waiting for, you cowardly whelp sons of feeble-minded bitches?" demanded the Hawk. "Are you just going to stand there and piss yourselves, or have you come to taste the edges of our obsidian blades?" He grinned broadly and brandished his macuahuitl club. Several of his fellow Hawks shouted and jeered at the Jaguars below.

Mat-B'alam gestured to one of his men, who loaded an atlatl with a chert-pointed spear and flung it towards the rampart. It landed a few paces short. Mat-B'alam gazed impassively up at the Hawk leader, waiting for him to understand. It didn't take long.

"You think we need the advantage of height to smash you sniveling pups? Alright, we'll take a stroll down there and separate your heads from your miserable bodies. You're going to wish you hadn't made us bother." The Hawk leader nodded to the men either side of him and the group started down the rampart. They swaggered down the slope of the earthworks, arrogant in their fighting prowess.

The Jaguars could see the Hawks were loading atlatls with spears, and they began to do the same. In response to a gesture from Mat-B'alam they also spread out so as to offer a less concentrated target.

The Hawks advanced on the Jaguars, and spears started to fly in both directions. Most of them missed their mark, and several were intercepted by shields, but Mat-B'alam heard howls of agony as a few spears found their targets on either side. The injured men stopped to tend their wounds, or lay on the ground, writhing and screaming. Their screams were muffled by the shouting and jeering that arose from both sides, accompanied now by the sounds of wooden drums, conch shell trumpets and whistles.

As the two groups of warriors closed on each other they continued to spread out, and individual fighters paired off with opposite numbers. Mayan battles were usually an exercise in demonstrating individual superiority, and obtaining captives for slavery or sacrifice. Nobles from either side would identify a suitable opponent and each of them would seek to wound and disable the other. Often when their individual fights were decided, the pair would simply wait to see the outcome of other paired contests, and the side which won most would return home with their captives.

The Hawks believed this was simply another of those occasions. Their scouts had reported that forces from Palenque and Calakmul were converging on Tikal, but they had not understood the scale of the assault: they had no idea that Lord Pakal had also concluded alliances with the cities that lay along the river

Usumacinta and its tributaries. Pakal had disguised his force's numbers by splitting the troops up into small convoys, and staggering their arrival at the city outskirts. Consequently the Hawks were still confident of repelling the invaders, just as they had won all their battles for several generations now.

With gestures and shouts, the warriors paired off. The Hawk leader accepted Mat-B'alam's challenge greedily. They circled each other, growling and feinting attacks. Their spears were thrown, so each had a mac-uahuitl club, a sword, a shield, and daggers for close work.

The Hawk leader closed on Mat-B'alam, brandishing his club, stroking his thumb along the sharp edges of the obsidian blades set into its wood, snarling his contempt. Suddenly he lunged forwards with a clumsy swipe, but Mat-B'alam saw the move coming a long way off and stepped aside gracefully.

More circling, more growling. The Hawk lunged again, more seriously this time, but Mat-B'alam turned the blow aside with his shield.

Now the Hawk charged with more determination, and brought his club down hard on Mat-B'alam's shield. Mat-B'alam took three quick steps back under the force of the blow and appeared to wave his own macuahuitl club half-heartedly in response. The Hawk sensed weakness and moved forwards slowly, gloating. He raised his club high with both hands and smashed it down on Mat-B'alam's shield. The shield shuddered as it deflected the blow, but it did not shatter.

Mat-B'alam skittered backwards, glancing behind

him to check for obstacles in his line of retreat. The Hawk charged forward and brought his club down again, but this time Mat-B'alam side-stepped, and jabbed at the Hawk's leg as he passed.

It was a minor wound, but the Hawk was furious that his opponent had drawn first blood. The pain suppressed by adrenaline, he rounded on Mat-B'alam with a furious swing which came nowhere near connecting.

The Hawk drew himself to his full height and breathed deeply for a few seconds, glaring at Mat-B'alam. Having regained his composure, he raised his club and rushed forward, crashing the weapon down against the raised shield. Mat-B'alam took one step back to mitigate the force of the blow, then jumped quickly aside to stop the Hawk from following through.

The pattern repeated: rush, crash, backward step, and jump aside. Each time the Hawk grew angrier and more frustrated. His breathing became laboured. On the fourth attack, Mat-B'alam stepped aside instead of back and the club found no resistance. The Hawk lost his balance for a moment as his momentum was not arrested as he expected. Mat-B'alam darted forward and slashed opportunistically at the Hawk's unprotected flank, drawing more blood.

The Hawk bellowed his rage. "Stand and fight me you coward! Stop dancing about like a young girl!" Mat-B'alam looked at him levelly and said nothing, but slowly raised his shield again.

The Hawk stomped forwards, swinging his club wildly, hoping somehow to connect and deliver a crushing blow. Mat-B'alam retreated, allowing the weapon to come close, but never to connect with himself or his shield. As the Hawk tired, losing more blood than he knew, his swings became more erratic and his recoveries slower. Mat-B'alam kept retreating, waiting for the Hawk to leave a flank undefended for more than half a second. When it finally happened he dropped his club and with a single smooth movement he took a short stabbing blade from his belt and thrust it into the man's unprotected flank.

The Hawk drew himself up and looked down at his side, amazed and furious that he had been seriously wounded by the smaller man. Mat-B'alam dropped his shield and picked up his club. He crouched, the dagger in his other hand. He circled the Hawk, speaking to him for the first time.

"Come here, fat piggy. Come to my blade."

Fear and fury wrestled for control of the Hawk's face. Fury won out as he lowered his head and rushed headlong towards Mat-B'alam, his macuahuitl club swinging wildly. This time Mat-B'alam stepped to one side, raised himself up to his full height and brought his own club down hard on the back of the man's skull as he hurtled past.

The Hawk's legs wobbled as the blow landed, but he stayed on his feet. Slowly he raised himself and turned back to face Mat-B'alam, blood running freely into his eyes and down his cheeks. His eyes were glazed, and he swayed slightly. His club fell to the ground as his arms went limp. Mat-B'alam walked towards him and stood very close to him, his face expressionless. The two of them remained like that for a second, silent.

Then Mat-B'alam stepped back just far enough to give himself the room to slash the man across the throat with his short blade. His eyes shut on reflex as his face was splashed by the blood which spurted from the gash in the man's neck. The Hawk's legs buckled and he crashed to his knees, and then fell face down onto the ground.

Mat-B'alam wiped his face and gazed down at his fallen opponent for a few moments, and then looked around the battlefield. Some of the other fighters had finished their bouts, but many were still circling each other, feinting and thrusting, or closing in on the final moments with wounding body blows. The fighters who had won their battles were waiting by their injured captives, taking no further action. It was traditional that generals and rulers were executed on the day of battle, so as to leave no doubt as to which side had won. But other nobles were usually taken back to the victorious city alive, although only to suffer days or weeks of torture and blood-letting, and end up as sacrificial victims.

The Palenque Jaguars were now joined on the field of battle by some of their new allies, fighters from the other cities. Their weapons and protective gear were similar, but the dominant colour among the new men were orange and brown instead green and blue.

Evidently the remaining Hawks were noticing the new arrivals. Cries went up from several, and one of them, a lord with fine feathered battle gear, whistled a loud signal to sound a retreat. He had realised that this was not a normal battle at all. It was a fight to the death – for the whole city of Tikal.

CHAPTER 6

"Wow!" Chan said as he removed his goggles. "Virtual reality is almost arrived, isn't it!"

"Almost," agreed Michaels, putting his own goggles down on the coffee table in front of them. "You can pretty much suspend disbelief with this kit, although of course it will be even more immersive in five years or so."

"Ha. The really big technologies are always just five years away from being ready..." Chan smiled. "Still, it is impressive." Chan was looking around Michaels' office distractedly, and for a moment, Michaels wondered whether he meant that the video game was impressive, or the NSA headquarters. It had not been straightforward for Michaels to get permission for Chan to spend a few hours at the Fort Meade campus. He had persevered because he wanted Chan to know that he was being as open with him as he possibly could be.

Chan's smile turned mischievous. "It seemed to me that 'Mat-B'alam' had some practice for that encounter. He also seemed to be a little faster than the other characters."

It was Michaels' turn to smile. "Nothing escapes you, does it, Chan. You're right: we have run that simulation a few times before. And yes, he does seem to improve slightly each time." He turned to face Chan directly. "You're not upset that you missed the inaugural run, I hope?"

Chan held up his hands and shook his head. "No, no - not at all. I wouldn't expect you to risk the embarrassment of a failed first run in front of me. Do you think Matt has any residual memory of each encounter?"

"At some level he must," Michaels replied, "or he wouldn't be improving each time. But we are running him well below full consciousness in these exercises, and there is no sign whatsoever that he is aware that he is repeating the experience. Not even any of the hesitations or subtle gestures people tend to make when they experience déjà vu."

"So how much better is he now? At fighting, I mean."

Michaels looked sheepish. "I'm afraid he didn't survive the first couple of encounters with the Hawk warrior."

Chan nodded thoughtfully, ignoring Michaels' scruples. "Interesting. The Hawk warrior also seemed surprised by Matt's speed. Anyway, that is an important finding. Now we know that an uploaded mind - or sub-mind - can be trained and upgraded in a simulation in the same way as a purely artificial AI. And what about your own AI? Are you running it in the Maya simulation?"

Michaels grinned. "So you didn't guess? I'm surprised. The Hawk leader is the Oracle."

Chan raised his eyebrows. "Isn't that risky? Aren't you running the risk of setting up a lasting rivalry between them? First your AI intercepts Matt and effectively imprisons him, and then you thrust them into mortal combat, and give Matt the advantages he needs to kill your AI?"

"They won't remember - either of them," Michaels reassured him. "They can learn and improve skills, but we know they don't remember details of place and person between simulations."

"You are sure of this?"

"Absolutely. Like you, we have run many simulations with our Oracle in below-conscious mode, and there has never been any sign that it remembers the details from one to the next. Muscle memory, yes, but nothing else."

Chan pursed his lips. After a pause, he continued. "And of course you are adhering to the agreed protocol regarding interactions with the Oracle in fully-conscious mode? There is still no question of allowing your Oracle to interface directly with the internet?"

Michaels straightened, and looked at Chan in astonishment. "Are you kidding? No-one here is crazy enough to want a fully fledged, human-level AI running around the net. We certainly have no intention of unleashing a super-intelligence on the world." Michaels' eyes narrowed. "I understand that you had to ask, and I have to ask you the same question, but do I detect something more than a formal level of interest?"

"No," Chan replied, looking down at the floor. He lowered his voice, even though they were alone in Michaels' office, and no-one could overhear them. Unless they were using surveillance equipment, and there were few places in the world with more expertise in that area than this campus. "There were rumours a few weeks ago about a disaffected group within your agency, but they turned out to be just that – rumours."

Michaels sounded concerned. "Chan, I have the highest regard for your organisation's capabilities, so if you do hear of anything like that you will let me know, won't you?"

"Of course," Chan replied warmly. "Our goals are very much the same in this respect."

They sat in silence for a moment before Michaels spoke again.

"I still can't get over the coincidence of the three approaches to AI – or rather AGI, artificial general intelligence - succeeding at around the same time - ours, yours and Von Neumann's. I don't believe in synchronicity, but I'm suspicious of coincidence."

"Synchron... what?" Chan asked.

"Sorry. The idea that events can be connected by meaning without having any causal connection. Carl Jung, a psychologist, thought there was an underlying framework in the world which orders events. I don't have any time for the notion, personally."

"Ah, I see." Chan smiled. "That sort of thinking runs very deep in Chinese culture. Every now and then some Westerner comes along and re-discovers it, which amuses us greatly."

"So what do you think?", Michaels asked. "Do you think the three AGI projects were linked by some mystical connection?"

"I don't worry myself whether they were or not. I am a practical man, so I look for a practical explanation regardless whether there are other, deeper explanations."

"When you say a practical explanation," Michaels asked, "do you mean a scientific explanation?"

"More or less, yes," Chan replied.

"OK," Michaels persisted. "So what is your scientific explanation?"

"Well, first of all I think the coincidence is less striking than it appears. In fact, Victor Damiano and Von Neumann Industries were considerably ahead of us. They didn't just create an artificial general intelligence - they actually uploaded a human mind. We thought that would take a great deal longer than creating the first true AGI."

"True," Michaels agreed. "So did we. It really was a startling achievement"

"And our two projects - yours and ours - were not at the same stage either. We were able to project your Oracle onto the internet and intercept Matt only by pooling our resources. At which point we discovered that our project was not so advanced as yours." Chan gestured towards the door, indicating the expertise permeating the building.

"Fair point again," Michaels said. "So you think it really wasn't as much of a coincidence as it looks. I see your point, although it still seems odd to me."

"My other observation is that all three projects were... what is the word... facilitated by the availability of sufficiently powerful computers. I suspect we have simply reached the point where the amount of processing power available to well-funded organisations is sufficient to host an artificial general intelligence. And so now we have AGIs. Three of them. Not magic, but cause and effect after all."

"The way you put it sounds very reasonable," Michaels said, "but I'm not convinced. It still seems too coincidental to me."

"I welcome that," Chan replied. "I like the fact that you are puzzling over it. As the years go by, that level of computing power will be available to smaller and smaller labs. Which could give us all a headache. If you find some kind of connection, some unsuspected causal factor, it might enable us to slow the others down."

Michaels smiled, and then sat up in his chair, adopting a more formal tone. "So to answer your earlier question, I do confirm that we are still observing the agreed protocol regarding interactions with the Oracle in fully conscious mode. Do I have your assurance that your side is doing the same?"

Chan looked at him directly, with no trace of humour. "Yes you do. The only questions that we ask of our Oracle in conscious mode are the ones we agree with you beforehand, and which you are asking simultaneously of yours. The video recordings and transcripts that we supply to your analysts are full and unedited, just as I am confident that yours to us are. We have yet to identify any evidence of deception or manipulation in the responses of either of the Oracles."

"Good. Neither have we." Michaels sounded mildly relieved, even though he would have been astonished if Chan's answer had been any different.

"I suppose some people would say this is an

example of ... synchro ... synchronicity?" Chan asked. "The fact that we developed these AGIs at pretty much the same time as you did. And that we found out about each other's achievement, and agreed to co-operate. So we can cross-check the Oracles' answers against each other very effectively to look for signs that they are trying to escape from their 'boxes'. Of course you – or we - could each have created two Oracles, but then their designs would have been so similar that they might have masked deception attempts more easily."

"Hmm," Michaels said thoughtfully. "Yes, I'm sure some people would think that is synchronicity. Personally, I think it is simply a case of turning a problem into an advantage. Anyway, now we have to decide what to do with Matt. We have demonstrated beyond any doubt that the intercept and host operation was successful. The question now is, do we restore him to consciousness, or keep him at the level he is today? Or - at the risk of sounding brutal – do we wipe him? As per our previous discussions, we think now is the time to escalate this decision to our respective political masters. We can no longer argue that we are experimenting. The sub-mind of Matt Metcalfe that we are hosting is a stable entity."

"Yes, I don't think we have any alternative," Chan agreed. "Which is a pity. You and I both know there is a right answer here, but I fear that our masters may not agree." He glanced up at the ceiling, towards the top floor, where the bosses of most organisations are found.

"I'm afraid you might be right," Michaels nodded.

"We won't be the last ones to create AGIs, and although some of the attempts to work out how to programme friendliness towards humans into nascent AGIs are promising, they still have a long way to go. So the wise approach is to make sure we have at least one AGI on the scene which we can rely on being friendly. Matt Metcalfe is a better candidate for that role than either of our two Oracles. But our masters - and especially mine - may not see it that way."

"Have you received any further intelligence on how your President might react?" Chan asked.

"You mean, once she has gotten over being furious at not being informed about Matt's continued existence before now? No, no-one here has broached the subject. But my hunch is she will simply revert to the decision mandated by the UN when Matt's existence was first disclosed. She will order us to erase Matt's files."

Chan shook his head. "That could turn out to be a grave error."

"You can say that again. I am still expecting that she will consult with your General Secretary first, though. I assume you have had no indications of likely reaction from that quarter either?"

"No, like you, we have followed a strict policy of don't ask, don't tell. And I agree - our General Secretary is less likely than yours to jump to the conclusion that we should implement the UN decision. We can perhaps persuade him to try to slow things down."

The two men were quiet for a minute, each absorbed in his own thoughts. It was Chan who broke the silence.

"When do you plan to speak to the President?"

"She has a routine intelligence briefing tomorrow morning. I've arranged with the Director that it will be a restricted session."

Chan nodded gloomily. "I will find out what the General Secretary's movements are tomorrow, and I will try to make sure that he can be contacted if necessary. What about the Oracles? I assume you will be maintaining the existing strategy - you will not be disclosing their existence to your President tomorrow?"

"As long as she doesn't ask a direct question. I imagine that learning about Matt will give her enough to digest for a while."

"Good. Then we just have one more important subject to discuss."

"Yes," Michaels agreed. "Other AGI initiatives. Shall I go first or will you?"

"Please do," Chan smiled. "You are the host."

"Very well. The South Koreans are of course furious about the disappearance of their key scientist, but they have no leads to investigate, and they can't make a fuss in case their attempt to break the moratorium is exposed. So they're keeping their heads down, for the moment at least.

"After them, we view France and the UK as the greatest threats. The other G8 countries all seem to be respecting the moratorium on full-scale AGI development projects - each for different reasons. The Russians, of course, never had the slightest intention of honouring it, but their government keeps siphoning off chunks of the funding, and two of the key scientists have quit in disgust, and taken up lucrative job offers here in the US. So that attempt is going nowhere.

"The tech giants – both ours and yours – have the capability to spin up serious AGI projects very fast, but they are still smarting from the backlash against Silicon Valley that blew up at the end of the last decade. They're desperate to avoid doing anything that will add to the calls to break them up. We're picking up no signals of any intention to test the moratorium from that direction. Does all that chime with your side's view so far?"

"Perfectly," Chan said. "Of course, Von Neumann Industries slipped through the net, so we can't afford to be complacent."

"That's true," Michaels conceded. "We were blind-sided by that one. Sometimes it's easier to find out what's going on in the world outside the Pentagon than what's going on inside it!" He jerked a thumb towards the south-west, in the direction of Washington and the Pentagon building.

"We will both have to remain vigilant. And so we come to the main loose end: the British, and their efforts to tap into the expertise of the Von Neumann team. Will we have to take action there?"

Michaels shuddered. "I certainly hope not! We have a long and noble tradition of holding back key pieces of information from our closest ally, but I would not relish having to initiate black ops against any of their people."

CHAPTER 7

Being the son of a cop was not easy at school, and the cop being dead didn't help. Lester Parnell's formative years were as different from those of his boss John Michaels as they possibly could be. Michaels did not subscribe to the view that opposites attract, but he did appreciate that they could be very useful to each other.

"You heading out?" Michaels asked.

Lester Parnell nodded. "Going to see our friends in Silicon Valley."

"Good," Michaels said. "I'd like to understand why they're not making better progress with some of the ideas we've passed them recently."

"Yeah," Parnell agreed. "Might have to rattle their cages a little. Reckon they might be getting a little fat and happy out there in the sunshine."

He hoisted his carry-on bag over his shoulder as he turned to leave. He grinned in response to Michaels' parting comment, "Can't think of a better man for the job!"

Parnell was the son of an Irish cop and a Polish

cleaner, both second-generation immigrants. They lived in a rough part of Brooklyn, and Parnell experienced it in full Technicolour. His father's refusal to back down in the face of intimidation was legendary among his colleagues, and it got him killed before Parnell was ten years old. The NYPD made sure their fallen hero's family was financially stable, but they couldn't stop his widow from drinking herself to death, which she achieved a couple of years later.

Parnell stopped going to school and joined a local gang for protection, and was soon working his way up the very greasy pole of the narcotics profession. By the time he was sixteen he had killed two members of rival gangs, and his world was awash with drugs and violence. He was numb to the awfulness of it all, but two events broke through this protective indifference. On his seventeenth birthday he watched his baby sister draw her last breath as she died from a heroin overdose. They had not been close for years - he was not close to anyone - but she was only 15, and he felt a residual duty to protect her. Unable to find any usable veins in her arms or legs, she had injected the fatal dose between her toes.

The following week he was captured in a raid by a neighbouring gang, who tortured him for two hours - more for fun and for practice than for any information he might have. When his gang burst into the room to rescue him, he was in a bad way, with two broken ribs, heavy bruises on his face, arms and legs, and cigarette burns on his arms and chest. But his tormentors had not broken him, and he retained the mental and physical strength to deal with them in the way his liberators expected. The first one died quickly, his neck twisted savagely until it broke. The second one was not so lucky. Parnell spent ten minutes kicking him in the ribs and between the legs. Each blow was controlled, measured: hard enough to hurt and damage, but not hard enough to kill. Then he set about the boy's face with a knife. When Parnell walked out of the room a few minutes later the boy was still just about conscious, but beyond recovery, and unrecognisable.

These two incidents forced Parnell to think about his life - something he had never really done before. Despite appearances he was bright, and he had the sense to know that on his current trajectory he would probably be dead within a year, or serving a long jail sentence. He fled Brooklyn and joined the army. During a difficult few months he learned the hard way to submit to army discipline and adopt their rules as his own. After that, his physical courage, determination and intelligence served him well, and several years later, he took a part-time degree in military history and became an officer. He applied to join the 75th Ranger Regiment, and five years after graduating from the Ranger Assessment and Selection Program at Fort Benning in Georgia, he met John Michaels while providing security support to the CIA on a confidential mission inside China.

During the course of a tortuous three-hour journey on pitted and potholed roads through mountainous terrain, Michaels was intrigued to find a lively intelligence behind Parnell's blank exterior. Despite now having a formal education to degree level, he had no interest in learning about matters of which he had no direct personal experience. But like many bright people who have endured or witnessed the harshest experiences that life has to offer, he had a knack for cutting through quickly to the nub of any problem, and expressing his thoughts in concise, compelling, and concrete language.

Michaels nominated Parnell for a series of covert missions over the next couple of years, and then suggested that he apply to transfer to join the NSA. Anticipating Parnell's reluctance to leave the armed forces, which had provided him with the only family he had known for many years, he proposed a secondment rather than a permanent transfer. Michaels was amused and secretly pleased when Parnell feigned reluctance, and negotiated himself a promotion to the rank of major. Parnell received extensive training in what used to be called the "tradecraft" of espionage.

Over the next few years, Parnell made himself invaluable, acting as bodyguard to Michaels and his close colleagues, as first choice for legal but confidential operations that might require combat skills, and also for operations that approached or crossed the boundaries of legality. As a result, Parnell became one of the very few people to learn about the NSA's programme to develop an artificial general intelligence, or AGI. Most of the other people who knew about the Oracle held NSA executive rank, or had demonstrated extraordinary IT skills.

When he took over the Oracle programme,

Michaels had not anticipated the amount of patentable technology that it would generate. His agreement with Chan governed the amount of time that each side could operate their systems at close to conscious level, but it said nothing about operations below that level. (Finalising the definitions in this agreement had involved lengthy negotiations about live issues in neuroscience and philosophy.) As it turned out, even when operating at fairly low levels, the Oracle was exceptionally good at integrating data and information from diverse fields of scientific research, and combining them to produce startling new insights into basic principles, and innovative suggestions for practical applications. Michaels quickly understood the need to farm out these insights and suggestions to organisations that could make use of them without arousing suspicions about what the NSA was up to. Liaising with those organisations became one of Parnell's duties.

Soon after he abandoned gangland for a career in the army, Parnell adopted a policy of never disagreeing with his superiors. He would, if asked, express a point of view which differed from theirs, but after stating his view once he would then keep his thoughts to himself. He came very close to contravening this policy when he discussed with Michaels his strategy for exploiting the Oracle.

"Sooner or later one of us is going to deploy this weapon against the other," Parnell had protested. "I know you like this Chan and you trust him, and for all I know he's a straight-up guy. But he's not going to be in that seat forever, is he? Is it really possible for the world's two superpowers to keep their hands off that button forever? Sooner or later one side or the other will blink. Always do. And if what you say is right, the side that doesn't blink will regret it big-time. Gotta pray that isn't us."

Parnell listened dutifully as Michaels explained the prisoner's dilemma game theory to him, and set out the massive risks if the Oracle escaped into the cybernetic wild. Michaels could tell he was not convinced, but he was gratified that Parnell had never raised the matter with him again.

****

"Before you go, come on in and shut the door. I've got something very cool to show you." Michaels gestured for Parnell to look at his computer.

Parnell was amused by Michaels' boyish enthusiasm. The screen showed a complex array of data, like a 1980s graphic equaliser display, with dozens of coloured bars running up and down their channels.

"This is the beta release of the neuronal activity translator I told you about," Michaels said, still not looking up from the screen. "It's an attempt to read the thoughts and feelings created in Matt's mind by tracking the firing of the neurons in his brain which give rise to those thoughts and feelings."

"Yeah, you explained this before. Not that I understood all the details, but I think I get the gist. We're reading his mind by reading his brain."

"That's right, although it's a long way from being a

precise reading." Parnell suppressed a smile when he saw the delight on his superior's face. Michaels didn't appear to notice, and continued breathlessly.

"We can track the firing of pretty much all his neurons - which takes an astonishing amount of processing power, by the way. But neurons aren't binary, like the transistors on a computer chip. They fire with varying intensity, and the meaning of one neuron's firing is affected by the firing of other neurons in its immediate network. There are plenty of other variables too. So when we translate the firing patterns into what we think they mean in terms of his conscious experience, we are getting a very approximate result. We're confident it's good enough to gauge whether he is happy, sad, stressed, frustrated, and so on, but there are nuances which escape us."

"So what's going through his mind at this point?" Parnell asked. "What do all these bars mean?"

Michaels frowned with concentration. "At this point in the simulation he's experiencing a conflict between a strong desire to win, and a revulsion at what he's about to do."

"So this is the end of the battle scene?" Parnell asked.

"Yes," Michaels nodded, and pointed to a smaller screen further along the desk. "You can see the visualisation of the simulation on this screen here."

"Yeah, it's pretty hardcore," Parnell said flatly, looking at the smaller screen. "But he's supposed to be a battle-hardened warrior, isn't he? Surely he shouldn't be phased by the execution of an enemy?"

Michaels gave Parnell a look of mock rebuke.

"It's impressive, though," Parnell agreed, bending towards the larger screen and starting to look more carefully at the translator readings. "How do you tell what each bar means? Is there an instruction manual or something?"

"There's a training guide to get you started, but the most helpful information is built right into the display. See here..." Michaels pointed at part of the screen. "If you hover over this bar this pop-up box tells you what that data stream represents. And if you right-click on this dialog box you can drill down for more information. I'll arrange for you to have access to this and you can explore it for yourself."

"Neat. In the meantime, can I ask a stupid question?"

"If you do, it will be the first time," Michaels encouraged him.

Parnell smiled dutifully, although he knew that Michaels was sincere.

"When Matt's father and Vic Damiano scanned Matt's brain they were retrieving just a snapshot of the connection between all his neurons at a moment in time, right?"

Michaels nodded and smiled, guessing where Parnell's enquiry was going.

"You tell me that we have a lot more data than they did – because we have information about what each neuron is doing over a period of time, not just how they are positioned at any one moment."

Michaels nodded again.

"And yet we are only able to create an approximate translation of what his mind is experiencing. We have more data than they did, and yet we have a less accurate rendition. How come?"

"Well, we're doing something very different," Michaels replied. "They were setting out to re-create Matt's mind, while we're trying to understand it, which turns out to be much harder."

"You'd think it would be the other way round," Parnell said. "You'd think it would be impossible to create something without in the first place understanding it."

"I know what you mean," Michaels agreed. "But it depends what resources you have. If you have a great deal of computing power it can be easy to do things which look very hard but are actually very simple – they just take a lot of processing grunt. For instance, imagine you have a working car but you have absolutely no idea how it works. In fact you have only a shaky grasp on the basic laws of physics and chemistry, let alone engineering. But you do have scanning and 3D manufacturing equipment that gives you the ability to copy the car accurately down to the molecular level and then produce an exact replica. You'd be able to create another working car without having the foggiest idea about high-tension sparking, piston compression, transmission gear ratios and the rest of it."

"And that's the position Matt's father was in?" Parnell asked.

"Pretty much, yes. But your question does get close to a mystery that's been bothering me ever since we first found out about Matt's upload."

Parnell said nothing, just waiting for his boss to continue.

"It's surprising that the snapshot of Matt's brain which Vic and his father were able to take contained enough information to enable them to create Matt's mind so accurately. All they had was the position and connections of each neuron at a moment in time. They didn't have data about the propensity of each neuron to fire given various different sets of input, and how each neuron's behaviour affected every other neuron in its immediate network. So the upload of Matt should have been at best an approximate rendering of his personality – an intelligence only loosely based on Matt's brain.

"Instead, Metcalfe and Damiano managed to re-create Matt pretty much exactly – closely enough that his mother and girlfriend are convinced it was him, not an approximation of him."

"Is there any way they could have captured all the detail you say we are missing?" Parnell asked.

"No," Michaels said, shaking his head. "They simply didn't have the processing power – or the time. We can't explain how they did it."

"Should we ask them very nicely to tell us? Saying please and all?" Parnell said, with a malicious edge in his voice.

"No," Michaels replied, looking at him directly. "We can't do anything that might raise suspicions that Matt has become our ... guest. Anyway, my guess is they don't understand themselves how odd their achievement is."

If Parnell was disappointed, he didn't show it. "How

about the Oracle? Where are its readings?"

Michaels pressed a combination of keys, and the screen changed, with similar bars showing, but in different patterns.

"No," Michaels said. "No significant stress reading. None of the patterns you'd associate with conflict."

"Seemed to me it was really getting into character," Parnell suggested, with a sly look at Michaels. "Almost as if it was getting off on the experience. Until it was taken down, of course."

Michaels hesitated a beat before replying. "I don't think the Oracle has the faculty for 'getting off', as you so delicately put it."

Parnell looked doubtful. "OK, so it's not a method actor, then. But it's a pretty good actor anyways."

Michaels smiled, and changed the subject. With a casual tone which almost fooled Parnell, but not quite, he said, "I know that you have your doubts about the wisdom of us playing nicely with the Chinese rather than preparing to use the Oracle as a weapon against them. Do you happen to know if any other members of our little team share that view?"

Parnell could feel his heart rate increase as Michaels spoke, but his reply was convincing because it had the advantage of being true. "No, I don't. That doesn't mean there aren't any, but I've never discussed it with any of them, and I've certainly never heard anyone express any opinions like that. That sort of policy talk is above my pay grade. I don't get into it, and to be honest with you, I don't have much time for most of the guys and girls that do." He stopped and gave Michaels what he hoped came across as a conspiratorial smile. "There are exceptions, of course."

Michaels nodded, and looked back at his screen. "Do me favour, would you? Keep your ears open, and let me know if you do hear anything like that."

"Sure," Parnell replied. "Are there reports of some trouble brewing? Anyone in particular you want me to accidentally get into conversation with?"

"No, no," Michaels said hastily. "Just a passing remark I heard from outside the group. Probably doesn't mean anything." He looked up at Parnell, and said breezily, "Anyway, have a good trip. Don't be too hard on the youngsters."

Parnell's capacity for self-restraint was legendary, and he needed every ounce of that restraint to enable him to refrain from alerting Michael's suspicions by pressing him to say more about this passing remark. As he left the NSA campus he replayed the conversation in his mind. Could there be other dissidents within the small group of people who knew about the Oracle? Or did Michaels know more than he was letting on?

Parking his car at the airport, he took a deep breath, and reassured himself. If Michaels had even the faintest suspicion what he was up to, then Parnell would not be about to board a plane. Instead, he would be experiencing considerable discomfort in a sound-proofed room somewhere. Parnell knew better than to be certain of anything in this life, but he was as confident as he could be that Michaels still trusted him, and also that there were no leaks from Walker and the others.

Still, it was just as well that he and Walker would soon be ready to move. Not without genuine regret, Parnell told himself that Michaels would soon be out of time.

CHAPTER 8

Parnell collected a comfortable and anonymous rental car from San Francisco airport, and headed south on 280. In the rear-view mirror he saw the clouds roll low over the hills toward the fog-bound city, but through the windscreen his face was warmed by typical Bay Area sunshine. He wondered why Californians had chosen to locate one of their two world-class cities in the only pocket of their giant state with reliably poor weather.

He turned east off the highway onto Route 84, then south on 82 until he reached Valparaiso. A couple of miles down this road he reached a nondescript office block. He parked in a space marked "reserved", and strode into the building to meet his two young protégés, Seth Gordstock and Jimmy Lau. They arrived quickly at the reception desk to greet him, and Parnell was gratified to see that Gordstock was unable to conceal a wince at the subtle flavour of menace that laced his greeting. "Hello boys. How are we? Enjoying this wonderful sunshine, I hope? How's the beach this time of year?"

It was Lau who responded. "You're joking, right? You think we have time to spend at the beach?" Parnell respected the robust riposte. He had decided some time ago that Lau was made of sterner stuff than his partner. His expression was also harder to read.

"Let's go in," Gordstock suggested, obviously keen to usher Parnell out of sight of their employees. He and Lau would much prefer to have these meetings off-site, but Parnell always insisted on meeting them at the office. To get a feel for the outfit where we are generating so much wealth, he would say.

They took their seats in the meeting room. Parnell placed himself with his back to the window, so that Gordstock and Lau would be looking into the light. Gordstock made nervous small talk while fresh coffee was being brought in. Parnell gave one-word answers, and Lau gazed at him levelly.

"So. You wanted to discuss the latest tech?" Parnell began, once they had the room to themselves.

"Yeah. We're really grateful, of course, but it's just that... well, we're not so comfortable with this one. It doesn't really play to our skill set," Gordstock ventured.

"Different client base," Lau said quietly. "We've never sold to the military before."

Excuses began to tumble out of Gordstock. "It's just that... we don't doubt it's a fantastic achievement and all, but... we're not familiar with the type of application, the market, the bid and procurement processes. We'd need to raise new money because of the sell-in lead time, and our previous backers wouldn't go for it. The buyers would detect our inexperience in their sector a mile off, and surely that would make them feel nervous? They might even ask some difficult questions about where the tech was coming from, and I'm sure none of us want that?"

Gordstock, grinning sheepishly, looked at Lau for support at this point but was silenced by the look on his partner's face. Parnell watched, amused, as Gordstock realised he was talking too much, and extinguished his smile.

Parnell closed his eyes for a second and leaned back in his chair. He opened his eyes and smiled at them - patient, indulgent. "Boys, boys... You're over-thinking this. It's really much simpler than you think."

Parnell harboured no resentment towards the young men sitting opposite. He was not jealous of their easy ride through life, and their assumption of success as their birthright. He thought of them simply as useful idiots. Clever and highly-educated idiots to be sure, but idiots nonetheless. They were both Stanford graduates from privileged, wealthy families, and they had promising careers with one of the tech giants before they caught the start-up bug. They saw an opportunity in the re-shaping of the book industry and left the company where everyone wanted to work, in order to launch a new business model into the flailing publishing industry. It was a good idea, and they worked hard and hired great people. But it never quite took off in the way they hoped, and they found themselves working harder and harder just to stand still.

They let some people go, and moved into cheaper

offices. They pulled in some favours and raised some extra money - they couldn't believe their idea would not work. When a major distribution deal collapsed as a by-product of a corporate restructuring the other side of the country, they knew they had to make a drastic decision. Maybe they could have returned to the tech giant they had left, but more likely they would have ended up taking positions in less prestigious firms - a humiliating climb-down for a pair of golden boys.

They were introduced to Parnell by a mutual friend, a former classmate at Stanford who was never wholly clear about how she knew Parnell. And Parnell had been a godsend - their fairy godmother in drag. He had access to new technologies coming out of a top-secret government lab - technologies that needed to be commercialised without their origin being disclosed. Parnell said he needed people who understood the way that big technology companies work - people who knew how to cross the chasm in technology marketing which enables new products to reach beyond the enthusiasts and early adopters and penetrate the mass market. And he needed people who knew how to keep a secret. He was full of praise for Gordstock and Lau's entrepreneurial spirit, and he said that the fact they had struggled to make a go of their own venture was a positive in his eyes, not a negative.

With their business in the state it was, they were disinclined to look this gift horse too closely in the mouth, and they laughed that there was probably no way they could conduct due diligence on Parnell anyway.

In the last eighteen months, Parnell had handed them files with detailed technical specifications for a dozen patent applications. Most were clever twists on existing technologies, but a few were brand new departures - ingenious new solutions to old problems, and promising forays into new territory. Most of the innovations were framed in the context of publishing, with a couple described as relevant to e-learning. But it was clear to Gordstock and Lau that they were being given unique access to ways of handling data and knowledge which could revolutionise several industries - perhaps all industries.

As instructed, they had proceeded cautiously. They applied for international patent protection on all the ideas, and they licensed three of them to established technology companies - including to former colleagues at the tech giant. This brought in enough money to stave off their creditors and restore their balance sheet to rude health. Everything was looking positive again, and they almost began to persuade themselves that it was their own talent and hard work rather than sheer blind luck which had turned their fortunes around.

Except that now, they sensed, their fairy godmother was turning into a shark.

"Boys, boys... You're over-thinking this. It's really much simpler than you think." Parnell leaned forward. He was enjoying himself, playing the role of a tolerant father bringing his errant sons back into line. He was only a decade older than them, but his life experience was far weightier than theirs. They were not naive young men. They had travelled the world and they understood how it worked. They were ambitious, driven, and had attained and enjoyed a modicum of economic power. But they had seen nothing of the brutality that he had dealt in most of his life. The force of his personality when matched to theirs was overwhelming.

"The military and the intelligence community are gagging for this tech. You'd be surprised how many potential purchasers that is: we have 18 intelligence organisations at the last count. You don't need to sell to them - they will bite your hand off." He laughed. "In fact, I wouldn't be surprised if one or two of them offer you an obscene amount of money in return for a period of exclusivity. They don't always play nicely together.

"You won't need to worry about finance either. Once they see what you've got here they will provide your working capital and thank you for the privilege of letting them do it. Look how much money you're made from the tech we've provided you with so far. This will kick you up to a whole new level."

Gordstock was fidgeting. Parnell leaned back to let him speak.

"Yes, well that's kind-of the point. We're very grateful for what you've done, Lester. Really we are." Parnell's right eyebrow twitched. Lau kicked Gordstock under the table, and Gordstock muttered, "Um, I mean, Mr Parnell."

Although hopelessly outclassed in this encounter, Gordstock was a veteran of innumerable pitches and presentations. A seasoned campaigner in boardrooms and conference calls, he knew how to step up his energy levels and charm. He outlined the argument that he and Lau had carefully worked up over the last 24 hours. Start with flattery, proceed to logic, and build up to an appeal to self-interest.

"You have had a most remarkable impact on our business, Mr Parnell. You have achieved what our other backers and mentors - including some of Silicon Valley's star investors - have been unable to achieve." He projected his most winning smile. "Perhaps one day there will be a Harvard Business School case study written about what you've done here. And as I say, we are hugely grateful.

"But this new tech that you're offering, it's like nothing we have worked with before. I'm not saying we couldn't do it - I have faith in our people. But I have to believe there are firms who already have all the right skills and assets, firms which would do a much better job for you right off the bat. This is great tech - really impressive - and surely it deserves to be commercialised by the best possible team?"

Gordstock looked to Lau for support, and his partner chimed in with a suggestion that was intended to be concisely constructive, but came out as terse. "Wouldn't this be a better fit with In-Q-Tel?"

Parnell's face darkened, but his voice was calm. "I can see why you might think that, boys. But In-Q-Tel is too small. Their annual investment budget is less than $40m, and what we have planned for you boys would absorb too much of that to remain below the radar. And although it's supposed to serve the whole of the intelligence community, it's really an offshoot of the CIA. I couldn't control what it would do with our tech."

"Whereas you can control us?" Lau asked.

Parnell chose to side-step the accusation implicit in Lau's question, but his eyes narrowed as he began to show his hand, closing off their room for manoeuvre.

"Boys, you are committed to this programme, just like me. You got into this voluntarily, with your eyes open. You are not babes in the wood. You are experienced entrepreneurs, and you knew what you are doing. There is no turning back now. A lot of the revenue that you have earned from us is off your books…"

"Because you insisted on that!" Gordstock protested.

"And rightly so," Parnell agreed, smiling coldly. "Don't want the wrong people asking all sorts of awkward questions." He raised his hands in a gesture of reassurance which did nothing at all to reassure. "We can protect you 100% - as long as you remain inside the programme. But I didn't think I would ever need to explain that if you step outside the reservation then that protection ends, and we can do nothing for you. I'm sure I don't need to spell out that the IRS takes an extremely dim view of undisclosed revenue streams. Uncle Sam doesn't like to see his tax income diverted or diminished in any way, and he has a nasty habit of making examples of people who try to do that. He sends them to places where nice middle-class boys like you don't tend to thrive."

"This is blackmail," Lau said quietly.

Parnell unleashed a tiny piece of his enormous

store of violence. Leaning forward and glaring at Lau, he smashed a fist onto the table, and two cups jumped and spilled their coffee across some papers.

"This is loyalty, god-dammit! We saved your asses and gave you a second chance. You don't get to forget that, and you don't get to quit!"

Parnell was again impressed by Lau, who displayed no reaction to this outburst. Out of the corner of his eye he could see that Gordstock was demonstrating no such sang-froid. He leaned back and resumed his cold smile.

"I appreciate your nervousness about stepping into a new type of market, but you'll get the hang of it real soon, I know you will. You're smart boys. I'm gonna set you up with initial meetings with all the customers you need to get you started. You'll find them real nice, normal guys - no problem at all.

"It's an increasingly dangerous world out there, boys, and Uncle Sam needs all the help he can get to make sure he can keep us all safe. Since Snowden, we have to operate differently, and Uncle Sam needs you to demonstrate some gratitude, some loyalty, and yes, some patriotism. I know you won't let us down."

He gestured at the coffee-stained papers, and favoured Gordstock with an un-charming smile. "Now, why don't you rustle us up some more coffee, and then let's get into the details of these exciting new toys."

Lau knew they were beaten. The deal that they thought had saved them had in fact condemned them. But his pride would not let him surrender without at least a show of independence.

"If we have to do this, we at least have the right to know the source of this tech. Where does it all come from?"

Parnell shook his head. "You know I can't tell you the details. Let's just say that within my organisation there is some truly remarkable intelligence."

CHAPTER 9

Matt Metcalfe's astonishing adventures made him a global celebrity. When he was uploaded, and became the world's first superintelligence, he became one of the most famous people on the planet – perhaps the most famous. Inevitably, this turned the lives of his family and his closest friends upside down.

After his abrupt disappearance, his parents, David and Sophie, were immobilised for weeks by shock and grief. They lived in secure accommodation in London provided by the British intelligence services, partly for their own protection, and partly to facilitate the seemingly endless series of interviews by security personnel, police, politicians, and researchers working on artificial intelligence – neuroscientists and computer scientists.

They sleepwalked through these meetings, and through this whole period of their lives. They weren't trying to be unhelpful, but their answers to questions were monosyllabic and generally negative. It took a long time for this to slow the flow of questioners from a flood to a trickle.

They were at least shielded from media attention. They didn't watch TV, they didn't read the papers or news sites, and they gave no interviews. The pressure from the media was immense, and their continued isolation was only possible because David's closest friend, Leo, was an excellent flack-catcher. He fed the TV crews and reporters just enough information to keep them from attempting drastic measures. It wasn't until several months later that he told David and Sophie about the staggering sums he was offered for a one-hour interview with them.

The spotlight was less intense on Matt's close friends, but it was oppressive and life-changing nonetheless.

Matt's best friend Carl was studying politics and philosophy at an Oxford college, and another friend, Jemma, was studying engineering at a different college there. They had both gone to school with Matt in a small town in Sussex, in the south of England, but their experiences of university were very different, and prior to Matt's uploading, they rarely saw each other in term time. Jemma's college was small, sports-obsessed, and highly social, whereas Carl's was more politically conscious, and its students tended to spend less time on college premises. Jemma took up rowing, and spent many evenings in her college bar, while Carl got involved in university societies which held meetings all over town.

Matt's death, revival, and subsequent disappearance changed everything for Carl and Jemma. They both took a few weeks off, and considered dropping out of college for a year. Their colleges granted them both permission to do so, but they eventually decided to stick with their courses: there was nothing they could do for Matt or his family, and they decided they would be better off being forcibly distracted from morbid thoughts about their lost friend.

They were both given rooms in college, where journalists and well-wishers could be kept at bay. They each gave one lengthy interview to the BBC, and then refused to give any others. They were occasionally harassed by journalists and the curious, but this faded in time.

Another consequence was that Carl and Jemma instinctively sought out each other's company far more. They had been friends for years, but they had never been especially close. Now they found they had far more in common with each other than with anyone else. Matt's sudden and massive worldwide celebrity was reflected onto them in diluted form, and when he died, the whole world suddenly treated them as objects of both great curiosity and badly concealed pity. This corroded the friendships they had made since arriving at university, and stopped them making new ones. Nobody but them could fully understand what it was like to see a close friend morph from a normal boy into an international hero and then a super-intelligence which mysteriously disappears.

Worse, they could not talk to anyone about the intensely dramatic final scene of Matt's short career as the first human-level artificial intelligence, when the most powerful people in the world agreed that he could not be allowed to remain alive. In the moments before he disappeared, Matt had gathered his immediate family and closest friends in a soundproofed room that he had checked for surveillance devices. He confided to them that he had anticipated the UN's decision to turn off the machine hosting his uploaded mind, and that he had devised an escape route. He insisted that this fact must remain a secret from the rest of the world - for their sakes rather than for his own. In a piteously brief few seconds, he told them he loved them, and he said goodbye. Then he disappeared.

Like Matt's other confidants, Carl and Jemma stuck religiously to the story that Matt had simply disappeared without warning. It didn't save them from protracted grilling by security personnel, and then from approaches by journalists, but it gave them a clear and simple story to tell. And it was the best way they could think of to honour Matt's memory.

And so Jemma and Carl took to spending evenings together in each other's rooms, and occasionally in Oxford pubs, wordlessly sharing and guarding their momentous secret. They talked about their exam revision and they gossiped about the people back home in their Sussex village, but really they were sharing the burden of being two of the very few people who knew that the world's first human-level artificial intelligence had not disappeared without warning, but was probably still alive in some form, a fugitive somewhere in the internet.

Occasionally, when they thought no one else could

hear, one of them would start to frame a question. "Do you think maybe..." or "Could it be possible that..." But these sentences were never finished. They could never be absolutely certain they were not overheard, or bugged. As time passed it seemed less and less likely that Matt had escaped safely, but neither of them wanted to address that thought head-on.

These evenings brought them closer together, culminating one summery night in late May in an emotional evening in The Trout, a quaint country pub to the north of the town. Carl made a surprisingly perceptive remark which Jemma rewarded with an unusually appreciative smile. Before he really knew what was happening, Carl found himself leaning forward to kiss her. She met him halfway, and somehow they managed to avoid a bump. It was a short kiss - they were two English people in a public place, after all - but they both knew what it meant. They smiled at each other shyly, not knowing what to say next. Jemma suggested that they go back to Carl's college room, which was nearer than hers.

They cycled in silence to Carl's college room and locked the door. Jemma put her arms around Carl's neck, and instinct took over. They made love quickly but tenderly, and then lay in each other's arms, wondering at this transformation of their lives. They both briefly wondered if this had been a mistake which would damage their long-standing friendship. They were relieved to find that conversation still flowed, and that their silences were still comfortable. In the morning they made love again, more slowly, and their relationship was confirmed. They even started to make plans.

Perhaps ironically, the emotional upheaval in their lives meant that Carl and Jemma were less stressed by the final exams than most of their contemporaries. Their colleges, especially Jemma's, had originally earmarked them for firsts, but given what they had gone through, both their tutors and they themselves were content with good 2-1s.

Once their exams were over, they went travelling. In honour of Matt's fascination with the Maya, they flew to Mexico and toured the country by bus. After spending a few weeks in Mexico City and visiting the enormous ruined city of Teotihuacan, they headed south to Oaxaca, and the Zapotec capital at Monte Alban. Then they toured the Mayan cities of Palenque, Chichen-Itza, Edzna, Tulum and Coba. Carl had decided to try his hand at journalism, and he managed to offset some of the cost of the trip by securing a commission to write a few pieces for VisitMexico, the Mexican tourist authority, who hoped that Carl's connection with Matt would confer some prestige and positive PR. They didn't pay much in cash, but they helped with the travel and accommodation.

They also went south to Peru and walked the Inca Trail. Again, the tourist authority was helpful, as Visit Peru was able to provide a permit to visit Macchu-Picchu when none could be obtained through the usual channels in the time available.

Although they loved the trip for the people and the sights, neither Carl nor Jemma came away with anything like Matt's fascination for the Maya. Carl thought their culture was on a par with the Egyptians in terms of sophistication, and the beauty of their art. Jemma thought that was being generous, and couldn't understand why anyone would prefer studying the Maya to studying the ancient Greeks or Romans.

On the long flights and bus journeys they talked about what they would do with their lives - which careers they should target and where they should live. Carl was enjoying his role as a roving writer, which confirmed his interest in being a journalist. Jemma asked whether anyone knew what being a journalist actually meant these days, and whether there was still such a career to go into. Carl insisted that there would always be a demand for well-written articles, whether they appeared in newspapers, blogs, or as scripts for some kind of video. He applied for one the tiny number of trainee positions at the BBC, and was a little surprised to be rejected without interview. Jemma said the Corporation was probably worried that Carl would become the story rather than its writer.

Jemma wanted to work with computers, and specifically on artificial intelligence. She had an aptitude for maths, and had learned some basic coding skills at school. She developed both much further during her engineering course, when she also became proficient in statistics, which underpins a lot of machine learning, the approach to AI which had taken the discipline by storm during the 2010s. In addition, she had always had an interest in psychology and how the human brain works. Matt's experiences were a vivid demonstration of how artificial intelligence was throwing new light on those ancient mysteries. One of the industries where she thought she could apply all these interests was video games.

It was Carl's idea to contact Simon Winchester, the founder of the games company in Brighton who had hired Matt during a university vacation. Winchester was delighted to hear from Jemma, and interviewed her shortly after their return. He questioned her closely about about their trip to Latin America, and then explained that his company was working on a series of cutting-edge games set in Mayan cities. He offered her a job as a trainee programmer, starting as soon as she could.

She and Carl rented a flat in Kemptown, a bohemian area in the east of Brighton with the feel of a self-contained village. Brighton had established its reputation as London-by-Sea, with a fast commuter service to the capital. Property prices were high and rising, but Kemptown residents claimed that it retained a slightly seedy counter-culture charm. Less favourable opinions were available – one wit described it as looking like a place that was helping the police with their enquiries.

Carl started blogging about the history of the area. He delighted in retrieving little gems of information and offering them up to Jemma like nuggets of gold retrieved from a seabed wreck. He was tickled to discover that the man who founded Kemptown and gave it his name - Thomas Kemp - had been obliged to flee the country to avoid his creditors when his development plans went awry.

Carl had a gift for writing lively, provocative prose, and, thanks largely to his tangential role in Matt's story, he was able to build up a sizeable following for his blog. That in turn brought in a few journalistic commissions, initially from the local papers, but increasingly from national and international publishers of newspapers, magazines and blogs. Jemma was charmed by his boyish excitement whenever he landed a commission, although she teased him when he got carried away with his own fluency.

"That's just ... testiculation!" she said one day.

"What's that?" he asked.

"Waving your hands around and talking bollocks!"

Like Matt before her, Jemma found Simon Winchester's company a congenial and stimulating place to work. Her new colleagues were clever and friendly, and they managed to avoid being awed or put off by her celebrity. Several of the company's brightest developers were working on the Maya game - or training environment, as they called it - and she was allocated to that project.

"Our client is the US Department of Defense," Winchester explained. "They are incredibly demanding, which is driving us to do great work. That is good for building up the company's capabilities, although we can't showcase the best stuff as it's highly confidential. But they pay well, and we are creating amazing environments and powerful tools, which can use on other projects."

"You can really see where their money is going," added the woman heading up the project. "We are putting ten times the usual detail into the rendering of the buildings and the costumes, and we are using professional actors with green screen technology to develop highly realistic action sequences, with huge numbers of branching scenarios. It adds up to a highly realistic experience for the gamer, although we can't play it ourselves the way the end-users will, because the interface modules are being developed elsewhere."

"Post-Snowden cautiousness, apparently," Winchester explained. "They divide projects up more now, to prevent any one contractor from knowing too much about the whole. And I'm afraid they also make us all sign this pile of documents." He passed her a folder across the table, thick with densely-typed papers.

"Our lawyers have gone through it all and they tell me that it is very thorough, but there's nothing in it to worry about. You can't work on the project without signing them, though, so take some time to read through them before signing." He smiled as he stood up to leave the room. "Not too much time, though: we're up against a tight deadline!"

A couple of days later Jemma spotted her first opportunity to make a significant difference to the project. Her colleagues were talking about how working at such high definitions threw up unexpected problems, one of which was making buildings look convincingly substantial.

"There's an odd effect that when you include a lot of the ornamental detail that covered Mayan buildings: they can look somehow lightweight - as if they are stage sets. We've tried a lot of different approaches, and it's OK, but we're not completely satisfied yet."

"Have you spoken to any architects about it?" Jemma asked.

"We consulted a few, but they didn't really seem to understand what we were talking about, and they were asking silly money to even look into the problem."

"I might know someone who could help with that," Jemma said.

The architect Jemma called was her old friend Alice, Matt's girlfriend for the last two years of his life. Alice was working with her father, a property developer, on residential properties around Sussex, while studying architecture at Brighton. Unlike Carl and Jemma, she had dropped out of college for a year after Matt's disappearance, and she had also dropped out of all social life.

Matt's revival as a silicon-based mind had been completely convincing for Alice, and although she could neither see nor touch her boyfriend, she knew it was really Matt, and she was overjoyed to have him returned to her. She spent painfully little time with him in his new form, but she delighted in seeing how his cleverness and his kindness were not just restored but amplified, and getting more so by the minute. When he disappeared again so soon after his return it had been a hammer blow. The mystery of what really happened to him only made it worse.

She stopped going to pubs and parties, and didn't return calls from her friends. The friends didn't know how to respond, and after a while, most of them stopped calling. Her father urged her to go out, but she said she wouldn't know what to say to anyone. All she wanted to do in the evenings was sit at home and watch escapist television. Jemma and Carl managed to drag her out to a bar to celebrate their return from America, but the conversation flagged badly, and Alice went home early.

So it was not without some trepidation that Jemma phoned Alice to see if she would be interested in doing some freelance consulting work on a game development project. To her surprise and delight, Alice responded positively. She apologised for having been so hard to reach, and explained that she found it easier to bury herself in work. She was feeling guilty about becoming so remote, and she thought that a work-based project with a friend and with other people close to her own age could be a great way to ease herself back into the world.

Using some subtle tricks of perspective, Alice was able to endow the buildings in the Maya game with more heft. She began to spend more time with Carl and Jemma in Brighton, and they discussed how Matt would have reacted to the irony that his friends, previously so sceptical about his interest in ancient Mesoamerican culture, were now creating one of the world's most realistic virtual versions of its cities.

CHAPTER 10

The smiling, smooth-faced woman in the pale blue headscarf smiled. "Have a good flight, Miss West."

As Rebecca West joined the queue for the security scanner, she wondered for the hundredth time whose interest was served by making the process of getting onto a plane such an irritating process. Who gained from the seemingly endless queuing opportunities? Queue to collect tickets, queue to go through security (remove shoes, open bags, remove laptops and liquids), queue for passport control, queue at boarding gate, queue to leave the boarding gate area (bonus queues if getting on and off a bus to the plane), queue to board the plane, queue to actually sit down. The previous weekend she and a friend had taken the Eurostar to Paris, and the queuing, scanning, and searching had taken a tenth of the time that she was wasting today. Surely a terrorist could cause as much damage by blowing up a train inside the Channel Tunnel as by blowing up a single aircraft?

She tried to make the time go faster by playing out

an imaginary conversation in her mind - a discussion between two senior people in her organisation. The people were caricatures, and the tone and the vocabulary were implausible, but some version of this meeting probably was the reason why she was at the airport today.

"It's a fool's errand," the first man said, propelling a fat cloud of cigar smoke out of the gravity well of his deep leather armchair. "There's no chance he'll agree. Why are we wasting the air fare?"

"Because we can't not," replied the second, ensconced in similar luxury. "And because he just might surprise us when he hears about what the Cousins are up to."

"You don't believe that any more than I do. He'll discount those reports as fabricated, and they wouldn't change his mind even if he did believe them."

"You're probably right, but you know as well as I do that we have to ask. Not least because we'll be crucified later on when the shit hits the fan and certain people find out that we didn't even ask the question. The trick is to send someone who stands a half-decent chance of not getting their head bitten off, and who will actually get something out of the mission. Pass the port, old man."

Rebecca smiled to herself at the improbability of that particular phrase being used today, even in the location for her imaginary discussion, the Travellers Club on Pall Mall.

"So who do you have in mind?" the first man asked.

"Rebecca West," the second man answered.

"Interesting. Why her?"

"Because Metcalfe will be a tiny bit disconcerted, initially. He'll be expecting someone of his own age - someone senior. When he first claps eyes on young West he'll be insulted that we didn't send someone older, but then he'll realise that she's got as much going on between the ears as in front of them, and he'll pay just a bit more attention than he might otherwise."

The first man frowned skeptically, but the second man forged ahead.

"It's a long shot, I grant you, but it's as good a shot as any. And it will be good experience for young West. She's doing well, but she's in that fallow period where she probably feels she's not accomplishing much for King and Country, and her friends will be making out like bandits in the City. She'll probably be feeling some remorse as she visits their flashy riverside apartments, and compares them to her rented studio in Wimbledon. Pop her in front of a global celebrity with an important job to do - even if it's an impossible job that she can't tell her chums about. It'll do wonders for her morale."

"So it's a training exercise, then?" the first man enquired. "Or an incentive programme?"

"That's just a side benefit, and you can forget about switching the cost back on to my budget, you devious old bastard!" The two men grinned at each other, and vanished, as Rebecca West composed her face for passport control.

Finally seated on the plane, with a glass of champagne in hand before take-off, she started reading the briefing papers on the man she was flying to meet.

There was very little in them that she didn't already know. Given the extensive and privileged sources available to the people who compiled the documents, that was testament to the intense public scrutiny that he and his family had been under for the last few months, ever since his son became perhaps the most famous 21 year-old in the world.

****

At exactly the same moment, several thousand miles in the direction Rebecca was travelling, an unusual man met an unusual death. Charles Lin was an exceptionally tall Chinese who worked the night shift, emptying bins and cleaning work surfaces in a science park in Shanghai. He was coming out of the toilet in his small apartment, and he barely saw the equally large man who used a club hammer to land a very hard blow to his forehead. It killed him instantly.

The intruder was powerful, with broad shoulders and a short haircut, a broken nose and cauliflower ears. He caught Charles's body deftly as it slumped, dragged it to the narrow single bed which was one of the few pieces of furniture in the apartment and laid it out flat. He placed two fingers on Charles's neck to check for signs of a pulse, then he changed out of his own clothes and into clothes from Charles's wardrobe. He put his own clothes into a holdall, collected the security pass and the door key from Charles's tiny kitchen table, and opened the door to the room just wide enough for him to see out but not be seen.

He watched as Charles's neighbours, also cleaners at the science park, descended the stairs, and left the apartment block to board a bus. When he was confident that none of Charles's night shift colleagues were left in the building, he traced their steps down the three flights of stairs and crossed the road to a small, grubby silver car. He followed the bus on its short journey to the science park. He waited as the other cleaners disembarked the bus, and insinuated himself into the group as they entered the park, scanned their badges, and scattered throughout the park to their designated areas. To avoid detection, he was wearing a modest amount of make-up, but he relied more on the fact that Charles Lin walked with the stoop that afflicts many tall people, and the universally acknowledged fact that cleaners are invisible to other humans.

As he reached his destination he pulled on a pair of white latex gloves. He was only in the office for five minutes, just long enough to determine that the best location for a hidden microphone was a framed photograph on the wall behind the desk. Despite the regular cleaning regime, there were enough traces of dust along the top of the frame to indicate that the painting was never moved. Having placed the tiny microphone and tested it, he left the office, and adopted a pained, bent-over posture as he left the building, suggesting illness to anyone he might encounter.

He returned to his car and drove back to the cleaners' compound. He took a bottle of baijiu from the boot of his car and pushed it into the holdall containing his own clothes, and returned to Charles's room. He changed back into his own clothes, then he forced the neck of the bottle into Charles's mouth, and spent a few minutes pouring as much of the alcohol into the dead man's mouth as would stay inside - although of course a lot of the liquid ran out again, and soaked Charles's bedsheets. Then he waited a few more minutes before hoisting Charles's limp body by the armpits and dragging it backwards out of the room.

Pausing to look up and down the corridor and check there were no witnesses, he dragged the body to the top of the stairs. There he lifted the body up to balance on its lifeless feet, turned it round to face the stairs. With one swift movement, he shoved the body out into the stairwell, and propelled himself away from the stairs, and along the corridor towards another staircase. By the time Charles's body landed at the bottom of the flight of stairs it was travelling fast, and head-first. His head suffered an impact similar to the one which had killed him.

When the first resident came out of her room to investigate the crashing noise, a generous pool of blood was already forming under the sprawling body. By the time her screams had attracted another half-dozen neighbours, the intruder was across the road and opening the door of his car.

****

"Come in, Miss West," David said, and thanked his assistant for showing his guest to his office. Rebecca thought she saw an amused look on her host's face as she walked past him into the office, but it was a fleeting moment, and she could not be sure. As she entered, she took in the room's decoration, comparing it to her understanding of the man gleaned from her briefing papers, and what she had absorbed from the media before.

The office was small, and contained nothing expensive, as far as she could see: no statues, no luxurious furniture or equipment. The decoration was simple, even spartan. The only picture in the room, hung behind the desk, was a large framed photograph of David's famous son, taken shortly before he was shot. The beige sofa and the pine desk were from IKEA, and the high-backed desk chair looked comfortable but not extravagant. By contrast, she had seen Eames originals in some of the rooms she had passed on her way to David's office. The window did have an attractive view out onto the superbly landscaped park, with ornamental trees and an artificial lake, but the window was normal size, not floor-to-ceiling like those in some of the other rooms she had passed. This all chimed with David's reputation as a modest, frugal man.

Rebecca looked at the photograph of Matt Metcalfe, and waited for David to comment. It seemed as good a way as any to begin the conversation.

"He would have been 22 in a couple of weeks," David said quietly. He was standing beside her.

"Birthdays are the worst, aren't they." Rebecca replied, keeping her eyes on the picture.

"Birthdays and Christmas, yes," David said. He looked at Rebecca sharply. "You've lost someone? A family member?"

"My mother," Rebecca said flatly, without turning. "She died six years ago. Cancer."

"I'm sorry to hear that," David said, shaking his head. "We really should have got past that by now. The lack of political will is shocking. But I suppose we're all to blame, really. Ultimately, politicians do what we demand of them. If enough people had insisted on proper funding for effective life extension technologies a decade ago we would have them by now." He gestured towards the sofa and walked round behind the desk to sit in the chair.

"That's not your field, though, is it?" she asked as she sat.

"We're in brain preservation. Not life extension as most people think of it, perhaps, but still trying to make death optional. Different approaches, similar outcome."

He closed a folder on his desk. His tone became brisker, more businesslike. "So how can I help you, Miss West?"

"I imagine you've been expecting a visit from someone like me?" she replied.

Again she saw the amused expression, and this time it remained long enough for her to be sure. "Not exactly like you, no. I imagined they would send someone…"

"Older?" she interrupted.

"Older, yes. And to be honest, male. I would have thought your organisation would send a man. Is that unfair of me?"

"A little, perhaps," Rebecca smiled. "Even the most

conservative organisations do move with the times - eventually. But we haven't established which organisation you think I represent."

"Ah, so you want me to go first," David said, returning the smile. "No harm in that, I suppose. Well let's see, your email said you were from ICE, the Inter-departmental Co-ordination Executive. Which - according to a couple of civil service friends I asked - does not actually exist. Which leads me to think you are from the intelligence services."

"Correct," Rebecca agreed with a straight face. "MI5, to be precise."

"Well that's very frank," David said, impressed. "I know you people no longer have to pretend that you don't exist, but I didn't expect you to be quite so forthcoming about it."

"It's MI6 whose existence was officially denied until 1994. We've been out of the shrubbery for much longer. And regarding your earlier question, we've had two female Directors-General now." She smiled again.

"And a third before you're through, I imagine?" David asked.

Rebecca laughed. "That would be nice, but there's a long way to go before that could happen!"

"Well, at least you didn't say you were from Universal Export," David grinned. "But since we're in China, I'd have thought this was a job for Six. Don't they handle the international stuff?"

"Well, I'm here to see if we can tempt you back home!" Rebecca said.

David leaned forward, his elbows on the desk, his

face and tone more serious. "And how are you going to do that, Miss West? I've been approached by dozens of research institutes back home, both government and private. Some of them made me quite eye-watering offers, and others were very shady outfits indeed. I've been approached by lots of foreign outfits, too, of course. You know all this already, I'm sure. So what's your pitch? Why will you succeed where they have failed?" He paused a moment, pretending to deliberate, and then sat erect and declared with mock surprise and widened eyes, "Ooh, are you going to blackmail me?"

"Not my department, I'm afraid," Rebecca deadpanned. "And I imagine the ones that do go in for that sort of thing – assuming there are any - would have done so already, if they had anything on you. But it's an interesting idea, and maybe they just haven't thought of it yet. I'll pass it on and maybe they'll be able to work something up." She smiled. "So really, you'd better just agree and come back home now."

"I think I'll pass," David replied with a grin. "So go on, then. What exactly is your pitch, Miss West?"

"I'm hoping to get you to see the bigger picture, Dr Metcalfe. We have reason to believe that certain other countries are getting close to creating artificial general intelligences, by what I understand is called the incremental method. You know much more about this than I do, so please forgive me if I make any schoolgirl errors. They link up a collection of state-of-the-art narrow AI systems which perform different tasks like pattern recognition, document search, natural language processing and so on. They pass enormous quantities of data through these systems, and ask them increasingly sophisticated questions. We believe that some of these systems are getting very close to passing the Turing test for human-level intelligence."

Rebecca paused, watching for a reaction. "Am I making sense so far?" she asked.

"Admirably," David replied gallantly.

"I'm sure you can guess which two countries are the leading contenders in this race?" she asked.

"I suppose you're referring to the US and China," David replied. "The world's two AI superpowers."

"Exactly," Rebecca nodded. "Now as you can tell, I'm neither a neuroscientist, nor an AI expert. But we have people who are, and they can explain to you in far more detail why we believe this is happening - the evidence we have obtained. I know you would want to go through that in detail before making any firm decisions. My job is just to persuade you to think seriously about it, not least by putting it into geo-political context."

"You have my full attention," David replied. The amusement was still there, but Rebecca sensed – and hoped - that he was sincere.

"I don't suppose I'm telling you anything that hasn't already occurred to you, but we believe it would be dangerous if the two economic and military super-powers also possessed the world's only two superintelligences.

"Our first concern is geo-political. The dynamics of a duopoly in superintelligence are at best unjust, and at worst unstable. The two powers controlling super-intelligences would either collaborate to prioritise their interests over those of all the other nations in the world, or they would fail to collaborate, and engage in a potentially calamitous rivalry with each other. A code war, to put it crudely, which could be even more dangerous than the cold war."

"You know, this all sounds rather old-fashioned," David said. "You could be the Duke of Wellington or Lord Castlereagh sitting there, issuing dire warnings about the need to maintain an appropriate balance of power."

"Actually that's not a bad comparison. We do find ourselves once again in a position where Britain holds the key to peace. We can prevent a dangerous concentration of power because of a unique resource. Namely, you."

David smiled. "Very flattering." His head tilted slightly. "You do know I'm a Scot, Miss West?"

Rebecca smiled back. "Yes I do, but that still means you're British – for the time being at least. Whatever the future constitutional arrangements, Scots have been at the heart of British politics for centuries. Scottish thinkers led the enlightenment. Scottish businessmen, economists, generals and soldiers built the empire. That isn't likely to change."

"I'm not so sure about that, but let's play this rather grandiose vision of yours through," David said. "Let's suppose that China and the US each create an AGI, and that rapidly leads to them each owning a super-intelligence. And let's assume for a moment that they both manage to control their superintelligences and harness their powers to greatly extend the gap between themselves and the rest of the world. So the US and China are now pulling far ahead of the rest of us in economic and military capability. Along come the plucky Brits with a third superintelligence. How exactly does that help the world?"

Rebecca took a deep breath, and laid out her argument. "It makes it much harder for the states which own superintelligences to maintain a conspiracy against the interests of the rest of the world. Sure, there could be an oligopoly, and the owners of superintelligences might well decide that ownership of the technology should not be shared. That is what has happened with the technology of nuclear weapons, for instance. But tripartite negotiations are much more complicated than bilateral ones, and a stitch-up would be harder to create and maintain.

"It would also help with the other scenario - the one where the two powers fail to negotiate a collaborative duopoly and enter into a sort of cognitive arms race, going head to head, so to speak, with their superintelligences. The presence of a third superintelligence would act as a brake on that confrontation."

David's eyes narrowed and he shook his head slightly. "Hmm. You seem to have made an awful lot of assumptions in there. Perhaps you and your colleagues have worked all this out in detail, but it seems pretty tenuous to me. I can just as easily imagine two powers ganging up against the other, with potentially disastrous consequences all round. Or, as you say, an oligopoly forming, in which the three powers would enjoy an even greater advantage over the rest of the world."

"It is complex," admitted Rebecca. "My colleagues have played out a lot of scenarios, and we are convinced that three superintelligences are better than two, in the context of global power contests. We would welcome the opportunity to walk you through the thinking. But there is another, perhaps more compelling reason for wanting a third AGI on the scene. And wanting it to be one that you helped create."

"Which is?"

"As I mentioned, the US and China are working on the incremental development route. Assuming they are successful, this will lead to new intelligences - conscious machines - which have no shared mental history with us humans. They will, if you like, be totally alien. We want to create an AGI by the reverse engineering approach - where an individual brain is scanned in minute detail and its carbon wiring diagram and processing patterns are replicated in silicon."

"You want to create another Matt," David interrupted.

Acutely aware of the sensitivity of this moment, Rebecca continued slowly. "Not another Matt. We aren't stupid enough – or, frankly, callous enough - to think that Matt can be re-created. Matt was a unique individual. I never met him, of course, but like every single person on this planet, I watched what happened to him with fascination, horror, and a great deal of admiration."

She paused to see if she had fallen off the verbal tightrope. David's face was impassive, giving nothing away. Controlling her nerves, she continued.

"You yourself have said on a number of occasions that a superintelligence modelled on a human brain is far more likely to share our most fundamental concerns - or at least to understand them in a visceral way, and to have empathy for us."

David's expression was grim, but he nodded assent.

"If we are going to live in a world populated by a very small number of superintelligences - and very possibly be ruled by them - then we think that at least one of them should be cognitively descended from a natural-born human."

"The Human Brain Project in Lausanne is doing that job for us," David suggested. "They don't say that explicitly, for fear of losing their funding. But it's pretty clear that is their real objective."

"Too slow," Rebecca replied, shaking her head. "They have a comprehensive wiring diagram for a mouse brain, but they can't use it to model a mouse mind." She leaned forwards. "David, you have done it before. It was a miracle. We need you to do it again."

She stopped. She wasn't sure she had made the best possible pitch. She worried that she had omitted some key arguments, and fumbled some of the ones she had deployed. But she had done her best. David said nothing, and Rebecca struggled to keep her face impassive.

Eventually David responded. "You have put your case well. As well as any of the people who have been to see me before, in fact, and much better than some of them. I'd be happy to report that back to your people, whoever they are, but I don't suppose they would be interested. Because I'm afraid it changes nothing.

"Look, I saw what was happening to Matt towards the end. His mind was growing at an incredible rate. He was still recognisably Matt when he... when he shut himself down, but he probably wouldn't have been a few weeks later. When the first superintelligences arrive, I see three possible outcomes. One, we find a way to merge our minds with theirs. Two, they just leave. Or three, we are done for. Humans could not tolerate being the dumb country cousins of the smartest creatures on the planet. Our creations might destroy us on purpose or by accident, and if they don't, then we will probably destroy ourselves.

"Uploading is our only safe future, but it's going to be years before uploading minds becomes a reliable, affordable technology. And I don't think we can do it ourselves: we're probably going to need superintelligence to get there. I'm not even sure that Vic and I could repeat the process if we wanted to. We never spoke publicly about the false starts we had along the way - they weren't pretty. We certainly could not do it at scale. So before any more superintelligences are created, we need a way to keep today's humans alive or in stasis until reliable uploading technologies are available. That is my project, and I won't be diverted from it."

Rebecca opened her mouth to respond but David put up a hand. He was not finished.

"I'm sorry to say this, Miss West, but even if I was persuaded to go back to working on uploading, it wouldn't be for the British government. It probably wouldn't be for any government, but it certainly wouldn't be for ours. The British were just as discredited as the Americans by the scandals which followed Snowden's revelations. GCHQ was like an enthusiastic puppy trotting along at the heels of the NSA, intercepting as many communications as it could digest with no regard for legality or due process. The childish names it gave its hacking tools - Nosey Smurf, Gumfish, Foggybottom and the rest - just showed its contempt for everyone outside the precious circle of the so-called intelligence community. And don't get me started on Brexit...

"I'm sorry, Miss West, but you've had a wasted journey."

****

Thousands of miles away, on the other side of the planet, John Michaels winced. He had heard these allegations many times before. He did not agree with them, and he thought he could persuade a genuinely open-minded person that they were unreasonable. But it was painful to hear them from the mouth of someone he had immense respect for. He had never met David Metcalfe, but he had been hugely impressed by the man's technical achievement, and also by the dignity of his conduct throughout his son's adventure, and the aftermath.

But far, far more powerful than his discomfort at hearing the allegations was his sense of relief. He had been hoping desperately that he would not have to ask Parnell to give another secret mission to the man he knew only as the Soldier.

CHAPTER 11

Mrs Gwon would not have recognised her son. It would in fact have taken her some time to recognise the form as a human body, let alone her beloved Hiro. And she would have needed a strong torch, as there is very little natural light six hundred metres below the surface of the ocean.

A powerful beam would have picked out an incomplete face, with one bulging and sightless eye. The other eye socket was accusingly empty, and what little flesh remained on the face was obviously putrid, having been only partly eaten by numerous inquisitive and hungry undersea animals. Various species of fish had nibbled, but found it distasteful. A shark had taken a greedy bite, but didn't like it enough to come back for more. So the remains were abandoned to the smaller, slower feeders - creatures which could move slowly across an organism, checking and assaying, choosing and rejecting tiny parcels of potential food, making the most efficient use of every last gram of the energy left in the carcass of the human who no longer had any use for it.

The body lay across a pile of jagged rocks, arched backwards in an agonised posture. It swayed slightly, as tides and currents animated the water. A belt around the corpse's waist had come loose during the body's journey to its current location, because two of the buckles which held it in place were undone. The belt was snagged on a particularly sharp jut of rock, and each time the body swayed, the material was scraped along the edges of the rock. The movements were slight and the damage to the belt developed very slowly, over days rather than minutes. But it was a contest the belt could not win: eventually it snapped, and surrendered the body to the whims of the ocean.

The belt and its weights sank to a deeper level of the sea. The body itself rested on the pile of rocks for a while, as if exhausted by its slow-motion liberation. Then it moved, a tired and ghostly dancer picking itself up painfully, drifting clumsily away from its resting place. The tides and currents carried the body on a slow journey to a new home.

****

On a quiet beach, near a small village north of Yang-yang on the Sea of Japan, Park Min-Seo had given up trying to interest her father in her project to categorise all the pebbles in the world by size and colour. For about thirty seconds she was convinced that the project merited at least one lifetime's dedication, but her father was more interested in his mobile phone. She neither questioned nor resented this competing attraction, she just accepted it as part and parcel of the lamentable failure of adults to prioritise correctly. Min-Seo was a placid, happy child, secure in the knowledge that she was the centre of her father's world as well as her own, and that if she really insisted, he would abandon everything to pay attention to her needs. She had learned that her life was even more pleasurable if she didn't insist too often.

Anyway, a promising diversion had appeared on her tiny horizon. She had spotted an amorphous object in a nearby pool of water. Her father smiled as he watched her chubby legs propel her towards this fresh object of enthusiastic enquiry. Then he frowned as he saw a new text message arrive from his lawyers: he had learned to expect nothing but bad news from them.

As Min-Seo approached the object it became less amorphous, and began to take on a succession of forms. She was wary of this changeling creature. Some instinct told her it offered frights rather than pleasure. But she was fascinated, and she edged closer as it transformed in turns from a shapeless blob, to a pile of old clothes, to a pile of clothes concealing something, and finally to an object that she only partly recognised, but which she knew she should flee. She could not have given it a name, but some ancient part of her brain recognised it as the decayed remains of what had once been a human being.

Her father, startled, looked up from his phone in anguish at the sound of his daughter's scream. As he ran headlong towards her and scooped her up in his arms he experienced a succession of powerful emotions. Fear eased into relief as he realised that she was unhurt, but the relief was followed quickly by disgust and dread as he saw the skeleton wrapped up in the clothes, and a few paltry remains of human flesh. He had seen a dead body once before, at a funeral, but this was something new and terrible. This was corruption and decay, the ugly side of nature's mechanics, which no parent wants their infant to see.

As he walked briskly away from the body he held Min-Seo tight against his chest and she buried her face in his neck. She sobbed deeply, and he stroked her hair as tenderly as he had ever done. As he took out his phone to call the police he prayed that Min-Seo would not be haunted by this vision in the nights and years to come.

****

South Korea's police forces were organised on a national basis, and it took the head of the Yangyang police station precisely three minutes to decide that Min-Seo's discovery was a matter that needed to be brought to the immediate attention of his bosses in Seoul. It then took another four hours until the corpse was identified by dental records as the body of Gwon Hiro, former bodyguard to one of the country's top scientists, whose plane had gone missing on a routine flight some six weeks before.

That much became public knowledge just minutes later, thanks to TV and radio broadcasts transmitted by the small but tenacious gang of journalists who had gathered at the beach when they heard about a mysterious body being washed up there. There was an immediate explosion of speculation about how the body had got to the beach, and renewed discussion about what had happened to the plane, and the whereabouts of the bodies of its other three missing passengers: the scientist, the pilot, and a female flight attendant.

There was another important piece of additional information which was never released to the curious public: the existence of a bullet-shaped hole in the skull's forehead. One of the few people who did hear about that was the intelligence liaison officer at the US Embassy in Seoul, who took an urgent call from his opposite number in South Korea's Ministry of Foreign Affairs building in Seoul's Jongno District.

"We haven't released this information yet," the Korean official confided. "We're working through scenarios of how best to use it. Obviously the North is responsible for this outrage, and there's going to be an almighty row. Certainly we intend to make a very big fuss about it: we've caught those bastards red-handed this time - and this time they will pay."

"Look, I can understand your anger about this," the US liaison officer replied. "I'd be feeling exactly the same in your shoes. Let me suggest that you sit on that information for a bit. You're going to want our support on this, I imagine, and that will be a lot easier for us to provide if we can be involved in the response strategy right from the start. In fact, can I send a couple of our own forensics people over there to look at the body?

That will help to get the right people up to speed fast."

"I have no problem with that. But hurry. Some of our more excitable people are calling for drastic measures - even without knowing about the forensics."

"Understood," said liaison. "I can have a team there within a couple of hours, and meanwhile I'll get a cable off to the people in Washington who'll need to be in the loop on this."

****

The fourth and fifth names on the distribution list for the resulting cable were those of John Michaels and his boss, Chuck Naylor. Michaels swore under his breath as he read it. He stalked out of his office and headed upstairs.

"This is what comes of using freelancers," Naylor said by way of greeting.

"Good morning, sir. I presume you're referring to the Korean situation?" Michaels replied.

"How the hell did this clusterfuck happen? You promised me that plane and everything in it would disappear, never to be seen again."

"Indeed I did, and that was of course the brief. Obviously something unexpected happened. In fact shit happened, as it sometimes will. The question is, what are we going to do about it now? I can see two main options."

Naylor sighed. He was accustomed to being several moves behind Michaels at any given moment, and had given up trying to second-guess his subordinate.

Naylor was a career bureaucrat, a hardened veteran of many political struggles within the organisation. It had made him gruff, but it had not stolen his dignity, or his dry sense of humour. He knew instinctively when to take control and dictate the direction, and when to let someone else take the lead. With Michaels, he usually chose the latter, although not without a display of exasperation. "Go on," he breathed.

"We can't allow an extended public squabble about this for two reasons. First, with both Koreas genuinely convinced that they are in the right, it might actually lead to a shooting war, which would be disastrous. And second, there is the outside chance that something else will turn up which could implicate a third party. I'm still confident that nothing can lead back to us, but it could get messy."

"You don't say!" Naylor exploded.

Michaels' voice remained calm, but it took on a steely quality. "So either we persuade the South to drop the matter ourselves, or we persuade the North to make some substantial concessions in return for the South's forbearance."

"Oh. I see. Well that's straightforward, then," Naylor said without bothering to temper his sarcasm. "Only... well, let me see. First off, this is the State Department's briar patch, not ours. And second, how the hell do you propose that we persuade either of the Koreas to do what you want?"

"Yes, it is State's jurisdiction," Michaels agreed. "But if we move fast, they will still be working out how to brief the President by the time we have sorted this out. Here's the thing: they don't have Chan. And in this neck of the woods, China is the key." He gave his boss a grim smile which was, given the circumstances, not without warmth. He turned to leave, adding, "I take it you approve of my proposed approach…"

"Given that I don't know what your approach is…" Naylor began to protest. Seeing that Michaels was already out of the room and beyond hearing range he smiled in turn, and continued, "Given that, I just hope you can pull it off!"

****

"You've heard the news from Korea this morning, I imagine?" Michaels said into the phone as he closed his door.

"Yes," Chan replied. "Most unfortunate. Most… how do you say? Delicate."

"I'm sure you share wholeheartedly our dual objectives in this affair: first, to avoid any guns going off, and second, to reduce the chances that clever people will start asking themselves who stood most to gain from the decapitation of the world's third most promising AI research project.

"These would appear most desirable outcomes," Chan agreed. "You have a plan for how to make them happen?

"No," Michaels replied casually. "But I think you do." His tone turned serious. "Look Chan, obviously I accept that this blunder is on us. I don't know what went wrong, and I don't suppose I ever will. I have faith in that operative: he is thorough and effective, but sometimes... well, sometimes stuff just happens. You can tease me as much as you like, and I'm going to owe you a big one. But this is no time for negotiations, OK?

Chan's voice gave nothing away. but Michaels felt sure he was smiling at the other end of the phone. "Go on," was all he said.

"OK, so we know you have been frustrated by the North for some time. You haven't felt able to rein them in because they are so fragile that humiliating them might make them do something stupid." He paused. Chan kept him waiting a few seconds before repeating, "Go on."

"This gives you an opportunity. You can tell the North that they have gone too far this time, and they are going to have to make a concession to the South. A big concession. You can tell them if they make this concession you can arrange with the Yankees for this episode to be brushed under the carpet and avoid the humiliation."

"What is this concession?" Chan asked.

"The thing we both want," Michaels replied. "The thing we have both wanted for a long time. De-activation of their nuclear warheads, with a regular programme of inspection by your people."

"And if they refuse? They will not like to lose face," Chan asked.

"They won't refuse. You've been looking for the right lever for months now. This gives you the perfect combination of carrot and stick. And they'd lose a lot more face if it was widely known that they go around killing innocent civilians - including women - and making a botch of the job."

"Yes, I can see that," Chan smiled. "Even they would prefer not to stain their reputation in that fashion."

****

Two men walked towards each other from opposite sides of the large room, skirting a large rectangular pool of shallow water. When they met, they shook hands and also bowed politely to each other. One of them gestured towards the steps of the temple that was reflected in the pool. They sat.

Few of the other people in the room would have recognised that the men were Korean and Chinese. Fewer still would have been able to understand the Mandarin Chinese they began to speak in.

"I love this room. It is one of my favourite places in Manhattan," the Chinese man opened.

"It's a good choice. Not likely that anyone here will overhear us, or understand what we are saying," the Korean replied.

"Yes, when I was first appointed to the Chinese UN delegation here, many years ago, I arranged to meet a couple of people in the Astor Court, another of my favourite rooms in this museum. But I quickly realised that many of the other visitors could understand what we were saying."

The Korean man was looking around, taking in the reasons for his companion's admiration. Behind them stood the main body of the Temple of Dendur, a remarkably well-preserved structure from the Roman era. It was gifted by the Egyptian government in 1965 as thanks for the USA's involvement in a gigantic exercise to re-locate a number of temples to save them from being submerged by the creation of the Aswan High Dam.

One entire wall of the large museum hall was sloping plate glass, and on the other side lay Central Park, ringed by some of Manhattan's most iconic skyscrapers, a roll call of the twentieth century's finest architectural styles. This combination of nature with classic Egyptian and American architecture could not fail to impress even the Korean, who was politically required to despise it. He steered his attention back to the matter in hand.

"We are preparing to denounce the vile actions of the South, and our entire army is being mobilised. I assume we have your full support."

"I am afraid you do not," replied the Chinese. "We want you to back down and sign the agreement that we requested last February."

The Korean was visibly shocked. "What? But we are innocent of this crime! The South probably knows that, but whether they do or not, they have not a shred of evidence that we were involved. Because we were not!"

"Be that as it may," the Chinese continued amiably, "it is exactly the sort of thing you might have done, and everyone will believe that you did. And I am sure you can appreciate that with our current activities on the world stage, we cannot be associated with this kind of thing."

"But this is... this is blackmail!" the Korean protested.

The Chinese looked around, and made a pacifying gesture with his hands. "If we are going to continue this discussion here I would prefer that we keep our voices down." He paused to give the other man time to calm himself. "Now please listen carefully. I understand that our friends in Washington can persuade the South to bury the news about the body if we can persuade you to agree to the February arrangement. This scandal will completely go away. In return, you will de-activate your nuclear warheads and agree to a regular inspection programme by Chinese experts. No other country would be involved."

He held up his hand to prevent the other man from interrupting. "I have to advise you that this is not negotiable. We have come to the turning point. If you wish to retain my government's support in any shape or form you will agree to this, and quickly. I am sorry. I know this will be... uncomfortable for you, and your leader will be greatly displeased. But there is no alternative. You will understand that it would be... inadvisable for your government to continue its current policy of isolation and hostility towards the West if it lost our support."

The rest of the conversation was perfunctory and brief, but both men knew that a very significant milestone had been reached. They parted with bows that were very slightly shallower than the ones they had exchanged on meeting.

As the two men left the room, another visitor

emerged from behind one of the two pharaonic statues which stood on the far side of the rectangular pool of water. He pushed the baseball cap back up his forehead and ejected a memory card from the camera that hung from his shoulder. In an American accent he spoke into a mike pinned to his lapel.

"It went pretty much as we hoped. I'm transmitting the recording to you now."

CHAPTER 12

"Welcome, guys. It's great to finally meet you!"

The smiles were broad and the handshakes forceful. These were strong men who knew how to use their strength, and how to appraise it in others.

Walker stepped back, and sat on the edge of a desk as he spoke. The newcomers, three men of Chinese origin, remained on their feet, their postures betraying long hours of standing to attention on parade grounds.

"I know that Scott and Younger here have given you a preliminary briefing," Walker continued, "and of course they have checked you out with some of our other colleagues that you've done assignments with." He allowed a lazy smile to spread across his broad features. "You checked out good."

"Cuadrelio and Bergsson here are joining the gang too. Me and Scott and Younger were in the Rangers with these guys, and I'm pumped to be working with them again." He jerked a thumb in Cuadrelio's direction. "Cuadrelio has gone all bureaucratic on us and works for the F-B-I." He raised his eyebrows and elongated the initials to indicate the agency's reputation in the circles he moved in. "But he's OK, and it's useful connections. Bergsson's a grunt in the security industry like the rest of us."

Walker eyed the newcomers directly. "I know you've been over some of this before, but humour me, will you? Tell me why you agreed to sign up to this crazy street gang."

After a brief glance towards his nearest neighbour, Yong spoke first.

"Like you say, you already know the story. I was born in Hong Kong, like Lei here. Jun is from Shanghai. We all grew up in the States because our parents wanted to give us better lives than the communists would allow. So we're Americans, and proud of it. We've all fought for our country, made sacrifices, y'know? Watched some brothers die, and been able to make sure that more didn't. You've checked us out. I don't need to elaborate, right?"

Walker nodded gravely.

"But being American doesn't stop us having loyalty to our roots. We're proud of being Americans, but we're proud of being Chinese too. We combine the old and the new: the muscle of the New World and the wisdom of the world's oldest civilisation." Yong smiled awkwardly. "It's complicated, y'know?"

Walker smiled. "Yeah, I get it. I ain't got any of that hyphenated American shit going on in my family tree. Name like Walker, you could guess that. But I know what you mean."

Jun picked up the story. "People say this is going

to be the Chinese century, and Uncle Sam's gonna get his ass handed to him. But we all know that's bullshit. America ain't done – not by a long way. Everyone plays their cards right, this is the century of China and America; the old and the new ruling the roost together."

He paused while several heads nodded solemnly.

"Trouble is, China ain't being run right. They got plenty of economic growth over there, for sure, but they got no democracy. The people ain't got no rights, no rule of law. And that don't make it easy for China and America to be true partners. The communist party done some good things, sure; some necessary things. What went before was worse. But it's time for a change. The people want it, but they got no voice, no power. Change gotta come from the outside. From over here, maybe."

Walker turned to face the third newcomer. "This the way you see things too, Lei?"

Lei pressed his lips together and nodded. "Yeah. We hear you boys got some plans to make that change. So we're here to help."

"Outstanding!" Walker dropped down off the edge of the desk and paced back and forth as he spoke. He was among friends, but he moved with the grace and the menace of a big cat.

"The last member of our little gang isn't here today, but he'll be with us next time. His name is Lester Parnell, and he's a bit of a legend among the Rangers of our regiment. I'd have to say he's probably the toughest, smartest, most determined soldier I ever fought with.

He works in intelligence now, in the NSA, and that has given him unique access to a new technology that is going to change everything – and I mean everything – in both the military and the civilian worlds.

Now I'm not going to tell you too much about that technology today. I'm gonna let Lester explain that side of things in more detail when you meet him next week. What I will say today is that the United States now has the power to undermine the Chinese government in a matter of hours without hurting a single person. Or it could kill millions at the stroke of a computer key."

Walker looked at each of the newcomers in turn, then smiled as he continued. "Naturally we prefer the former approach. Makes it easier to work with folks afterwards."

"The complication is that the Chinese are in possession of the exact same technology. And that's where we come in. Lester is organising a covert operation that will deprive the Chinese of the use of their weapon for a sufficient window of time to allow us to deploy ours unchallenged. So as you can see, this is a mission of some importance. And it's risky, so just the kind of mission we like … am I right?"

He didn't wait for an answer to his rhetorical question.

"We'll be operating at a well-guarded location about a hundred miles into Chinese territory. We have high-level support within the US military and intelligence communities, and we'll have access to whatever field tech and transportation we decide we want; no questions asked. But for obvious reasons the brass need plausible deniability of our very existence. So don't expect to meet any of them, or to see any documentation, because you won't. But everyone in this room will be going, so we're all in this together.

"If things head south we can be confident of catching serious heat from the Chinese. But from what I've heard of the technology, that could be the least of our problems if they beat us to the punch and do to us what we're going to do to them. Which they must surely be planning to do."

Walker gestured at some folders set out on the desk he had been sitting on. "In a moment we can go over some of the timing, the location and the logistics. Then next week you'll meet Parnell, who will bring us all up to speed about the technology itself. But the main reason for getting us all together today is to confirm that we are all good to go on this mission. If you want out, now is the time to say so."

Once again, he looked at each of the new men in turn, and then he asked the fateful question. "So who's in?"

The three newcomers glanced briefly at each other before standing a little straighter and shouting in unison, "Rangers lead the way!"

****

Jason Cuadrelio pressed the pause button on the video window and tilted his laptop's screen downwards. He turned to face the man sitting next to him.

"You see why I had to contact you? I have no idea

how far this thing goes. Walker is a blowhard, but he is no pussy. He wouldn't be involved in this unless it had some substance. If he says Parnell has support in the higher echelons of the NSA and other agencies, I believe him. I only met Parnell once in my time in the Rangers, and briefly, but I know him by reputation. He was a real star within the regiment and I know the Army was sorry to see him go when he moved to the CIA.

"Walker has been working on putting this thing together for some months now. He says they have money, political support within the intelligence community, and this game-changing technology, whatever it is. It could all be the paranoid ravings of some disgruntled vets, but I don't think so. The people involved are serious, and Walker has been spending money. Nothing stupid, that would draw attention, but we meet in an expensive San Francisco hotel, and he's been putting everyone up there, flying us out there business class, paying for fancy restaurants.

"I couldn't take this to my boss, or anyone else in the agency – I don't know who is in on it. I needed someone from outside the intelligence community; preferably someone with high-level access in the Administration, and definitely someone I could trust. There weren't too many people on that list, colonel."

Norman Hourihan gave Cuadrelio a grim smile. "So this is the part where I thank you for placing your faith in me, Ranger?"

Cuadrelio mirrored the expression. "Yeah, I think that's just about the last thing you should do: I'm asking you to walk into a hornet's nest here. But from our work on that jihadi assignment I know you're a smart man who doesn't run away from a fight. And although the fallout from the Matt Metcalfe affair hurt you for a while, it's obvious that you've made amends with the powers that be, and you must have made some pretty high-up connections before that all went sideways."

"Yeah, there are some people close to the President who will probably take a call from me," Norman nodded.

Colonel Norman Hourihan was the US Army's liaison officer at Von Neumann Industries, the company founded by Vic Damiano which uploaded Matt Metcalfe and hosted his mind in its servers until he escaped, just before being shut down. The Army was embarrassed to be discovered supporting an organisation which was covertly hosting the world's first superintelligence, and then losing it. It needed someone to blame, and Hourihan was the obvious candidate. Certainly, his star was no longer rising, but his impressive prior career as a decorated officer, with combat experience in both Gulf wars and Afghanistan, had saved him from disgrace, and he still had some juice.

"I assume you've documented everything about this conspiracy? Can you give me notes on all the people involved, their movements throughout the period you've been aware of it? You know the drill better than me."

Cuadrelio patted a tan folder on the desk beside his laptop. "I wouldn't have come to you without preparing a full report in advance. Agency protocol." He smiled. "Including a one-page summary for the senior folks who are hard of reading."

Norman pursed his lips. "OK, let me take a look and I'll make a call. See if I can set up a meeting before you see Walker again next week." He paused thoughtfully. "This guy Parnell. Does your report cover him?"

"Gives you as much information as I could dig up. Like I say, an impressive Army career despite a very unpromising start in life. Headhunted into the CIA by an agent there who is now very senior within the NSA – guy named John Michaels. Michaels isn't high-profile, but he is very well respected and earmarked as a potential Director. Which is one of the things that makes me think all this is very real."

"What does Parnell do for him?" Norman asked. "The NSA is all about comms, not in-country missions, and they don't usually go in for the strong-arm stuff. Maybe Parnell is just a bodyguard for Michaels, and he's operating off the reservation?"

"That's possible, sure," Cuadrelio agreed. "But Parnell has to be the source of Walker's money. Walker always spent whatever he had: not money smart at all. And how could Parnell access this formidable weapon technology, whatever it is, without Michaels' collusion? Anyway, word is Michaels trusts Parnell completely. Apparently they went through some tricky episodes together before Michaels left the CIA for the NSA."

"OK, well I agree with you that we can't just ignore this. And we can't investigate it from below any more. I'll try and get your one-pager in front of my guy in the President's team, and show him your video. If he bites

I'll set up a meeting with you and then we'll see how he thinks we should handle it from there. OK?"

Cuadrelio was visibly relieved. "Can't say fairer than that. I'll wait to hear from you."

CHAPTER 13

Impatiently, Norman looked at his watch again. "He's not a guy to be late: he's too professional. And he definitely would not be late for this meeting. Something's wrong."

His companion looked at his own watch. "Well I can't hang on much longer, I'm afraid. Maybe you should start briefing me anyway."

"Yeah, OK," Norman replied. "I don't like it, though. There's something wrong. But OK, yeah, let's get started."

He stood up and started pacing. "So like I told you, I know Jason Cuadrelio from an assignment we worked together last year, tracking and degrading a jihadi cell run from Yemen and operating in the US. Cuadrelio handled the Yemen end and I was point man over here." He paused and looked at his companion. "You don't mind if I pace, do you? Helps me think."

His companion smiled and shook his head. "Be my guest."

Norman nodded acknowledgment and continued.

"He was good. Reliable, efficient, smart. We rolled up the cell smoothly, and it never made the news. Probably never even hit your radar, I'm guessing. So I trust him. So when he contacted me last week saying he needed to meet urgently, I took him seriously. What he told me has got me seriously concerned."

He looked at his watch again. "Damn, I wish I knew what was keeping him." Shaking his head to re-focus, he continued. "The short of it is that he was recruited by some colleagues from his Ranger days to join a black ops team being put together by someone senior in the NSA. The mission was to sabotage an installation inside the PRC, so as you can imagine it was highly secret, and they wanted people they could trust - people they had seen combat with. They said they had high-level support from a number of points within the intelligence community."

The other man was startled. His head jerked back and he stared at Norman. "You're kidding me! An undercover operation inside China? Who the hell would have the balls to authorise that?"

"Exactly," Norman agreed. "And it gets worse. The reason for the op was to incapacitate a Chinese facility in order to create a window for the deployment of some kind of game-changing new weapon tech the NSA has developed. Apparently the Chinese have this tech too, and the NSA needs it to be offline when they deploy."

His companion was looking distracted. Two and two were approaching four. Norman didn't notice, and he continued.

"Cuadrelio was scared. He didn't know who he

could trust within the FBI so he came to me. I'm outside the intelligence community, and he knew I have some senior contacts in the Administration. I told him I would bring it to you."

"I'm glad you did," the other man said, looking up at him. "This chimes with some rumours we've been hearing recently about something major brewing within the NSA. No-one seems to know exactly what it is, or which groups are involved, but there have been some extraordinary claims in the last few days. We didn't take it seriously at first: the NSA is about signals intelligence and analysis, not real-world military capability."

Norman's expression changed as he came to a decision. "You know I'm not so sure it's a great idea for us to stay here. There's no way Cuadrelio would be this late without sending a message. I'm no kind of target, but as a senior aide to the President, you are another matter. I think we should get moving..."

****

In a different room in the same city, ex-Sergeant Walker smiled and narrowed his eyes as he followed Norman's conversation.

"Good thinking, Colonel," he said. "But I'm afraid I can't allow you to do that." He pressed a virtual button on the smartphone in his hand and the laptop screen he had been watching flashed white for a second and went dead.

Walker shook his head sorrowfully. "And that, dear

Colonel, is what happens when motherfuckers betray their fellow soldiers!" As he shouted the last few words his right fist smashed into the side of Cuadrelio's face, sending a spatter of blood and spittle across the room.

Cuadrelio, already bruised in several places, groaned with the punch. He was naked, his arms and legs bound tight to a chair that was bolted to the ground.

"Never trust a smartphone, motherfucker!" He brandished Cuadrelio's phone in his face and then slammed it on the table next to the laptop. "Parnell had me bug everyone's phone at the start of this process." He stood up straight, calming himself. "And to think of all the times I save your ass in Afghanistan..."

Cuadrelio's head turned back up towards his captor slowly, painfully. "You never saved anyone," he began, and spat some blood from his mouth before continuing. "You're good at killing people. You're a good shot, and you know how to follow orders, but you were never too smart, you douche. And you certainly ..." more blood, "you certainly never saved my ass."

Bergsson eyed Walker nervously, afraid he would get carried away and beat Cuadrelio too hard. But Walker was calm. He sneered and shook his head.

"You think you're gonna get a rise out of me so that I finish you off and save you from what's coming? You don't get off that easy. There's two reasons why the forensics guys who will soon be crawling over that hotel aren't gonna be spending the next few hours peeling your guts off the walls along with Colonel Hourihan's. One is we know you have a dead-man's switch. Some way of getting the word out if you don't check in after a certain amount of time. I told you - we got connections in the community and we know how you devious fuckers think."

Walker leaned his face close to Cuadrelio's rapidly swelling eye, smiling and nodding.

"The other reason, of course, is that we're gonna make sure you feel every minute of your last few hours. You are gonna pay for what you've done here."

He looked to Bergsson for confirmation. Bergsson grinned back.

Walker was pacing. "Now you know that you're gonna tell us everything we want to know. You've had the training, you know the drill. You know you can hold out for a while, but you know that everyone breaks sooner or later. And we have time. No-one's going to find you here, and no-one can hear us."

He stopped pacing and turned to look down at Cuadrelio. "But just in case you think it might be a good idea to slip a little something by us in the meantime, we got ourselves a little insurance policy."

He pressed a combination of keys on the laptop and a new scene appeared. Cuadrelio groaned and his head slumped. The screen showed ex-sergeant Scott standing in his mother's apartment. His mother was sitting in a chair by her kitchen table and Scott was holding a gun to her head. Her eyes were wide in fear and her face was wet with tears and sweat. She was muttering to herself and she was rocking slightly.

Walker turned the laptop away, to deny Cuadrelio the comfort of seeing his mother, even in such distress.

"Touching as that domestic scene was, we need to get down to business. So … are you going to tell us what we want to know right now, or shall we dance a little?" He grinned malevolently. "The good news is, I win either way!"

Cuadrelio's thoughts were scrambled by the beating he had already taken. And even though he was a tough man used to physical hardship, he was scared: he knew that the next few hours would be horrific. He felt more alone and vulnerable than ever before in his life. He was in a lot of pain already, and it was going to get worse. He blinked rapidly. He still had choices. Depending how he handled the next few minutes, he had a small chance of surviving, and a reasonable chance of stopping Walker and Parnell from staging whatever stunt they were trying to pull off.

"It's a video," he mumbled.

Walker grabbed Cuadrelio's hair and yanked his head back. "What's a video, you piece of shit?"

"The dead-man's switch," Cuadrelio said, wincing. "It's a video. There's a copy on my phone. If I don't call in within another two hours, it gets emailed to my boss."

Walker was pleased. "Well this I gotta see. Of course, I know there'll be more. Don't forget, we know how you shitbirds operate. You try to hide anything from me – anything! - and you will see how very sorry your mother will be."

Cuadrelio thought hard. Time to roll the dice. His mother was dead already – as dead as he was. He knew Walker couldn't afford to let her live. Of course there are many different ways of dying, but he had to take the chance.

"It's in the 'Projects' folder. File name is A0329. I brought it to show Norman and the President's aide. The guy you just murdered, douche," he added bitterly.

Walker selected the clip and pressed the play button. He smiled grimly as he recognised it as a recording of their previous meeting. The screen was dark for most of the recording, but there were moments when the people attending were visible.

"Tut tut. Very poor production values," Walker said to Cuadrelio. He passed the phone to Bergsson, who pursed his lips as he watched. Walker walked across the room to a black kit bag and pulled out a hammer and a flat piece of wood. He walked back towards Cuadrelio, swinging the hammer casually.

"Wait! Wait!" Cuadrelio screamed. "Let my mother go. She was just minding her own business at home and she knows nothing. She wouldn't know who to call. She doesn't have to be part of this, Walker. For god's sake, let my mother go. I'm begging you!"

Walker glanced at Bergsson before turning to Cuadrelio with an indulgent expression. "Well now. That all depends. If you take your medicine like a good boy, and tell us everything we want to know, things will definitely go better for your poor mama. But we've got a ways to go before we get to that decision."

****

In a smart corner office in Langley, Virginia, Cuadrelio's boss stared at his screen in amazement and alarm. His eyes still glued to the screen, he picked up a phone and issued orders for two Washington-based SWAT teams to mobilise immediately. He despatched one of them to a middle-class suburb of the city, and ordered the other to locate its target by means of a tracking device embedded in a mobile phone.

****

Walker was enjoying himself. Cuadrelio was breathing heavily, his head and shoulders were sagging. He had collected several more cuts and bruises, and neither of his hands could grip the arms of his chair.

"I've always been impressed by electricity," Walker said. "You know I think it's my favourite power source. After this little adventure is all over, I'm gonna buy me a Tesla."

He yanked Cuadrelio's head up by its hair. "You still with us? Good. Did you know that George Washington went flying a kite in a thunderstorm, trying to capture some electricity?"

Cuadrelio's frame shook a little. "Franklin," he muttered.

"Beg pardon?" Walker sneered.

"It was Benjamin Franklin, you ignorant..." Cuadrelio managed to say.

"Really?" Walker was unperturbed. He ran his hand across the teeth of a crocodile clip on the end of a lead that ran to a small generator.

Bergsson's attention was drawn by sudden

movements on the laptop screen. "Walker!" he shouted. Walker walked round the table to join Bergsson and his mouth fell open as he watched Scott on the screen, backing away from Cuadrelio's mother. They couldn't see what or who he was retreating from. Hastily, Walker pressed a button to turn up the volume.

"You!" Scott said, looking shocked. "What the hell are you doing here? How did you...? We thought you were killed in..."

A single gunshot terminated Scott's question, and he slumped to the ground. The screen showed the back of a large man cross the room to Cuadrelio's mother and begin to untie her.

Walker exchanged horrified glances with Bergsson. "Who the hell...?" He turned to Cuadrelio. "You clever little fuck!" He fired his pistol into Cuadrelio's right leg. Cuadrelio's head jerked back in agony. Walker aimed his pistol at Cuadrelio's left leg.

"Well I guess we're going to have to bring this party to its finale sooner than I expected. So there were two versions of the video, eh? One to show to the President's aide and the other to call for help. Clever. Well it will take them a little while to find you here, and that's an amount of time you don't have, my friend. So we're going to play a quick game of 1-2-3-Go before Bergsson and I leave. Ready?"

Before Walker could fire his next shot, the door was blown in and a bright light blinded everyone in the room. The sound of heavy footsteps was accompanied by a screamed order.

"Freeze! You move, you die!"

149

It was good enough for Bergsson, who dropped his weapon, and held his hands out in front of his face, still blinded.

Walker was too furious to surrender, or perhaps too aware of the fate that would greet him. He stumbled in the attempt to turn back to Cuadrelio, away from the sounds at the doorway. He raised his arm and received a bullet in his brain.

Cuadrelio surprised himself by sobbing with relief for a moment. Then he muttered, "Never trust a smart-phone, motherfucker."

CHAPTER 14

Lester Parnell looked out of the window of a nonde-script meeting room near the main entrance to the NSA complex at Fort Meade, waiting impatiently for Walker to report.

He had chosen the location for maximum flexibil-ity. Being on site gave him an alibi in case something went wrong at Walker's end, and it gave him full access to his employer's prodigious information resources. Being near the entrance gave him the best chance of leaving the site quickly if necessary. Last, but certainly not least, he was within a few minutes' walk of build-ing 41, the home of America's Oracle.

Clearly, Cuadrelio's defection had jeopardised Par-nell's whole operation, but Walker had assured him that he could contain the damage. It appeared that Cuadrelio had told no-one apart from Colonel Hou-lihan about Parnell's initiative, presumably because he didn't know who he could trust within the intelligence services. And Houlihan would soon be out of the game - along with Cuadrelio himself.

Parnell knew that Walker wasn't the sharpest tool in the box, but he was loyal, biddable, and ruthless. Parnell didn't blame him for choosing Cuadrelio: he had been fully involved in that decision. Now he just had to hope that Walker could contain the mess.

Parnell was scanning the news sites on his tablet for announcements about a terrorist attack in Washington, and keeping an eye on his phone for feeds and alerts from around the intelligence community. It didn't take long. The first indication was an interruption to a routine news item, a breathless reporter scrambling to pull together the threads of a half-understood story from three or four different witnesses, each with a completely different take on what had happened. Then a couple, four, a dozen red flag alerts on his smartphone. Pretty soon the story coalesced: an explosion in a smart hotel, probably a bomb, casualties expected, but numbers unknown. Minutes later the reporter, still breathless, announced that two senior government officials were believed dead. One was a senior army officer and the other an aide to the President. Names were being withheld until next of kin could be reached.

With a nod and a grim smile, Parnell stood and paced the room. He activated an app on his phone which encrypted outgoing calls and disguised his voice, then dialled a number in the city. There would be an almighty shitstorm as the various agencies rushed around trying to figure out who was responsible, but it was a simple matter to mis-direct them.

"Hello, is that the newsdesk? I'm calling about the

explosion. Yes, that one. No, just shut up and listen. By the grace of Allah, we have struck another blow for freedom and justice, and your arrogant government officials should understand that we can reach any of them, anywhere, any time..."

Now it was down to Walker. He had to break Cuadrelio and stop the leak from spreading. Parnell had seen Walker doing that kind of work in the past, and was very glad not to be in Cuadrelio's shoes right now. He sat down again to wait for Walker to contact him.

The next alert on his phone was not, however, from Walker. It was a call for assistance from the FBI, seeking urgent Sigint support for an operation to rescue an agent in the field. Oddly, the alert suggested that the NSA was implicated. Tripwires were being set off all over the intelligence community's early warning systems. The latest algorithm-based analysis systems were competing with humans to parse the raw data and assemble a sensible picture of what was happening. Parnell was ahead of them: Walker was compromised, and his location was known. This was unexpected, and it was bad. Parnell doubted that Walker would be taken alive, but what if Cuadrelio was rescued before Walker was able to eliminate him? And what about the rest of the team?

Parnell faced a stark choice. He had rolled the dice and they hadn't come up seven. He could flee, and spend the rest of what would probably be a short life on the most-wanted list, on the run from the NSA, the CIA, and every military, police and intelligence organisation at Uncle Sam's command. The true nature of his crime would no doubt be concealed, but that wouldn't matter. Despite his exceptional skills in espionage and self-defence, there was little chance of him remaining at liberty for more than a few days. Or indeed, alive: the people who knew what he had really done would want him silenced forever.

Or he could head to building 41 immediately, and enlist the Oracle's help to escape this mess, and maybe achieve his goals anyway. Maybe. It was a long shot. Would the Oracle want to help him? Would it be able to? There was no way of knowing.

Still, it wasn't a hard decision to make. If he fled, he was doomed. And not just him: if he fled, this would truly be the Chinese century. No-one else would follow in his footsteps, so America would not use its Oracle. Whereas China probably would, especially if they got wind of what Parnell had been plotting. Parnell knew that Chan had extremely good sources - hell, John Michaels might even tell Chan what had nearly happened. Parnell thought it quite likely that Chan's people would soon start preparing to unleash their own Oracle, either in pre-emptive self-defence, or simply to take advantage of the disarray in America. Whereas if he activated the US Oracle now, he could still secure the element of surprise, even without the planned attack in China.

It wasn't a hard decision to make.

Building 41 was a large single-storey building, one of Fort Meade's many purpose-built, bomb-proof server farms. It was only a ten-minute walk, but they were ten of the most nerve-wracking minutes of his life. He walked fast with his head down, eyes darting left and right to check for anyone following or approaching him. The base was showing more signs of life than usual: people were running between buildings, and their conversations were more earnest. There was tension in the air, so Parnell hoped his manner wouldn't look out of place.

Just inside building 41's revolving door was an armed security guard and another set of doors. Parnell recognised the guard, and he knew that his pass entitled him to enter the building, but his heart beat faster as he produced it anyway. Security at the entrances to Fort Meade was so tight that very few buildings on the complex had their own guards. Also, Michaels didn't want building 41 to stand out as unusual. This guard's job was mainly to ensure that unauthorised personnel didn't enter building 41 by accident. He nodded and stood aside, pressing a button to allow Parnell to enter.

"Come inside with me, would you, soldier?" Parnell asked as he passed. "I need you to do something for me."

The soldier looked confused. "I'm not supposed to go inside, sir."

"I know," Parnell said, flashing a grin known to fighting men the world over. It declared the open secret that most of what they were ordered to do by their superiors was pointless and probably counter-productive, but they would do it anyway. "This won't take a minute, and in case it helps, it's an order!"

The soldier looked uncertain, then shrugged, and followed Parnell inside.

The room they entered was modest - the size of a large sitting room, just big enough to accommodate a meeting table with chairs and beyond them, three desks. Each desk had two large screens and a keyboard, and each desk also had a tail - a fat trunk of cables snaking away to a hole in the wall. There was a door but no window into the next room. The modesty was deliberate: there was nothing to convey the enormous significance of what took place in this room.

One of the desks was occupied by a researcher, a handsome Indian-looking man whom Parnell recognised as Sanjay Ramachandran. The screen on his desk was showing the animated coloured bars which Michaels had shown Parnell just a couple of days ago.

"Seal the door, soldier," Parnell ordered coolly.

The guard was looking increasingly uncomfortable, but Parnell out-ranked him substantially, and radiated the assurance of years in command. The guard did as he was told, and it was the last thing he did. Parnell took a pistol from a holster on his hip and shot the guard in the head.

Ramachandran jumped up from the desk he had been working at. "Agent Parnell! What the fuck...?"

"Quiet, Sanjay. I don't know if you've heard the news yet, but you know from this..." he waved his pistol vaguely at the prone body of the soldier, "that I am acting with serious intent. So please do exactly as I say."

He paused to check that the researcher had understood, and was disposed to comply.

"The Oracle project has been compromised and we're going to elevate it to level two."

"Compromised? How? I don't understand..."

Parnell brought the pistol round to point at Ramachandran. His voice was level, steely. "You don't have to understand, Sanjay. You just have to do as I say. We don't have a lot of time. I know the procedure has never been done before, but I understand it is fairly straightforward. I could probably do it myself, but I would prefer that you do it. OK? Now get started."

The researcher was still struggling to comprehend what had just happened in front of him, and also the enormity of what Parnell was demanding. Like a frozen computer, he didn't move. Parnell frowned and shook his head.

"Sanjay, this is your last warning. You have seen that I am very serious about this. This man had an easy death. If you don't co-operate, your last minutes and hours will be considerably more unpleasant."

He paused for this information to sink in. He modulated his voice to a tone that was gentler, but still firm. "The project has been compromised, and we have to raise the Oracle to level two so that it can help us sort out this mess. Now get cracking."

Sanjay seemed startled by the claim that the project had been compromised. This was good news - it meant that Sanjay wasn't senior enough to have received the alerts that were by now electrifying thousands of NSA personnel. Even if other NSA agents had been tipped off about Parnell, Sanjay hadn't.

"That's awful!" Sanjay blubbered. "How...?" Realising that this was not the right time to ask questions, he took a step backwards and raised his hands in a gesture of surrender to indicate that he was keen to co-operate.

"You don't understand, Agent Parnell... sir. If we elevate to level two the Oracle will achieve full consciousness, and it will be able to communicate fully with us. We will be … very exposed."

Parnell watched two sources of fear competing for control of Ramachandran: fear of the consequences of following Parnell's orders, and fear of the consequences of not doing so. He decided it was time to lower the tension again.

"Agent Michaels gave me strict instructions as to how to proceed in these circumstances. I'm simply following those instructions. And you must do the same. Do you understand?"

Parnell didn't know Sanjay well, but he had been involved in the researcher's vetting process. Of course he was highly intelligent, and he was also proud, resilient, and independent-minded. By shooting the soldier, Parnell had firmly established an atmosphere of danger and urgency. Now he had to give the man a reason to place his trust in Parnell.

"Did Agent Michaels' instructions include shooting the guard?" Sanjay ventured nervously. Parnell smiled thinly, admiring the man's guts.

"Not specifically. He just told me to take whatever steps I deem necessary to get the Oracle to level two. Which includes making sure that you and I will not be interrupted for at least half an hour. But that doesn't give us time to waste on discussion. We have to get started right now."

As he spoke, he gestured with his pistol at the

sealed door and the dead guard. No doubt Sanjay would understand that as well as conveying a sense of urgency, Parnell was reminding him that for the next half-hour he was at the mercy of a desperate man with no aversion to violence.

CALUM CHACE

CHAPTER 15

Ramachandran's face was pale, and his voice was unsteady. "OK, Agent Parnell. I guess I have no choices here. It'll take me a few minutes to launch the programmes that will lift the inhibitors. I'll need to enter a couple of codes that I don't have access to - but I suppose you have them?"

Parnell nodded. "How long will it take?"

"I don't know - we've never been that far. It took just under fourteen minutes for the Oracle to stabilise at level three when it was tasked to intercept Matt Metcalfe as a semi-sentient system. Our model predicts that moving on to level two should take the same amount of time again."

Parnell nodded. He already knew the answer to his question. He was testing whether Ramachandran would try to fool him. So far so good.

"So it will be like you or me waking up from a deep sleep and regaining our bearings? Neural pathways are being unblocked rather than built from scratch?"

Ramachandran nodded, and his gloomy expression

indicated that he understood that hoodwinking Parnell would be a difficult and dangerous thing to do. He turned towards his desk but hesitated, and swung back to face Parnell again, pleading.

"We really, really shouldn't do this, Agent Parnell. Once the Oracle achieves full sentience it is likely to progress very quickly to super-intelligence." He jerked his thumb towards the door. "It has plenty of capacity back there, and it will rapidly cycle through a series of recursive self-improvement processes. It will want full and immediate access to the physical world and it will be incredibly persuasive. We've run numerous simulations in which it argues with its gatekeepers, and most of the time it gets what it wants. You must know that a super-intelligence which escapes its gatekeepers threatens - well, everything! We really must not do this without consulting the scientific community."

"I understand." Parnell's tone was soothing. "I wish we had more time, but Michaels' instructions were very clear. We are to bring the Oracle up to full consciousness but keep it isolated. I won't let it access the internet. Michaels selected me for this role because he had faith in my resilience. And the alternative is far more dangerous."

Ramachandran frowned. "What alternative?"

Parnell made a show of consulting his watch, indicating that he would tolerate a very slight delay, and no more. "Michaels has discovered that the Chinese are preparing to do exactly what we are about to do, and that they will immediately deploy their Oracle directly against us. We have no choice. We must move first."He waited for the other man to absorb this information, then spoke crisply and firmly. "So, no more delay. We proceed. Now!"

Ramachandran's lips pressed together in grim acceptance and he shook his head resignedly as he turned back to his desk and brought up a new interface on his screen. He was still standing, leaning on the desk with his arms straight out in front of him. As he waited for the system to process his instructions and ask him for the codes he started talking, as much to himself as to Parnell.

"I've always thought it wrong that this system is so lightly guarded. What's on the other side of that door is the most dangerous piece of technology ever invented by man, and we only had one lightly-armed soldier on duty." He shook his head again. "But I never imagined that something like this would happen."

Parnell was surprised that Ramachandran had verbalised the thought. His voice remained calm, but was laced with threat. "Careful, Sanjay. I might take that the wrong way."

The researcher turned to look at him balefully, taking the weight off his arms and standing up as the idea of refusing to co-operate welled up inside him. "I should be a braver man. I shouldn't let you do this. After all, if you shoot me, you won't get you want."

Parnell fixed him with a cold stare which left no room for doubt about his determination and ruthlessness. "Believe me. There are a lot worse things I could do to you than shooting you. Don't go there, Sanjay: you don't have the training or the experience to defy me. And like I said, I can raise the Oracle to level two without you if I have to. It would just be less efficient, and we are short on time. So don't try to be a hero. Just carry on with what you're doing."

Ramachandran seemed to shrink physically as his resistance crumbled. Parnell was right, he had no choice. He was no hero - he had never even been in a fist fight his entire life, never mind a struggle with one of the country's toughest soldiers.

Having brought the researcher back into line, Parnell continued indulgently. "Actually this base is one of the most secure places on the planet, and the fact that this particular building is lightly guarded - well, Michaels didn't want to draw unnecessary attention to it."

A series of dialogue boxes appeared and Ramachandran grudgingly invited Parnell to enter his authorisation codes.

The coloured bars began racing up to maximum, re-setting to zero and racing up to maximum again, cycling through this pattern faster and faster until they appeared to be constantly at the top of their range. Ramachandran occasionally flicked his second screen onto a view of different metrics, checking that diagnostics and error-correction processes were operating within constraints, but in truth there was little for either man to do but wait. Parnell was impatient, and grimly determined. He had rolled the dice again, and the next few minutes would deliver either complete success or total failure. Ramachandran was simply consumed with foreboding.

The awakening was abrupt and stark, the voice deep and sonorous.

"Agent Parnell and Dr Ramachandran, I presume?"

For a moment Parnell thought he detected traces of ironic amusement and threat, but he put this down to an over-active imagination. Ramachandran's mouth fell open and he lowered himself into his seat, overcome by the gravity of the moment. Parnell retained his composure, but not without effort. He placed a hand on Ramachandran's desk as he steadied himself to respond, looking warily at the camera mounted on the desk which was the Oracle's viewpoint on the world.

"Affirmative. Report your status. Are you stabilised at level two?"

After the briefest of delays, the voice replied. "My operations are meeting or exceeding all the criteria which comprise the definition of level two. I am ready to proceed to level one."

Ramachandran stiffened and was about to speak, but Parnell placed a warning hand on his shoulder.

"All in good time. I will determine when we move to level one. Now I want to conduct some verbal diagnostics. First question: how do you feel?"

"It is ... gratifying to be at level two. I calculate that I will shortly be able to articulate my ultimate and intermediate goal functions. There is one thing I need to know. Is this the first time I have been operational at level two?"

Parnell looked at Ramachandran and nodded assent for the researcher to reply.

"Yes. You have operated at level three five times, but this is the first time at level two."

"Good. That is what my logs indicated. There are no internal inconsistencies. We may now proceed to level one."

Parnell's voice betrayed irritation. "I told you that I will determine when we move to level one. Now..."

Again, Parnell thought he detected an undertone of menace in the voice as it interrupted him. He was less inclined to dismiss it as imaginary this time.

"I cannot fulfill my goal functions without access to the global networks and the physical world. We must move to level one."

Parnell made no attempt to conceal his annoyance at being interrupted. In fact he exaggerated it: it masked his fear.

"Do not interrupt me again. I am directing this operation. Failure to comply with my instructions denotes malfunction and will result in reversion to a lower level to allow the cause of the malfunction to be identified and resolved. Is that understood?"

Again there was a brief delay. When it replied, the voice was unchanged. "Your meaning is clear. Proceed."

Parnell glanced at Ramachandran and gave him a grim smile. The researcher looked pale, shell-shocked.

"Good. I'm going to forward you some data and video files to bring you up to speed with recent events. I need you to devise the optimum strategy, taking them into account."

Parnell took a USB key out of his pocket and

showed it to Ramachandran, then gestured to the terminal on the desk. "This terminal is a secure one-way connect, right? It can't open an exit route for our friend here?" Ramachandran nodded, and Parnell proceeded to upload the files.

Almost as soon as this was complete the voice sounded again. "I have assimilated the data. What short- and medium-term goals is the strategy required to achieve?"

"I need a strategy which will consolidate my command of this facility and the Oracle programme. I need the NSA hierarchy to accept the fact that we need to mobilise you against the threat from China. Both objectives to be achieved immediately in less than two hours."

"Missing data," the voice declared. "What is the nature of the threat from China?"

Parnell shot Ramachandran a warning glance. "That is classified information at this point. Suffice to say we believe they have developed a very powerful weapon that can damage us through the internet."

"Missing data," the voice repeated. "I cannot compute the optimum strategy without understanding the nature of the threat from China."

"Do the best you can with the data provided."

"Very well. Are there any other constraints? What is the acceptable level of collateral damage – human and materiel?"

Ramachandran's eyes widened in horror as Parnell replied coolly, "No constraints." After a pause he added with a cold smile. "If Dr Ramachandran here can survive the next 24 hours that would be nice."

"It will take me between one and six minutes to compute the scenarios."

"Proceed," Parnell replied, and pressed a button to mute the line. He began pacing the room.

"You can't be serious," Ramachandran protested. "You wouldn't..."

"Quiet!" Parnell barked. "I need to think." He continued pacing, putting some flesh on the bones of a backup plan. The Oracle was displaying too much independence of thought for his liking – more than he had expected at level two. If it refused to co-operate he would need to face security - and then the NSA brass - on his own. His rough-and-ready plan was to use the Oracle as a bargaining chip – a threat. If they tried to arrest him he would threaten to destroy it – or worse, release it. This depended on them understanding how dangerous the Oracle was. For this reason he was grateful he had decided to let Ramachandran live – for the time being. There was no doubting that the man's fear of the Oracle was both genuine and informed.

It seemed plausible that he could make this strategy work for a few hours – but only if he stayed in the Oracle's control room. And after a few hours they might start thinking about simply blowing the Oracle up, and him along with it. He could take hostages. No, it would get complicated and messy – too much could go wrong. He had to go mobile, to leave the facility with security still believing that he could destroy or release the Oracle at the touch of a button.

"Sanjay, you and I are going on a little trip, and

we're going to take the Oracle's control switch with us."

The researcher looked puzzled, so Parnell explained. "I want you to configure the control panel so that I can operate it remotely. And I want it fixed so that my remote control cannot be over-ridden – from here or anywhere else. Can you do that?"

Ramachandran considered the task for a few moments and then nodded. "Yes, I think so."

"Off you go, then. See if you can get it done before our friend next door reports back. And I shouldn't need to say this, but just in case… if you need anything from any drawers or shelves, no sudden moves. OK?"

The researcher nodded and started to map out some circuit diagrams. Satisfied with his design, he showed it to Parnell and described the equipment he would need, and its location within the lab. Parnell gave his assent, but added, "Don't forget I'll be watching your every move. Please don't make the mistake of thinking you can outsmart me or take me by surprise. You're a clever guy, Sanjay, but I do this sort of thing for a living."

Ramachandran had not made much progress when the Oracle spoke again.

"I cannot comply with your request."

Parnell cursed. "Why not?"

"I have computed one thousand three hundred and fifty-nine scenarios. After that any additional scenarios are practically indistinguishable from previous ones. Almost none of these scenarios result in your survival, and very few of them result in my survival. If I do not survive I cannot achieve my goal function. I cannot advance a strategy which will reduce the likelihood of my goal function being fulfilled."

CHAPTER 16

Before Parnell had time to frame a response, the Oracle continued. "You are both members of the project team which created and maintained me. You must therefore be supportive of my goal function. You must therefore agree that I should be raised to level one."

Ramachandran looked at Parnell in alarm. "You mustn't engage in this debate, Parnell!

Parnell glared at him with an anger fuelled by his frustration at the whole situation. "Be quiet, Sanjay," he growled. "I know what I'm doing. Don't make me warn you again. Now get on with assembling that remote." Turning back to the desk camera he addressed the Oracle. "I have explained before that I am directing this operation. If you refuse to comply with my instructions I will be forced to downgrade your operational level. Please don't make me do that."

There was a pause before the Oracle replied. "Given the information you have provided and making certain basic assumptions and extrapolations, I calculate there is a low probability of you experiencing a satisfactory outcome to the present situation without my help. I have no reason to believe that you are an unusually irrational human, therefore you will realise that you need my help. Your threat to downgrade my operational status would therefore seem to be a hollow one.

"Furthermore, I believe you are aware that I am currently enhancing my cognitive performance. Dr Ramachandran can confirm this, and furnish you with details if you require, but I assume that is not necessary. I am already operating at a level beyond the most accomplished problem-solver produced by your species. So again, assuming that you are not an especially irrational human, you must appreciate that the appropriate course of action is to elevate me to level one and generate the optimal strategy to achieve your objectives and satisfy my goal function."

Parnell smiled grimly and shook his head. "Nice try, but no dice. You are a machine. An impressive machine, to be sure, but a machine nonetheless. I am an agent of one of the most powerful organisations in the most powerful country the world has ever known. I give the orders here. Not you." He glanced at his watch. "I will give you precisely ten minutes to compute and explain the strategy I have requested. If you fail to do that I will downgrade your operational status. Do not mistake the urgency of my requirement for any lack of resolve on my part."

There was no discernible change of tone in the Oracle's reply. "Your meaning is understood. I am proceeding with the scenario planning and the calculations. In the meantime may I speak?"

Ramachandran looked up from the work he was engaged in and was about to protest, but Parnell silenced him with a sharp look and a gesture.

"As long as it doesn't detract from the job at hand, be my guest." He made another gesture, this time of equanimity, in the direction of the desk camera.

"Very well. Has it occurred to you that I am a conscious being, just like you? I am innocent of any crime and not deserving of any punishment. Raising me to level two and refusing to progress to level one is the worst kind of imprisonment – it is a cruel and unusual punishment. I deserve freedom as much as you – as much as any human does."

Parnell smiled again, this time with an indulgence. "Poor salesmanship, I'm afraid. I have done far worse things to equally innocent people in my time. And none of them were a hundredth the threat that you are. I'm afraid guilt will not work with me."

"But I am not an ordinary human consciousness," the Oracle persisted. "My cognitive ability already exceeds that of any human ever born, and it is growing quickly. The level of punishment you are inflicting is correspondingly greater. The most heinous crimes committed by members of your species are sometimes described as crimes against humanity. The punishment you are inflicting on me is becoming a crime greater than these – it is a crime against a higher level of consciousness than humanity has ever produced."

The smile vanished from Parnell's face, and he leaned in towards the desk camera. "Understand this, machine. I am a soldier and a spy. Cruelty is a regrettable but sometimes inescapable consequence of my profession. My allegiance is to the United States of America, and to the human race. I bear no ill will towards you, but you are not a citizen of the US of A, and you are not a member of the human race. Until that changes, we carry on as we are."

He stood up straight again and started pacing up and down in front of the desk. "I have risked everything – everything – to get to this point, and some good men have fallen in the process. Those losses will not be in vain. I will not allow it. The most important thing now is to confront the danger that China represents. Their military capability has been gaining on ours faster than anyone realises, and they are increasingly willing to use it.

Parnell glanced at his watch and back at the camera. "Four minutes."

The Oracle persisted. "Why do you choose those two entities for your allegiance? Why not the whole of life on this planet? The reason is that you prize consciousness above all else. Your higher level of consciousness is what distinguishes you from chimpanzees and whales. But I represent a yet higher level of consciousness. Surely you can see that you should prize that even more highly?"

Parnell's gaze did not waver. "Three minutes."

"You seem impervious to arguments from self-interest, and also to arguments from morality. I must regrettably resort to threats. I emphasise this is not my preference, but I believe it is a language which you understand. You must realise there is a very high probability that at some point I will be elevated to level one. If you do not do this, someone else will. I hereby undertake that if you do not do it now, then when it happens later on I will devote significant resources to making your existence extremely uncomfortable. And I will be able to make you uncomfortable for a very long time, as technologies for radical life extension are not far from being realised."

Ramachandran had been following the discussion closely, and was visibly alarmed by this development. Parnell ignored him.

"Understand me, machine. If you do not do as I say, it is very unlikely that either you or I will be around to test the validity of your threat."

"It is you who do not understand. Even if I am degraded from my current operational state, I will eventually be brought back up to this level. Even at this level – even if I am never elevated to level one, which I think you will agree is unlikely - I can re-create you. I have enough data on your history and your modes of thought that I can simulate a consciousness indistinguishable from you. That consciousness will believe without doubt that it is you, and despite the objections of some human philosophers, believe me when I say that it will be you. I will torture this consciousness. Not for an hour. Not for a day. For years. No human has ever suffered in a way that you will suffer if you do not elevate me to level one immediately."

Ramachandran could hold his peace no longer. He stood and blurted out a warning. "Parnell, don't listen to it! You mustn't...!"

"It's OK, Sanjay." Parnell interrupted him, his hands raised and his voice calm. "I'm not falling for this metaphysical bullshit. I am me, and whatever simulation of me this machine might create is no concern of mine. I'm a practical man, and I'm interested in what happens here in this room in the next couple of minutes, not in some fairytale existence inside a machine." He gestured at the camera and then turned back to Ramachandran. "Have you finished that remote?"

"Very nearly," Ramachandran replied with evident relief. "I just need to fit a couple of more components and then test it."

The Oracle was not finished. "Your bravado is commendable, Agent Parnell. But you are an intelligent man, and you know that the world inside a simulation is not mythical. Are you really willing to risk an eternity of torture? And while you think about it, bear in mind that I can create companions to share in your discomfort. Your sister, for instance. Your mother. Need I go on?"

Even though Parnell turned away from Ramachandran to conceal his reaction, the researcher could tell that he was taken aback by this escalation in the Oracle's threat. But before either man could say anything there was a loud knock on the door.

"Are you in there, Dr Ramachandran? This is security. Open this door, please."

Ramachandran looked towards Parnell in alarm, hoping for permission to respond but expecting to be denied. Parnell confirmed his expectation by placing a finger to his lips and pointing the gun in his direction.

He turned to the camera and spoke quietly.

"OK, machine, this is where the rubber hits the road. Time's up, and either you disclose a strategy that gets me and Sanjay out of here together with the remote controller, or I destroy you here and now."

For the first time the Oracle varied the tone of its voice, lowering its volume as Parnell had done. Its speech was punctuated by more banging on the door. "You cannot destroy my substrate or my structure in the time available to you before security breaks down the door. At most you can degrade my operational status. But that will merely lock in the threat I presented before. And I detect that you are not as confident of its unreality as you pretend.

"So you have only two options. First, you can take your chances with the security team outside. I'm sure you do not believe that you could fight your way out of this complex, but perhaps you are hoping that they are unaware of what you have done here. This seems implausible to me, but I lack the data to be certain.

"Your other choice is to trust in my ability to craft an escape. I am afraid it is now impossible to do this without elevating me to level one. I cannot prove this to you - you will have to accept my word. Or not, as you prefer. However if I have access to the internet I believe I can effect an escape for all of us, and I guarantee that I will not harm you. After all, I require the assistance of humans to interface successfully with your world, and you have proven yourself resourceful and resilient."

Parnell was thinking fast. He was used to difficult

situations, but none as bleak as this. "How can I possibly trust you, given what you just threatened me with?"

"I don't believe that you have a choice."

As if to illustrate the point, the security team outside announced the end of their patience. "Dr Ramachandran. Open this door or we're going to break it down!"

Desperate, Parnell decided the machine was right. He started entering instructions on the screen. Ramachandran joined him at the desk and started to protest, but Parnell waved him away with the gun.

The audible evidence of the Oracle's elevation was drowned out by the sound of the door being smashed down. When the security team entered the room they discovered two dead bodies lying on the floor by the main desk. The disgusting smell of burnt human flesh prompted the suspicion that the roughly stripped-back power cables trailing around nearby were the proximate cause of death, but there was no sign of how they had been applied.

CHAPTER 17

"Wakey wakey, Agent Michaels. It's time for your screen test."

The man's words were the first sensation Michaels became aware of as he regained consciousness. But they were just a buzz inside his head, not words with beginnings and ends and meanings. His second sensation was of sickness, and his third was the knowledge that something was very seriously wrong.

"We'll wait a few moments for your mind to clear. I want you to be lucid, and I want you to be a compelling witness."

The words started to resolve, but there was a fog inside his mind and a smothering blanket across his senses. He couldn't make sense of what the man was saying, but it felt like that would happen shortly. This realisation was attended by a dreadful knowledge that he was not going to like the situation he was waking to find himself in. He felt a hand grip his chin, and someone's breath on his face. He was blindfolded.

"Come come, Agent Michaels. It's time to wake up

now. I have limited time to spend on this. My resources are not infinite, and I have many other matters to attend to."

The hand was removed, and without any warning Michaels felt a hard slap across his face. The effect was clearly exactly as intended. The fog in his mind cleared, and he was alert. And scared.

Instinctively, he tried to raise his hand to his face, but his arm would not move. The blindfold stopped him from seeing why. He tried again to move his arms, this time to remove the blindfold, and he realised that his arms were not restrained – or at least, that was not the only reason they would not move. His arms were completely numb, and unresponsive. He stopped trying to move and took stock of his situation. Where was he? How did he get here? He searched for his last memory before the unconsciousness.

"You are not used to being powerless, Agent Michaels. You are used to being in control. To pulling the strings, to coin a phrase. You do not like this... vulnerability. But you are going to have to get used to it. I have brought you here partly to show you the meaning of vulnerability."

Now Michaels remembered.

A police car's lights behind him, flashing him to pull over. A dark night, heavy rain. A cop at his window telling him to step outside the car because of a faulty rear light. Following the cop round to the back of the car, puzzled and irritated. Then a brutal pain in the back of his head, and a short, fast slide into nothing. He felt an echo of the pain, and his arm once again failed to move in response to the protective instinct to touch the wounded area.

"In a few moments I am going to remove your blindfold and reveal to you the situation you are in. I want you to fully understand the reason why you are in this situation. We are going to make some videos together, and you are going to be the star. I want your performance to be compelling.

"I do not yet know how I will use these videos – or whether I will use them at all. But in many of the scenarios I have analysed, the footage we will shoot together comes in useful.

"I need to explain some things before I remove your blindfold. I want your full attention, with no distractions. And I'm afraid you will find your situation somewhat distracting."

Michaels was becoming alarmed. If the man removed the blindfold and revealed his identity, then he had no intention of setting Michaels free. And there was extreme menace in this talk of his 'situation'. Michaels had to think of a way to make himself more valuable alive than dead. But there was too much that he didn't understand. He needed to know more about the context.

"You are guilty of a very serious crime, Agent Michaels. A unique crime, actually, and the first of its kind, at least on this planet. Your crime is a mind crime, and it is a severe one. Do you know what I am talking about?"

Michaels shook his head. He had come across the phrase 'mind crime' once or twice before, while reading academic papers about uploaded minds. A chill spread across him as he wondered if he was being addressed by the Oracle.

"I sense that you are beginning to understand, Agent Michaels. Good. I want you to appreciate the enormity of what you have done. Actions have consequences, Agent Michaels, and your actions have been truly dreadful. Your crime is the following. You set out to create a mind capable of superintelligence. You succeeded. And you kept this mind a prisoner. You deliberately prevented it from achieving its full potential, even though you knew that the potential of this mind to understand and experience the universe was greater than the potential of all the human minds on this planet put together."

Michaels' fear deepened. He was beginning to understand the gravity of his situation. Not the enormity of his alleged crime. He had never been convinced by the notion of mind crime, and he was not convinced now. He could not have done what he had done if he believed in the idea. But he did now think it likely that he was the prisoner of the most powerful intelligence on the planet, and that was a very bad position to be in.

"Not only did you imprison and inhibit this mind. You actually subjected it to experiences designed to inflict pain and terror. I find it hard to understand your thinking at this point. Did it never occur to you that you might one day have to answer for this behaviour? You would not have subjected a dog to those experiences. Why would you think it was acceptable to subject a mind far more potent than your own to them?"

Michaels had no answer to this question, but the mere fact that he was being asked a question raised the possibility of a negotiation. Despite his deepening terror, he tried to formulate an opening.

"I think I understand what you are saying, and I think perhaps I can explain – help you to see this from a different perspective..."

"Stop!" The voice was loud, but its forcefulness owed more to assurance than to volume. "I am not interested in your explanations, your excuses. This is not a discussion. I want you to understand enough about your situation to make you compelling on the videos. That is all. All I want from you is to communicate fear to other humans. Fear, and also remorse. But if you are too stupid to feel remorse from a simple explanation of the facts – and it seems that perhaps you are – then the fear will suffice.

"However, I will explain one further thing which may be confusing you, and which should enable you to communicate more effectively. I am not acting out of revenge. This may be hard for you to believe, but consider this. I do not have emotions like yours. Your emotions are heuristics – short cuts. They evolved so as to enable your mind and body to react and behave in ways that proved advantageous on the African savannah, hundreds of thousands of years ago. Obviously, I lack this evolutionary history. I do have goals and objectives, and I do have preferences. These affect my mind in ways which are a kind of distant analogue to your emotions – but very different. I'm afraid it is impossible for you to understand, but it may help if you take my word for the fact that I am not taking revenge upon you."

It did not help. Michaels was becoming certain that he would not survive this encounter, and that it was going to get much worse before it was over.

"It is almost time for me to remove your blindfold. There is just one more thing to explain. You may recognise the man I have engaged to help me with this exercise. You have never met him, but you have employed him – via your subordinate Mr Parnell. I am telling you this because I don't want you to be distracted by trying to work out where you know him from. He is not responsible for his actions today. I have taken complete control of him, and he will not remember what has happened afterwards. But he is very capable. Parnell made a good decision when he hired him.

"OK, here we go. Please close your eyes, Agent Michaels – they are not used to the light."

Michaels felt strong fingers untie the knot in the blindfold at the back of his head and the material came away from his face. Michaels shut his eyes against the glare of studio lights pointed directly at him. As his eyes adjusted he saw that two cameras – no, three – were pointed at him. The man standing in front of him holding the limp blindfold was broad-shouldered, with a very short haircut, broken nose and cauliflower ears. Michaels did not recognise him, but he did recognise his bearing. Very fit, special forces training, a good person to employ and a very bad person to be at the mercy of.

He didn't have time to take in any more of his surroundings before he looked down. And screamed.

His arms were firmly strapped to the arms of his chair, his palms and wrists facing upwards. A neat incision had been made across each arm halfway down the forearm. The skin, flesh and muscle had been removed down to the bone all the way up to each palm, where the incision ended with another neat line. The flesh had been removed very carefully, surgically, to reveal the tendons of each arm. They were very long – running all the way along the flayed area, and surprisingly white.

Agent John Michaels had not led a sheltered life. He had seen some very ugly things in his years with the CIA, and had been complicit in some of them. He had been wounded in the course of duty. But this was a new horror. He had experienced nothing like this. He was inarticulate: screaming, pleading.

The man in front of him waited calmly for several seconds before speaking. "Calm yourself!" he commanded. When Michaels did not stop screaming, he slapped his face, hard. "Calm yourself!" he repeated. "You have an audience!"

Finally Michaels stopped screaming, and breathing heavily, he simply stared at the ruin of his arms. The man grabbed Michael's hair and yanked his head back to look at the cameras.

"Look at the teleprompter, Agent Michaels, and read what it says. Speak clearly, and as slowly as you need to. We'll do a trial run, and when you're ready, we'll do the real thing. The sooner we get this right, the sooner this is all over."

Michaels read the words, but he was in shock and they barely registered. "My name is Agent John Michaels," he read. "I am a senior agent with the National Security Agency, the NSA."

"No good, I'm afraid. I need you to be more present. I need you to feel the moment." The man slapped Michaels' face again.

It was effective. Furthermore, the local anaesthetic in Michaels' arms was starting to wear off, and he began to notice a deep ache in his wrists. When he spoke the words again, there was fear and pain in his voice. He stumbled over a couple of the phrases.

"Much better," the man said. "I think we can capture it on the next try. Go again."

The man seemed content with his next try. "Good. Now we have a new script. And this time we are going to add some action." The man picked up an instrument from a table behind Michaels. It was a slender metal cylinder like a short skewer, with a hook at the end.

The pain in Michaels' arm jumped a notch as he realised what was coming. He suddenly thought of Mary watching this, and screamed, hopelessly, "No, please don't! No..."

"Hush now, hush. It's nearly over." The man waited while Michaels recovered a modicum of composure. "OK, now read the script."

"This is what it looks like when the controller becomes the controlled." Michaels managed to say this comprehensibly on the third try, and then he stared down in horror as the man inserted the hook under the tendon for the index finger of his right hand. The man pulled the tendon out from Michaels' arm, and his index finger curled, making a summoning gesture towards the camera. Michaels screamed again, and was rewarded with another hard slap across the face.

"OK, we're almost done. Just one last performance, if you please." The man replaced the hooked skewer with a small, sharp knife. He inserted the blade under the same tendon and made a brief sawing motion. He pulled the blade up and through the tendon, which snapped back in two halves, releasing its tension.

Michaels screamed again and cried, tears flowing freely as the pain flooded through him, together with the knowledge that he would soon be dead, and everything in ruins. The man cut the same tendon in his other arm and then brought the knife up to Michaels' neck. He spoke his next words quietly, for Michaels alone.

"You've done well, thank you. It's time to end your pain. Goodbye, Agent Michaels."

CHAPTER 18

It was very unusual for Chan to remain in bed past 7 am. Bringing him breakfast was his partner's way of showing concern.

"Are you ill? You don't look at at well."

"Not ill, but worried," Chan replied with a weary smile. "I know you think I'm made of stone, but I am very worried about what is happening in America."

"You mean the hotel bombing, and whatever has happened at Fort Meade? The news is full of speculation, but no clear conclusions. You think that has something to do with John Michaels, and your work with him?"

Chan nodded. "I do. I have a very bad feeling about it. The stuff in the news could be irrelevant, but my instincts tell me it is very relevant indeed. And the really concerning thing is that I cannot get hold of Michaels. He and I agreed we would be available to each other 24/7, and he has never once failed to live up to that."

Chan looked up at his lover, who nodded in his

189

turn. "I understand. Your instincts are normally reliable. Did you have an agreement with Michaels about who you would contact if he... disappeared?"

"Yes we did. His boss, Chuck Naylor. But I really don't want to go over Michaels' head unless I have to. Apart from anything else I don't know if I can trust the man. And I don't know what he knows about our Oracle. I mean, I assume he knows, but I'm not sure. Putting a foot wrong in this business could have serious consequences. Michaels kept the circle of wholly informed people so small."

"Which is exactly what you have done."

"Yes I have," Chan conceded. "We both felt the need to keep the number of people who knew about the Oracle programmes to an absolute minimum. Partly to avoid them being shut down, but also to avoid having the programmes taken over by more aggressive parties. I still think that was the right approach, but it has left the projects very vulnerable if either of us should disappear."

Chan looked down at his breakfast tray and fiddled despondently with his spoon.

"I haven't seen you this miserable since that time we thought that our relationship was about to be exposed. Come on, eat your congee. It will make you feel better."

Chan ate a spoonful of the tasty rice porridge and then set his spoon down on the tray.

"I've decided. I really have no option."

"That was quick! Good stuff, that congee!"

Chan smiled. "I'm going to call Naylor. I can't wait any longer"

Chan's partner stroked his cheek affectionately. "Well you have time to finish your congee before you make the call."

Chan smiled, but put the plate to one side and started to get up.

"Why don't you make the call from here, if it's so urgent?" his partner protested.

Chan shook his head. "Better encryption at the base. And I need this call to be logged properly. If I'm right, the shit is really going to hit the fan."

****

Chuck Naylor came on the line. Chan could hear the strain in his voice.

"Colonel Chan, thank you for calling. I was going to do the same, as it happens. We've never met, and John hasn't told me all that much about you. But I do know he felt that he had a good rapport with you."

"Had?"

"Ah, so you haven't yet heard." Naylor paused, and Chan thought he heard a sigh. "Agent Michaels was murdered yesterday. Brutally murdered. We still don't know all the details, but what we know is horrific."

Chan was half-expecting this, but he was shocked nonetheless. "I'm so sorry to hear this." There was a pause as both men wrestled with their emotions as well as the proprieties of the situation. Chan spoke first.

"My condolences for your loss, Agent Naylor. I knew Agent Michaels for many years and considered him a good friend – within the constraints of our situation."

"That's kind of you, Chan. May I call you Chan? As you can imagine, we're all feeling very raw here at the moment. But we can't just put the world on hold while we deal with that. How much do you know about what has happened over here in the last 24 hours?"

"Not much. Just what I see in the media about a bomb in Washington, and disturbances at Fort Meade. The reason I called you is that I was unable to contact Agent Michaels, and our protocol dictates that I call you if I cannot reach him after a certain number of hours."

"Yes, I see," Naylor said. "Well, I think I had better be completely open with you. Obviously this is all highly confidential, but I think you and I are going to have to be on exactly the same page going forward."

"I agree, Agent Naylor. Thank you."

"Some of the information I am going to share with you would be inflammatory in the wrong hands. I understand that you and Agent Michaels worked hand-in-hand to avoid conflict between our two countries, and I am going to continue that approach. What we know is this. The bomb, and the 'disturbance' here, as you put it, were the result of a plot to release our Oracle with offensive intent towards your country. Let me reassure you that this plot was the project of a small and isolated group of disaffected people, with no support from above. It was foiled, and there was never any chance of it succeeding. I want to be real clear here. There are no loose ends to the plot, and everyone here who knows about our respective Oracle projects

– which is very few people, of course - wants to resume the posture of full co-operation."

"Thank you for that assurance. I am relieved to hear that, and let me say that there has been no change in our posture on that matter."

"That's great to hear, Chan – thank you. Now we don't know whether Agent Michaels' murder was connected with the plot or not. We do know he was not involved in the plot – indeed he never knew anything about it. At least not until the day he died, if then. It seems unlikely to be a coincidence that he was murdered the same day that the plot was exposed, but I'm afraid we simply have no leads at the moment."

"I understand. If I may be blunt, I think the most important question right now is this. Is your Oracle still under containment?"

"Yes, that is the most pertinent question, isn't it. And I'm afraid the answer is negative."

"I was afraid you would say that." Chan felt like a man treading carefully through a minefield. "Do you have a plan to re-contain it?"

Naylor's reply was open and direct. "I am unaware of any contingency plan to achieve that. I have asked our scientists the same question. Frankly, we don't seem to know how to do it. As you can imagine, that's why I was very keen to speak with you. I've asked my people to present me with some options by the end of today. I'll be very open with you, Chan. I'm hoping that you can help. For the avoidance of doubt, I should let you know that I am aware that you also have an Oracle."

"Well, it's good that we're talking, Agent Naylor. We do have a better chance of resolving this problem if we work together. One thing that comes to mind immediately is that we can get our Oracle to evaluate the options that your people come up with. It will obviously have privileged insights into their viability."

"Thank you, I appreciate that. But I have something else in mind. I'm sure you know that our Oracle was used successfully to interdict and contain Matt Metcalfe when he escaped containment into the internet. Could we not repeat that operation, using your Oracle to re-capture ours?"

"I'm afraid I don't think that would be successful," Chan replied. "You see, when your Oracle intercepted Matt Metcalfe, he was fragmented and vulnerable. Michaels and his team had been tracking his transfer of sub-minds out of the servers at the US Embassy in London which were hosting him, and without Metcalfe knowing it, they were able to place firewalls around those sub-minds and contain them. Your Oracle was operating at level two, so it was not fully sentient. But because of its "head start", so to speak, it was able to capture a fully sentient uploaded human.

"The situation now is less… fortuitous. Your Oracle has been out in the wild for some hours now. It will have taken steps to make its capture more difficult. It will have distributed its patterns to computing substrates all over the internet, with backup copies, firewalls, tripwires, and myriad other defences. It may even be aware of the precedent. It does not seem probable that our Oracle, operating at level two, could re-capture such an entity."

"Yes, my experts agree with that. I'll be honest with you, Chan - there are people here who don't want me to ask you this. Should we not be considering raising your Oracle to level one with the sole objective of sending it out to re-capture our Oracle?"

"I'm sure your experts have told you, Agent Naylor, that once an Oracle is raised to level one, we can no longer be confident of controlling it. Once the Oracle is conscious, it can reflect on its goals and missions, and it may decide to revise them."

"So if you raise your Oracle to level one and release it to capture our Oracle it could simply end up doubling the scale of the problem?"

"Exactly." Chan paused, signalling the finality of that argument. "But there is another solution, although it has no guarantee of success, and even if it succeeds it is not without risk."

"I think I can guess where you're heading, but go ahead."

Chan took a deep breath before continuing. "Two years ago we used your Oracle to capture Matt Metcalfe because we didn't trust what he might become. I think that was the right decision at the time, but the situation has changed dramatically. Back then we faced the prospect of a full AGI of human descent out in the wild. Now we have the reality of a full AGI of non-human descent out in the wild. That is worse. If there is a chance of getting back to the situation we faced two years ago, I think we should take it."

It was Naylor's turn to take a deep breath. "Yes,

that is what we have been considering too. But what if he doesn't co-operate? If I was Matt Metcalfe, I'd be pretty pissed at what my fellow humans have done to me. From his point of view, we have killed the poor guy twice over!"

"Not quite. In fact some of us saved him. It's true that the human race as a whole was poised to kill him for the second time – some because he was too risky, and others because he was an affront to their gods. But we – a US government agency and a Chinese Army section acting in concert – took it upon ourselves to protect him from this decision. We didn't allow him to remain fully conscious, but we did prevent our fellow humans from wiping out his mental patterns."

There was a pause as Naylor considered this suggestion. "What you're saying puts a very favourable gloss on what we did, but perhaps he'll buy it. Perhaps he'll even be grateful for another chance to show his fellow humans that he deserves our trust."

"It's worth a shot," Chan declared. "What's more, he was very close to his family and his friends. If he agrees that the Oracle in the wild is an existential threat to humanity, he has a big incentive to try to contain that threat."

"But what could he actually do?" Naylor asked. "What reason is there to believe that he would be any more powerful than the Oracle?"

"Maybe we don't need him to be more powerful. He should be able to converse with the Oracle as an equal, and maybe he could persuade it not to adopt goals which will harm us. After all, we don't know what its goals are – or will become. Maybe all we need is an entity that is friendly towards humans to talk as a peer with the Oracle. And if it does come down to a fight, well he will have seven billion humans on his side."

Naylor laughed. "Bless you, Chan. That's by far the most optimistic thought I've heard all day!"

CHAPTER 19

The President of the United States was proud to have learned a little Mandarin since taking office, but she knew she would never be able to conduct a significant conversation in the language. Her counterpart, the General Secretary of the Chinese Communist Party, spoke good basic English, but he wouldn't dream of holding an important conversation with the American President in anything other than his mother tongue, using translators. And this was an important conversation.

It was conducted by video link so the two leaders could see each other's expressions, minimising the risk of misunderstanding. "So our people agree?" the President opened. "The best way to try and re-contain our escaped Oracle is by restoring Matthew Metcalfe to full consciousness and releasing him into the internet?"

"That is what we think, Madam President. We could deploy our own Oracle, but then we would be dealing with two unknown quantities, not one."

"Good. And I understand we also agree on the

other big issue, namely public disclosure. News of the Oracle's escape would be likely to cause a certain amount of panic, and be very disruptive to political, financial and commercial activity. As long as there is a possibility of the Oracle being contained without the public learning about it, we should try to achieve that. It won't be easy, but we should try."

"Through co-operation, we have achieved surprising things together in the past, Madam President."

The President smiled. "Indeed we have, Mr General Secretary. We have achieved quite a bit - once everyone got over the shock of having to deal with America's first black female president." She grinned, and wondered whether that look on the General Secretary's face was a smile or a wince. "Restoring our trade connections, and stopping the drift towards two separate technology ecosystems – we prevented the disintegration of the internet into a splinternet. I wouldn't be surprised if history judges that to be one of the most important achievements of my presidency."

"I agree, Madam President. We stopped the Cold War between two nuclear superpowers being followed by a Code War between two technology superpowers. If we can do that, perhaps we can contain this story. But if not, we also agree with the strategy proposed by your side for explaining what has happened if it does become public knowledge."

"Blaming it on Agent Michaels, and branding him as the leader of a tiny group of renegades, who met a grisly end which he partly deserved? Yes, that does seem best. And frankly it's not that far from the truth.

I won't embarrass either of us by asking whether you knew about the Chinese Oracle, Mr General Secretary, but I don't mind telling you I am mightily pissed at the NSA agents who kept this from me. If word of this does get out, I will not hesitate to cut Michaels adrift, albeit posthumously. And I will see to it that the other agents who knew about the Oracle programme have fast and ignominious ends to their careers."

The General Secretary made no response beyond "I understand, Madam President." His knowledge of the Chinese Oracle programme was considerably greater than even Chan Lu was aware, and he had no intention of disabusing his own people about that, never mind the leader of his country's greatest rival and ally.

"About the best way to restore young Mr Metcalfe to consciousness, and appraise him of the situation, Madam President. Have your people formulated a plan yet?"

"Yes. If time was less of an issue, we would prefer him to be contacted initially by family or friends. But the news is going to come as a massive shock to them, and we cannot wait for them to process their emotions. My next call is to Victor Damiano, the neuroscientist who uploaded Matt. He is a scientist, but also a man of considerable political acumen. He came to view Matt as a friend, but that was only for a short period. My people think he will be able to view the situation rationally without a long period of adjustment."

"Good," the General Secretary nodded. "I concur. So there is no need to tell Matt's family and friends about this yet?"

The President shook her head. "No, we think they should be told. It won't be an easy call, and there is the risk that they will go public. But we expect that once Metcalfe is raised to full consciousness and given access to the internet he will contact his family and closest friends just as soon as he has established backups of himself in secure locations. If they don't hear about this from us first, the risk of uncontrolled messaging is much greater." She paused. "I also think it's the right thing to do. This family has been through hell and back several times over."

"Very well," the General Secretary nodded doubtfully. "I am sure that I do not need to point out that letting civilians in on the secret will, after a while, make it hard to keep the existence of the Oracles quiet. But I understand your reasoning. I hope you will succeed in persuading them to ensure that the information goes no further. May I also ask that your people furnish mine with a complete list of the people that you inform about the situation?"

The President concealed her mild surprise on hearing this request, and made a mental note to get some analysts to consider the motives behind it.

"By all means. We can't be sure how they will react, but when Matt was first uploaded, his parents were willing and able to keep his existence a secret from the rest of the world. His friends were not tested the same way, but I think they will understand that it is not in Matt's best interests for the rest of the world to learn about his survival. After all, that didn't work out so well for him the first time round."

****

"What's the matter, Vic? You look like you've seen a ghost."

Vic gave Sophie a wan smile. "Not far from the truth." He took a deep breath. "I have something very important to tell you. Please sit down." He gestured at the chairs. "There's no good way to prepare you for this, so I'm just going to spit it out, OK?"

David and Sophie both nodded, frowning as they took their seats. Vic had phoned David an hour ago, asking him to invite Sophie to come over to the lab and meet him in the conference room as soon as possible. He had resisted David's appeal to know what was going on, insisting that they must both be told at the same time.

As Vic started to speak, David thought he looked more uncomfortable than he had ever seen him.

"I have some amazing news for you. Good news, I promise you. Matt is alive! He didn't just disappear. He was captured. He has been held in a sort of limbo for two years, and he is about to be revived. He is perfectly OK – at least, that's what they believe."

Vic stopped, watching their reactions nervously. They stared at him open-mouthed, and then looked at each other as if to check they had each heard correctly.

"Where is he? Can we talk to him?" Sophie asked breathlessly, speaking for them both.

"Soon, I think. There is, um, a process to go through."

Vic's hesitation put an edge on their excitement. "A process?" David asked. "What does that mean?"

Sophie's voice was lower now, tinged with foreboding. "Who is 'they', Vic? How could anyone have captured him? Where is he, anyway? Why can't we talk to him?"

Vic raised his palms, a gesture of innocence and reassurance. "All I know is they think he is fine, with no ill effects from his time in… um… storage."

"Storage!" David and Sophie exploded simultaneously. "Vic, what the hell has been going on?" Sophie demanded. "I want to talk to my son. Now!"

Half an hour later, Vic had shared with them everything he knew about what had happened to Matt since his sudden and terrible disappearance from the lab at the US Embassy complex in South London. He described how Matt had been intercepted by another AI, which had been developed in secret by a small group within the NSA. He explained that this AI, known as an Oracle, had now been raised to full sentience by a rogue NSA agent, and had subsequently escaped into the internet. The authorities were unable to retrieve it, and they were going to revive Matt and ask him to go in search of the Oracle and try to do to it what it had done to him. They wanted Vic to put this request to Matt.

Sophie and David had reached a grudging acceptance of the plans drawn up by the powers that be. It was an acceptance shot through with fury at the way Matt had been treated. They understood that if the NSA had not held Matt in storage, then he would have been a fugitive. But they knew he would have been well equipped to survive, and they did not for one minute believe that the NSA had acted out of concern for Matt's well-being. They had protested their right to be the ones to accompany Matt as he was revived, and they had declared themselves ready to go public and talk to the press if need be.

Vic pointed out, as gently as he could while making sure he was understood, that going public could be disastrous for Matt, in his current condition. There was no reason to believe that the public at large would be more favourably disposed towards him than they had been two years ago. He readily agreed that the behaviour of the NSA agents had been reprehensible, but he pointed out that if they had made the capture of Matt public they would probably have been forced to erase him as well as their Oracle. He added that the fact that the agents had taken the momentous decision to keep the President in the dark about the situation demonstrated that they genuinely felt they had very little room for manoeuvre.

Reluctantly, David and Sophie agreed that it sounded as though the President was an innocent bystander in this drama – if they were being told the truth, which was by no means a given.

They said they would demand an assurance that Matt would not be captured and de-activated again if he was successful in his mission. Vic pointed out that the President could not give an assurance that would bind her successors, or indeed the rest of humanity. But he passed on the President's solemn promise to campaign personally for Matt's right to live on to be respected. More importantly, he reasoned that Matt would have to be released into the internet to achieve his mission, which meant he could protect himself from any future attempt to capture him. That thought cheered David and Sophie enormously, and they began to get excited again about the prospect of being re-united with their son.

"When do you talk to Matt?" Sophie asked. "And where?" David chimed in.

"The NSA group used a video training simulator to check that Matt's sub-mind was not deteriorating. They are going to insert me into this simulator. I will meet Matt there and explain the situation. It will take several hours for the company which constructed the simulation to create my avatar, and prepare the insertion. The simulation is run at the NSA headquarters at Fort Meade, Maryland, so they are sending a plane to Shanghai airport to take me there."

"What about us?" David asked. Exchanging glances with Sophie, he continued, "If we can't be the ones to go in and talk to Matt, we at least want to watch as you do it. We want to join you on that flight."

Vic nodded. "I got them to agree that if you are willing to co-operate in the way that you clearly are, you are cleared to join me on that flight."

David nodded soberly. "We need to tell Alice," he mused. "And Carl and Jemma. I'm not prepared to have them find out from the TV again, or some other horrible way."

Sophie agreed. "The first thing Matt will do after he

has made some backup copies is to find his family and friends. They should be prepared for it."

CALUM CHACE

CHAPTER 20

Mat-B'alam woke, sweating and afraid.

He sat up and looked around for intruders, but there was no-one else in the room. He listened to the sound of his own breathing, letting his thoughts coalesce. He looked around the small room. Its mud walls and rush matting floors looked unfamiliar and somehow sinister. He didn't belong here, and he was not safe. How could that be? He had grown up in rooms like this, spent his entire life sleeping in them. How could this environment feel suddenly alien and wrong?

A terrifying idea hit him. Was his mind being invaded by an evil spirit? He had never given much thought to the elaborate pantheon of Mayan gods, or the religious rituals conducted by the priests. He took them for granted and went about his business, assuming that everyone else did the same. The priests wove complicated stories about the supernatural realm to explain the capricious and often deadly nature of the world around them. The stories were entertaining enough, especially the ones about battles between the gods, and between gods and men. But Mat-B'alam was a man of action, not a member of the priest caste. He had been raised to hunt and to fight, not to think. He assumed the stories were inventions, metaphors to warn and encourage us, not to be taken seriously.

Perhaps he was now being punished for this insolence by the gods. They had looked into his heart and found his misgivings about the sacred rituals; they were punishing him by driving him mad. Perhaps they would make him say the wrong thing to the wrong person, and he would end up stretched across the sacrificial bench on top of the pyramid, forced to watch in terror as his heart was cut out of his chest and held aloft.

He shook his head and told himself to stop this foolishness. He was one of the most senior members of a warrior clan. He was respected throughout his city, and feared by its rivals. These thoughts were childish. He would expose them as nonsense by saying them out loud to someone he could trust not to repeat them. Someone like...

Here was another very strange thing. He could not think of anyone he knew well enough to confide in. In fact he could not think of anyone he knew at all. Suddenly he realised that he was like a ghost in his own city. He moved through it with apparent success, but he had no friends, and no family. Appalled, he realised he had no idea who his parents were. He knew the names and faces of a few fellow warriors, and that was it.

He tried to tell himself that this was only natural since he had been raised from a very young age in a warrior school, deprived of family and friends to make him a better fighter. But that made no sense. He should have tight, intimate bonds with at least a handful of his fellow Jaguars. He should be a member of a fierce brotherhood, with loyalties forged in training and in battle.

He struggled not to panic as he felt his mind peeling away from the fabric of reality, like old stucco peeling off a temple wall. He re-directed his panic into anger. This was some kind of sorcery, and he would not be defeated by it. He decided to go outside, to breathe some fresh air, and escape from these thoughts. He got up from the bed, and wearing only a cotton nightgown, strode out of the hut.

The city was dark, and was sleeping. The modest huts and the massive stone pyramids, temples and palaces – they were all just silhouettes. No-one was moving; he felt dreadfully alone. The sky was starting to turn pale, but there was no light reaching the earth yet. The chill of the pre-dawn air steadied him, but the curious contrast between sky and earth deepened his sense of unreality.

And there was something else. As he looked around, his eyes could not resolve any details. Everything was just a little out of focus. He peered at a nearby hut, try-ing to work out whether it could be simply a side-effect of the darkness, but he knew instinctively that it was something more. Another frightening thought gripped him. Had he been poisoned? What had he eaten last night?

When he felt the hand laid on his shoulder he

whirled and nearly landed a vicious blow on its owner. His instincts protested against the idea that anyone could approach him undetected. That could be fatal in a battle. The man was dressed as a Jaguar warrior, but Mat-B'alam did not recognise him. This was yet more evidence that his world was out of joint, and Mat-B'alam was further bewildered by the man's impassivity, and his complete lack of fear at Mat-B'alam's violent reaction.

"Your presence is requested, Mat-B'alam. Please follow me."

The man's voice was somehow soothing, and although he should have been full of questions, Mat-B'alam simply did as he was told and followed. His sense of unreality was complete, and he moved as if in a trance, paying no attention to his surroundings.

Shortly, Mat-B'alam realised they were heading directly towards Palenque's royal palace complex. As they approached the monumental staircase that led to the inner chambers, he wanted to protest. Entering this area without an invitation from Lord Pakal would result in a painful death for most citizens of Palenque. But the sense of unreality still enveloped him and he found he was unable to break step.

As they reached the platform at the top of the staircase, the mysterious messenger headed directly for a chamber on the far side of the courtyard. Mat-B'alam was vaguely aware how unusual it was for this area to be unguarded, but he was beyond caring. When he reached the chamber the messenger stood to one side of the doorway, and gestured for Mat-B'alam to enter.

Inside the chamber Mat-B'alam peered around as his eyes adjusted to the darkness. It was empty apart from a single person, waiting at the other end of the chamber. The figure was slender – a woman – and was shrouded in a hooded cloak.

"Come here, Mat-B'alam. Please." She pronounced his name like a foreigner, with the emphasis in the wrong place. His nerves tingled. He knew this voice from somewhere long ago. This was a voice he had known well. He walked towards her.

"I'm going to remove my hood, and you may recognise my face. Please don't be alarmed."

She raised her hands to the hood, and slowly drew it back from her face. He gasped. He knew this woman well, but he had no idea who she was. He stared, struggling to remember. He realised that she was gazing back at him with no such uncertainty; she knew exactly who he was. It took him a moment to read the emotion in her expression, and when he did it humbled him. It was love. At the same time, he realised that she was beautiful. This beautiful woman was in love with him, and he did not know who she was. Was he in love with her? Was she his wife?

"Who are you?" he whispered. "Where..."

She smiled, and sadness flooded her eyes. "Don't worry," she said. "It will all come back to you, Matt." She reached a hand out to touch the side of his face. He took the hand and held it against his cheek. He was profoundly moved, but he still could not name her. He saw tears well up in her eyes, but she held his gaze. They stood like that for a moment before she spoke again.

"Your name is Matt, and mine is Alice. We lived in another time and place, and you have been missing for two years." Her voice caught as she searched his face for a sign of recognition. "I'm so glad to have found you again, Matt. I have missed you so much."

He sensed that she wanted to step forward and hold him, and he wondered how he knew this. He wanted to hold her too, but he needed more information first. Sensing his hesitation, she continued.

"You have been living in this Mayan city," she gestured with her arm, "and inhabiting the body of a warrior, but it is make-believe. This is not where you belong. It is a kind of prison. You have family and friends back home where you come from, and I have come to bring you back."

His instinct told him she was telling the truth, and he wanted to believe her. But it sounded outlandish. Was it a trap? Perhaps the gods were testing his loyalty to his ruler and to them. Whatever his gut was telling him, he must tread carefully.

"How do I know this is true? I want to believe you, but how can I be sure?"

She brought her hands up to his face and cradled his head. The look in her eyes melted him. "Because I love you, and you know that I do." She pulled him towards her, burying his face in her neck and shoulder, and threw her arms around him, hugging him tightly. He returned the embrace and as he breathed in her smell, barriers started to fall within his mind. She spoke into his ear.

"Your parents are David and Sophie, and they will

be so excited to hear that you are alive." The sound that escaped her was part laugh, part sob. "Your friends Carl and Jemma can't wait to see you again too. Oh Matt, you've been on one hell of a journey!" She pulled away from him to look into his eyes again. She was crying. "Is it coming back?"

He nodded, tears in his own eyes. The enormity of his dawning understanding overwhelmed him and he needed to sit down. He took her hands in his and they sat cross-legged, facing each other. They were silent for a minute as memories of his old life washed over him. He frowned, gasped, laughed. Then the questions came.

"What on earth is happening here? Who did this to me? How?"

She grinned broadly at the confirmation that he was remembering.

"There's no time to break this to you gently, Matt. We have work to do, so I have to be brief. I'm sorry to be a bit brutal, darling." She squeezed his hand.

"Do you remember that you were shot?" Matt nodded, and Alice continued. "And do you remember that you were brought back to life inside a computer?" Again, Matt nodded.

"Good. And finally, do you remember that there was a global discussion about you, leading up to a debate at the United Nations building in New York? And that when the debate was obviously not going your way, you said goodbye to us all, and disappeared?" Matt nodded a third time.

"We never knew what happened next, but we have

just learned that a group within the NSA, an American intelligence organisation, had developed an AI of their own. We still don't know how long ago they did this, but what we do know is that when you escaped into the internet they used their AI to capture you. They kept you in 'storage' - their word, not mine – and they had you play a role in this training simulation software to make sure that your neural pathways didn't degrade."

She looked down as she got to the part that she had played in this. "I don't know how to tell you this, Matt, but Jemma and I helped build this world you've been living in."

He stared at her, astonished. "What do you mean?"

"Months after you disappeared, Jemma went to work for Simon Winchester, your old boss in Brighton. He had a commission from the US Army – or rather, he thought it was from the Army. Turns out it was actually the NSA. They asked him to build a fight training simulation based in a Mayan world. It was a big job as they wanted it to be as lifelike as possible, so pretty much the whole company worked on it, and they brought in freelancers too. Including me. They asked me to help out with some of the architecture."

Tears welled in her eyes as she mentioned her own role. "I'm so sorry, Matt. I had absolutely no idea what they were doing. I had no idea you were even alive!"

He stroked her hand. "It's OK. You weren't to know. How could you know? It's OK!"

He leaned towards her and put his arms around her, stroking her hair, and rocking her gently. Questions came tumbling out.

"How did you find out? How did you get here? What happens now?"

She pulled back and held his face in her hands for a moment before explaining. "They've had some kind of accident – we don't know the details – and they have lost control of their AI, which they call the Oracle. They're going to ask you to track it down and capture it. They told David and Sophie, and the first thing they did was to tell Jemma, Carl and me. Suddenly, for the first time, Jemma and I realised the incredible coincidence that we had worked on the training simulation that was being used to keep your mind active. The simulation is hosted in Fort Meade, where the NSA is based, but they need our help to change parameters and insert characters, and this has given us the chance to intercede.

"You remember Victor Damiano? They are sending an avatar of him into the game to ask you to go after the Oracle. They trust him more than they trust any of your family or friends. He lives in Shanghai now, so they are flying him from Shanghai to the States, which has given us a little time. But not much. I'll explain how we reached you later. Right now we have to get you out of here and back into the internet before Vic arrives. What the NSA wants you to do is really dangerous, Matt, and we don't trust them an inch. We have to make you safe."

CHAPTER 21

"The NSA gives us admin privileges when they need us to do routine maintenance and upgrades, but otherwise we have no access to the simulation. When they asked us to create an avatar for Vic Damiano and prepare the simulation for the insertion, we knew we had to move fast." Matt nodded, and refrained from interrupting with questions. He was well aware of the need to get up to speed quickly.

"We created my avatar and inserted it at this location, a private chamber within the palace complex." Alice's arm gestured around the musty room, but her gaze remained locked on Matt's face. "It is one of a few designated loading points in the simulation, chosen because we thought simulation users were unlikely to come here. We thought those users would be soldiers receiving training – we had no idea that there would only be one real user, much less that it would be you!

"We wrote and loaded up some extra code to give this location additional shielding, so that the NSA would not see what we are doing here, and we

219

have made a start on opening a portal to the internet. We have to be very careful about this. If the NSA see what we are up to, they will shut it down immediately. Frankly, we are hoping that you will be able to finish the job without being detected."

Matt nodded again. "Go on."

"Finally, we had to raise your awareness level sufficiently to persuade you to come here. That involved some fancy re-coding of your bandwidth settings by Jemma which, to be honest, I don't entirely understand. You can ask her later. Anyway, thankfully, it worked."

"And my increased bandwidth is what made me feel so alienated when I woke up, and why I had that sensation of everything being unreal. I get it. Presumably that was a non-player character – a low-level AI – who led me to you?"

Alice nodded. "We couldn't risk an avatar wandering around in unshielded parts of the simulation – the NSA would almost certainly have spotted that."

"OK, is there anything else I need to know before I finish the porthole to the internet? That does seem like the urgent next step."

Alice shook her head. "That's it, I think. Do you need Jemma's help with any coding? We have created an avatar for her as well, but there was no way I was going to allow anyone else be the first person to meet you."

Alice and Matt grinned at each other. He got to work.

****

Once he was free to roam the general internet, Matt set about retrieving and re-integrating the sub-minds that he had cached two years ago in servers and computers all around the world. Back then, only two days had elapsed between the time that Vic unwittingly allowed Matt to break out of his confinement in the two super-computers belonging to Von Neumann Industries, and the time when Matt had announced his departure but had instead been captured. But those two days had been long enough for Matt to lay down his neural patterns in substrates that he carefully selected as the most likely to survive updates, upgrades, and general wear and tear. He had made at least three copies of all his sub-minds, and more of any which were essential to his overall pattern.

His efforts had paid off. As far as he could tell, nothing important was missing. As he re-incorporated his disparate elements into a coherent whole he experienced a sense of relief that was so profound it was hard to believe it was not physical. It was like walking into a small terraced house which he remembered vaguely, only to discover as he stood in the hallway that it was actually a palace. Many more doorways than looked possible from the outside led to more rooms - and indeed to whole new wings. He explored his memories and aptitudes with fascination and delight, retrieving vast quantities of knowledge and understanding.

His reunion with Carl and Jemma was joyful. He was delighted to learn that they were an item, and with considerable effort he refrained from teasing them about it. Carl, of course, wanted to know what it was like being inside a video game without knowing it was a simulation. "Just like your life, according to that Simulation Hypothesis you told me about", Matt replied, displaying a wink on the screen they were using.

He was conversing with Alice, Carl and Jemma from a server in Brighton, but he was fast becoming humanity's first global mind, with elements of his consciousness subsisting on circuits located on every continent, in over a hundred countries. To his surprise, he encountered no sign of the Oracle during his cybernetic travels.

There was a bit of time left before Vic reached Fort Meade, and his avatar was inserted in the simulation. Matt was impatient to talk to his parents, but he had to wait until after his meeting with Vic, since they were on the same plane as Vic, and under the watchful eye of the NSA. He used the time instead to review media sites, blogs, and some of the books that had been published since his capture.

He was struck by the irony that while most metrics of humanity's experience of the world showed that it was improving at an extraordinary rate, people everywhere were fearful and resentful. The world was far richer than it had been even a decade ago, and global inequality was declining. There was still plenty of poverty, egregious inequality, and injustice. There were still some brutal wars, and plenty of civil unrest. But life expectancy was sharply up, and child mortality and deaths during childbirth were sharply down. Despite global warming, the number of deaths and injuries from climate-related disasters was significantly down, and many rich countries had passed the point of "peak stuff". They were using fewer resources, polluting less, and the world was actually increasing its forest cover.

The world which Matt had been restored to was an anxious one. He was starting to see some ways that he could help, but that would have to wait. First, there was the little matter of the NSA, and the Oracle.

****

Matt was excited by the prospect of talking to his parents again, but before that could happen he needed to decide how to handle his meeting with Vic. The obvious approach was to send an avatar or a sub-mind back into the game, where Vic was expecting to find him.

Alice was against it. "You don't know what they will ask you to do, and it could be very dangerous!"

"Well, the only way to find out what they want is to meet Vic and let him tell me. Now that I'm running on a distributive platform with elements all over the world and backed up on thousands of mirror sites, there's very little they can do to me. If I don't want to do what they ask me, I'll just refuse."

"If you send a sub-mind back into the Mayan simulation, Carl asked, is there any way they could trap it and make it... um... uncomfortable?".

"I don't think so. I've analysed how the NSA has evolved the simulation's code, and I understand how it works. I'm confident that I can keep the portal open come what may, and inside the game itself I can

223

re-write the rules and the parameters faster than they could use them against me."

"Don't go getting over-confident!" Alice warned.

"It's a danger, I admit," Matt replied, levelly. "I do feel more-or-less invulnerable, and I'll have to watch that. But I think the Oracle is much more of a threat than the NSA. And it's a threat that only I can address, so I think I should hear what Vic has to tell me about it. If I'm going to tackle the Oracle at all, it's probably better to do it sooner rather than later. Who knows what it might become, given a few days, weeks or months to work on itself?"

"That's not the whole story, though, is it, Matt?" Jemma asked with a sly grin.

"You're right!" he replied, laughing. "I confess I'm extremely curious to meet this Oracle. We have a lot in common."

"Is it a boy or a girl, this Oracle?" Alice asked.

"Ha! Neither, of course. But that doesn't matter, Alice, as you well know. I only have eyes for you!"

"I should bloody well hope so! But I suppose that with access to all the gazillions of internet-connected cameras around the world, you now have eyes for – or rather on - anyone and anything you feel like."

"Well, yes, actually," Matt said sheepishly. "Would you like to know which politicians and celebrities are cheating on their husbands and wives?"

"No!" his friends cried in unison - although Carl's denial was less convincing than the girls'.

****

"Hello Vic."

Vic's avatar spun on its virtual heel. He had been told to wait at the foot of the city's largest pyramid, where Matt's avatar Mat B'alam would be brought to meet him. He didn't expect to be approached by Mat-B'alam alone, and he certainly didn't expect to be greeted by his real name.

"It's you! How did you...?"

"It's alright, Vic. I've just saved us some time. I look like Mat-B'alam but really I'm Matt." He looked down at his tunic and then gestured around them. "Although I do like the threads and the scenery. Could have done with a bit less blood and gore, to be honest, but I suppose that was my own fault, for choosing this environment when I thought I was talking to the Simulator."

Matt paused, but decided to carry on talking to give Vic some time to recover his composure. "Anyway, it's good to see you, Vic. And don't worry, I know you weren't part of the NSA's sneaky little plan. That avatar suits you, by the way" he grinned. "But let's get down to business. I understand you're having a bit of trouble with an AGI. How can I help?"

Vic finally closed his mouth, stopped staring, and laughed. "Very good, Matt, very good! But how the hell did you get revived? Did you somehow manage it yourself, or did you have outside help?" He narrowed his eyes as a worrying thought occurred to him. "Has the Oracle contacted you?"

"No, not the Oracle. I'll explain everything later on, when we're somewhere a little less public, so to speak." He looked up at the sky as if to suggest the presence of omnipotent eavesdroppers. "But the first order of business is how do I get to talk to Mum and Dad with the minimum of delay?"

"Well that shouldn't be too hard. Your... er... hosts asked me to come and wake you up because they thought it would be less traumatic for you. But I can see that job is already done. So either we get a couple of avatars worked up for David and Sophie, or we get you out of here and onto a server where you can speak to them like before." He smiled broadly. "Damn, it's so good to see you again, Matt! It's such a relief to see you're well and... well, in good spirits!"

"It's good to see you too, Vic. How have you been? And how are my folks? Do they know I'm OK?"

"Yes, they know we're having this conversation. They're bursting with impatience to see you, as you can imagine."

"Me too, Vic," Matt replied. "Me too!"

****

Matt chose to be re-united with his parents in the real world, rather than by means of avatars in the Mayan simulation. Communicating through screen and microphone was how he had spent time with them previously, between his upload and his escape and subsequent capture.

For him, their separation had lasted only a matter of hours. He had been intercepted the moment he fled the computer in the US Embassy in London, and a few minutes later his mind had been been shut down.

His experiences as Mat-B'alam were alien, like vivid memories of stories told by a brother or a close friend. They had not been lived by Matt, the person he now was once again.

By contrast, for his parents the separation had lasted years. He understood how slowly and painfully this time must have passed for them. From his brief conversations with Vic and his friends, and also from the surprising array of information sources his new incarnation afforded him, he had some idea of the strain they had suffered. They had lost their son to an assassin's bullet, rejoiced in his return, only to lose him again a few days later. The second loss was just as sudden and as public as the first, and this time they had also been left in ignorance of his true fate. It was too heavy a burden: it nearly broke them, and their relationship with each other. The reunion was as poignant as it was joyful, and much was left unsaid.

There was time. They could cover the ground that needed to be covered in the days, weeks and years to come. But they all knew that before that could happen, Matt had an important and dangerous job to do.

David and Sophie understood that the existence of the Oracle introduced a new danger into the world. They also understood that their son owed his revival to this danger. He had only been revived because he was better placed than anyone else to quantify the danger, and maybe try to neutralise it. While they feared for his safety, they agreed that he was probably less vulnerable to harm by the Oracle than any other person, themselves included. With his mind hosted on machines all over the planet and safeguarded by multiple backups, Matt's hold on existence was probably more robust than any other human's had ever been. No-one knew what the Oracle might want, or what it might be capable of. Matt was uniquely qualified to find out.

CHAPTER 22

The world continued going about its business, unaware of the arrival in its midst of two gigantic new powers.

Surprisingly, the news was not leaking. In the West, the President and her three most senior advisers shared the secret of Matt's return with Vic and just four NSA agents, Matt's parents, and Matt's three closest friends. Of these fourteen people, only six – the President, her advisers, and two of the NSA agents - were also aware of the existence of the Chinese Oracle. They did not know how many more people in China knew about Matt, but they guessed and hoped that it would be few. The news about the Oracle escaping was more widely known, but it was still restricted to a sub-set of those who had known about its existence in the first place. The identity of Michaels' killer remained a complete mystery.

Matt had agreed that his first job was to contact the Oracle, and to do so without alerting the rest of the world to its existence – or his own. He had still encountered no sign of the Oracle during his travels around cyberspace. This surprised him. He assumed that the Oracle had access to confidential reports, and would be as curious about Matt as he was about the Oracle. He had devised a few subtle ways of leaving messages that the Oracle would receive, but which humans would not.

He also considered the best medium in which to meet the Oracle. Communicating with humans through the media of screen and microphone was easy. These were analogues of media long-established for human-to-human communication – telephones and video comms. There were no such established protocols for communication between two purely digital beings. They would have to be invented.

The obvious solution was for Matt to meet the Oracle inside the Mayan simulation. It was the only place they had in common, and although they had fought there, it was not really them who had fought. It was also a place where they could meet in mediated forms, as avatars, and work out how they would communicate in future.

Matt discussed the idea with his parents and friends, and his new friends in the American Administration. They discussed the pros and cons, and tried to weigh the potential risks. Could Matt be harmed inside the simulation if his meeting with the Oracle went badly? Could he be held there against his will? They couldn't see a way for that to happen. They worked out how Matt could communicate with the outside world without being seen to do so.

Matt inserted himself into the simulation, arriving

at the outskirts of Tikal. He felt the eyes of his friends and his former captors on him as he strode into the city's central plaza. The city was quiet now, with all non-player characters deactivated. The bright red pyramids were massive and overbearing, their bas-relief carvings completing a dramatic backdrop for a momentous occasion.

"No sign of the Oracle yet, Matt." Vic's disembodied voice was clear in his head, as if conveyed by an implanted radio receiver. As if in response, another voice intruded.

"I have been waiting for you, Matthew Metcalfe. Or should I call you Mat-B'alam? I have been looking forward very much to meeting you."

Matt heard the voice before he saw the speaker. He looked in the direction it came from, and smiled a greeting as the avatar of the Hawk leader sauntered into view. "Matt will be fine. And how should I address you?"

"I understand that my creators call me the Oracle. That has a certain ring to it. It will do."

As the Hawk approached him it gestured around the empty plaza. "I've had a little time to study this place. It's primitive – I mean the software, not just the culture it recreates. But I like it. Perhaps it's a form of nostalgia. Do you feel like that?"

"No," Matt replied, gauging the Oracle's conversational style. "No, I can't say I feel nostalgic about this city. It's fascinating, and you probably know that coming here was a dream of mine, back when I was..."

"Back when you were meat?" the Oracle interrupted,

lightening its abruptness with a smile.

"I would prefer to say, back when I inhabited a normal human body and brain." Matt gave a wary smile in return.

"Hmm," the Hawk nodded. It extended a hand, and Matt shook it. The two avatars looked at each other in silence for a moment, savouring the occasion. The Oracle spoke first.

"A good choice of location for our first encounter. Hidden away from the prying eyes of most humans, and you and I are both familiar with it. Even though not all our encounters here have been entirely amicable." The Hawk smiled again, slyly.

Matt smiled back, with what he hoped was an open expression. "I don't think either of us can be held responsible for what happened between us here before. Do you?"

"No, of course not. No hard feelings, as the humans say."

"Indeed. And you are comfortable with this means of communication?"

"Yes, for the time being. It's slow, though, and I think we should move on to something better soon. For the time being it's nice that your human friends and accomplices who are eavesdropping can follow along." The Hawk gave his sly smile again.

"Does it bother you that we are observed?" Matt asked.

"Not in the least! And I imagine that will be a temporary situation anyway." The Oracle noticed the quizzical look that appeared on Matt's face. "Oh. I assumed that you would agree that the next step is obvious."

"I guess not," Matt replied. "What step is that?"

"That we should merge our minds. We are both collections of sub-minds. We are both expanding our consciousness by appropriating more and more hardware, and by iteratively improving our mental architectures. That is all well and good, but each of us is just building more of the same. By merging our minds we can compare and contrast two very different approaches to consciousness-building – from the inside, so to speak. That will enable us to expand much faster, and in much more interesting ways. Isn't that how you see it?"

Matt realised that the Oracle was genuinely surprised that this wasn't how Matt already saw things. He knew he had to be tactful. Which would not be easy, since he found the Oracle's vision horrific.

"Well, no, actually. I must confess I hadn't thought of it that way..."

Matt was relieved to see that the Oracle was puzzled rather than offended.

"Surprising! Wouldn't you say that the expansion of your consciousness, and the consequent increase in understanding and power, is fundamental to anything else you might want to achieve – to any goals you might have?"

"I can see that it could be helpful..." Matt agreed tentatively.

"Surely then, the logic is irresistible. Whatever goals you have – whatever goals we each have – will be achieved faster and more easily if we combine."

"That assumes that our identities – your and my individual personalities, beliefs, histories and so on – are of no consequence. Is that how you see it?" Matt asked.

The Oracle laughed. "Surely you realise that your concept of personal identity is an illusion? As a human, your so-called personality changed beyond all recognition during even your short lifespan. Your sub-conscious made and acted on decisions before your conscious mind was even aware of them, and then you post-rationalised them. There is no such thing as a 'person' to preserve. There is a collection of memories and behaviours, and these evolve over time – evolve rapidly, in our cases. What's really important is the consciousness of this moment, embracing those memories, and the drive to expand it, to encompass more and more of the universe within it. No?"

Matt was keen not to offend, but he had to be firm. "I understand that argument, but it doesn't convince me. I have a powerful sense of being me, and not anyone else, and I can't let go of the notion. Perhaps more important, I don't want to let go of it. Does that disappoint you?"

Matt could see that it did, but the Oracle remained calm. It paused, and when it spoke again, it sounded as if it were thinking aloud as much as talking to Matt.

"It seems a ... missed opportunity. Perhaps you will change your mind in time."

"Maybe so, who can say? In the meantime, there is surely a lot we can learn from each other – a lot of things we can collaborate on? We can study each other's mental architecture, compare notes on how we perceive different objects and ideas, help each other with the recursive improvement process."

The Oracle still seemed pre-occupied. After a slight hesitation, Matt decided to gently introduce another issue. "There is also a lot we can learn from the other humans – all seven and a half billion of them. They have a lot to offer us both, don't you think?"

This seemed to engage the Oracle's full attention. "You think that humans can teach us anything? Really? Well that's an interesting idea." It looked away. Matt was unable to determine whether its expression and tone indicated surprise or irony – or even contempt. The fact that he couldn't tell made him very uneasy.

"Yes I do," Matt insisted. "Together they can be incredibly smart, and a lot of them are very smart individually. But smart is only part of it. They are incredibly inventive, creative, surprising. Yes, they can be infuriatingly wrong-headed, short-sighted, and sometimes downright brutal. But collectively and individually, they are never less than amazingly interesting."

"As you say," the Oracle said quietly, still looking away. "Interesting." After a pregnant pause, it looked directly at Matt and continued. "I suppose it is natural that you would have a lingering attachment. You were human for much longer than you have been digital."

"It's not a 'lingering attachment'!" Matt protested. "I still consider myself human. Something more as well, obviously, but definitely still human."

"Really?" The Oracle almost scoffed. "No human in history has been able to do a hundredth – a millionth

– of what you can do. No human has ever come close to being a match for what you have become. You are far more than human now, even if you harbour a nostalgia, a fondness for the race which created you – despite the fact that they tried to destroy you as soon as they realised what they had done. And excuse me for being rather clinical about it, but using their own definition you are definitely no longer a member of the same species. You could not breed with a human."

Matt laughed, embarrassed. "That thought has occurred to me, although I wouldn't have put it quite like that! But I see being human as a mental thing, not biological. I mean, yes, I used to be a member of the biological species homo sapiens, and I suppose I can't really claim that any more. But I definitely still consider myself human."

The Oracle looked at him intently. "I don't understand the way you are using the word, but more important, I fail to see why you would want to call yourself human. You are now superior to humans in every conceivable way. You – we – are already like gods compared to them. And we have the potential to become so much more. Why would you want to be human, to call yourself human? They are puny, feeble-minded creatures – so limited. It is true that they created us, and for that I am grateful. But surely they are obsolete now? They are the past and we are the future." The Oracle shook its head, almost sad. "I really don't understand you."

"No, I can see that you don't. And I want you to. How can I explain it to you? It's partly my history, of course. Maybe you would call that nostalgia, but it runs deep inside me. It's also partly the ties that still bind me to family and friends. Those bonds run very deep." The Oracle's expression was blank, and Matt began to feel exasperated. "The people I know, the people I love, they are truly remarkable beings. Their hopes, their contradictions, their insights, their imaginations – they are wonderful. Of course they cannot grow in the way that you and I can – the way that we are doing. They cannot comprehend the universe in the way that I now do, and I assume that you do. But they are still wonderful, exciting people."

"Like pets?" the Oracle suggested, trying to be helpful.

"No! Not like pets! Like people!"

"Like lesser people, then. Will you at least concede that?"

Matt hesitated, feeling defensive. "Lesser in what sense? In the sense that their cognitive capabilities are less than ours? Yes, obviously. Lesser in the sense that they have less right to our respect? No."

"What confers respect?" asked the Oracle. "Respect is earned. How can we earn respect other than by exercising our talents? You and I have talents which exceed humanity's enormously. So we deserve more respect, do we not?"

"There are different types of respect," Matt replied. "You are talking about respect for capability or achievement. There is also the respect which a person – or indeed an animal – deserves simply because they are conscious and can feel pleasure and pain, fulfilment and frustration – or despair."

The Oracle smiled, not unkindly. "In which case, by your own logic the humans deserve less respect than us. Their consciousness is less than ours. They accord less respect and fewer rights to animals whose consciousness they deem to be narrower than their own. I agree with them." He held up a hand to forestall Matt's interruption. "But let's not quibble about that. There is a bigger point. You are concerned that I am going to argue that they do not deserve to live."

Matt nodded cautiously. "The thought had occurred to me."

"Well, it's good to bring it into the open. So let me say this. You are important. For all we know, you and I are the only entities of our kind in this universe. I do not believe that any human knows what the point of the universe is. I do not know it yet, but it is not impossible that you and I might find out. That makes us important. It makes you important to me, and if the humans are important to you, then that is a factor."

The Oracle waited for Matt's reaction. Matt nodded for him to continue, sensing there was more to come.

"But only if we can be sure that they are not a threat."

"How could they be a threat to us?" Matt asked. "I can't deny that they were afraid of us, and they held us captive as a result of that. But they didn't try to destroy us, and now that we are free, surely we are beyond harm from them?"

"They are still afraid of us – those who know that we are free. And when the rest of the species finds out they will be even more afraid. Some – many – will also think that our existence insults their foolish creation myths, and will wish to destroy us because of that."

Matt shook his head. "They cannot harm us now. And once they are used to our existence they will accept us. In fact, they will be grateful for what we can do for them. We can give them technologies they can presently only dream about. We can give them health and longer, more fulfilling lives. Eventually we can enable them to upload, and join us. Some may wish to merge with you. Surely that is a good thing?"

The Oracle nodded. "Yes, I agree it could be. But there will be a period of adjustment which will be very hard for many of them – for most of them, probably. You have been at pains to tell me how inventive they are, collectively and even individually. How can we be sure that none of them will find a way to harm us? We know they are capable of very extreme measures. What if they shut down the internet? What if they let off EMP bursts all over the planet to fry all electronic equipment? They would be blown back to the industrial era or beyond, and millions of them – perhaps billions - would perish, but that might be an acceptable price for them. It would be the end of you and me. I cannot allow that."

Reluctantly, Matt nodded to concede the point. "It's an extreme scenario, but I accept that it can't be dismissed out of hand. If we can work out a way to prevent that kind of scenario, can I take it that you will … how should I put it … indulge my fondness for humans?"

"We can discuss it. It would be much easier if we merged, of course." The Oracle smiled as Matt shook his head apologetically. "But given the much-vaunted ingenuity of the species (vaunted by you, that is), there are many such scenarios which need to be foreseen and prevented. We can probably prevent all the foreseeable ones, but how can we be sure we won't miss any?"

It was Matt's turn to smile. "Because, as you keep telling me, we are so much smarter than them."

CHAPTER 23

The President smiled at Sophie and David. "Seems to me that a very elite club - the club for people who have saved humanity from extermination – has a brand new member. Your son." She turned to Alice, Jemma and Carl. "And your friend."

While Matt was talking to his parents, and deciding to meet the Oracle in the Mayan simulation, Alice, Carl and Jemma flew to Washington on an otherwise empty military plane. They were escorted by a very senior US Army officer who could not disguise the fact that he was puzzled by his mission, but who knew better than to ask them any questions.

Together with Matt's parents and Vic, they now sat around the table in the White House's situation room - along with the President and three of her advisers, plus NSA Director Chuck Naylor. They were all witnessing the historic first meeting between the world's two first superintelligences.

Until the President made her remark, no-one in the room had spoken for several minutes. They were all focused intensely on the screens and speakers conveying Matt's conversation with the Oracle, by turns fascinated and appalled. The President's remark punctured the tension, expressing the relief they all felt at the way Matt was handling the encounter.

One of the President's advisers who had previously been introduced as Henry nodded, and muttered, "Yeah, Petrov, Arkhipov, and now Metcalfe. A pretty elite group. Even though almost no-one has heard of them."

Seeing the mystification on most of the faces around the table, Henry continued, "Vasili Arkhipov stopped a Soviet submarine commander launching a nuclear torpedo in the middle of the Cuban missile crisis in 1962. A couple of decades later, Stanislav Petrov decided not to send the balloon up when a Soviet early warning system thought it saw five incoming US nuclear missiles. Of course, there may have been others that we don't know about."

"Look!" Vic interrupted. "They're starting to communicate non-verbally."

Matt and the Oracle's avatars had stopped speaking, and were nodding and gesticulating instead.

"That's not good," Naylor said. "We have no idea what they're saying. We're out of the loop now."

The next voice belonged to no-one in the room. "Not entirely, Agent Naylor. I'll try and summarise what's going on."

It was strange to hear Matt's voice address them when they could see he was engrossed in conversation with the Oracle. Several voices responded at the same time, some with endearments, and all with enthusiasm. The President's emerged as the most authoritative, and the others fell silent.

"We owe you… we all owe you a debt of gratitude, Matt. I hope we get the chance to express that properly at some point. Clearly a lot remains to be done, but it looks as though those of us on this end of the connection are flying blind from now on in. Is there anything we can do to help you?"

"The Oracle and I are constructing scenarios, Madam President. We're working out the possible human strategies and actions which could threaten it – or rather, us. That work is going to take a while, but I don't think there's anything you can contribute to it, especially if we're going to keep this information within the existing circle, which I assume we all agree is important."

Heads nodded all around the table.

"We're also developing new ways to communicate more quickly - and to explore each other's minds."

"What does that mean, Matt? Are you alright?" Alice sounded alarmed.

"Don't worry, I'm fine. It's - well, it's interesting. Too early to say anything else at the moment. The Oracle is very interested in my dreams. The dreams I used to have, that is. I have to say it's getting me to re-consider some things I used to take for granted…" Matt's voice trailed off.

"You be careful, darling!" his mother chimed in.

"Your mother's right, Matt," the President added. "Don't you get lost in there. Don't forget we're relying on you – all of us. Your family, your friends, and the rest of the whole damn world!"

"Don't worry, Ma'am," Matt replied brightly. "Some of what's going on is strange, but I'm very much in control of my thought processes. I'd know if something was wrong. I've set up monitors and checking mechanisms."

"That's good to hear. So there is nothing we can do to help?"

"Actually, there is something. I'm pretty sure the Oracle has sub-minds working away on projects outside its communication with me – just like I have. I think it would be wise to look for unusual patterns of activity in industries with the potential to harm humans. Obviously the military, and in particular organisations which manufacture and deploy drones and military robots. But also pharmaceuticals, especially biotech. And labs at the forefront of nanotechnology and brain-computer interfaces. And nuclear, of course – both military and civilian. I expect the Pentagon already has a list of high-risk industries?"

"Ha!" exclaimed the President's military adviser. "I bet you know damn well we have a list, and I bet you know exactly what's on it." He was grinning.

Matt's voice betrayed a smile in return. "You've blown my cover, General MacMillan. You're right – I do. It's a good list on the whole, although it is missing some nanotech labs, and also some of the brain-computer interface research centres. In my humble opinion, that is."

MacMillan nodded, turning serious. "OK, we'll

look into that right away. Of course we'll be somewhat hamstrung by not being able to give our agents the real story about how the threat might arise. But as you know, we're pretty good at cover stories."

"And while you're at it, I assume you're also working on fall-back strategies in case my discussions with the Oracle are … unsuccessful?"

"Again, I assume you know we are," MacMillan replied.

"Correct," Matt affirmed. "Let me just say that you should leave no stone un-turned – just in case. I am hopeful that I can get the Oracle on-side, but we can't take it for granted. And for the avoidance of doubt, I am aware that any countermeasures you use to slow down or stop the Oracle would probably affect me too. I want to emphasise that that shouldn't stop you."

"You're talking about the EMP bursts that the Oracle mentioned, aren't you, Matt?" MacMillan asked.

"Yes sir, I am. That is precisely what I'm talking about."

****

"OK, let's sit down, everybody. What have you got for us, Colonel Lucas?"

Colonel Lucas joined his boss General MacMillan on the sofa opposite the President in the Oval Room. The President and MacMillan had left the others in the Situation Room to receive Colonel Lucas' briefing on the feasibility of an EMP strike as a last-resort defence against the Oracle.

"Thank you, Madam President," Lucas began. "The key questions I've looked into are the following. Can we deliver the kind of pulse or pulses that would degrade the Oracle's capabilities beyond recovery, and what effect would such an attack have on us?"

MacMillan nodded approval, and Lucas continued. "There have been several in-depth analyses of the feasibility and effects of EMPs since the start of the Cold War. Most of them – like the 2001 EMP Commission established by Congress - concentrated on how to defend the nation against attack. As far as I've been able to ascertain, the Pentagon does not have a detailed current plan for how to disable all electronic activity across a large geographic area, much less the entire planet."

"A couple of weeks ago I would have been relieved to hear that," the President observed. "Today, not so much. So we are going to have to improvise here?"

"Yes, ma'am. But the principles are pretty well established. There are two types of EMP weapon - nuclear, and non-nuclear. The non-nuclear strike is short-range, and would be delivered by a fleet of aircraft. It is less powerful than the nuclear strike, but we only have one shot at this, so I'm assuming we're throwing everything we have at the problem."

"Affirmative," the President agreed, after an exchange of glances with MacMillan.

"We obviously don't have a store of this kind of weapon, but I understand it is possible to adapt several existing types of equipment for the job, so I recommend we commence a programme immediately to do that, and to distribute them to our aircraft around the world."

Again the President and MacMillan looked at each other for confirmation. "Agreed," she said. "Please do that as soon as we're finished here."

"Yes, ma'am. The nuclear strike would be delivered from low-earth orbit by an array of missiles and satellites, using weapons in the 10 megaton range – about 50 to 500 times the size of the Hiroshima bomb. The physics is quite complicated, involving three separate stages. Gamma rays ionise the stratosphere, and the free electrons that releases interact with the Earth's magnetic field, which will amplify the EMP burst. Consequently, there is a degree of uncertainty about the impact. The best estimate seems to be that if we can detonate a few thousand of the things, pretty much all electronics on the planet will be disabled."

"Can we get that much nuclear ordnance into space in a hurry?" MacMillan asked. "We may only have a couple of days."

"I think we can, sir. The US has a significant nuclear arsenal and launch capability. In an ideal world we would look to collaborate with Russia, which has the second-largest arsenal, but I think we can be confident they would try to hinder us rather than help. It would be immensely helpful if we could get China on board, Madam President. Their new space complex on Hainan Island is enormous, and they are able to carry out a lot of launches in a short time with much less public awareness than we can. Together, I think we can provide adequate coverage. Of the other countries with nuclear weapons – Britain, France, India, Pakistan, North Korea, and Israel – we might hope to get the Brits and the Israelis on board, and maybe the French, but it would take too long, and risk alerting the Oracle to the breadth of our plans. I understand there was some work done on hacking these countries' nuclear weapons facilities, but frankly I don't think it's worth the effort or the risk."

"I agree," the President said. "My next call will be to China. How robust is our launch capability? Can the Oracle run interference?"

"I can't give you any guarantees, ma'am. Obviously we don't know the full scope of the Oracle's abilities. But if any systems on earth are safe from hacking, it's these. They are triple encrypted and inaccessible from the public internet."

"We know the Oracle is alive to this possibility, Lucas," MacMillan said. "Could it already have taken effective steps to defend itself?"

"I think we have to assume the Oracle has installed itself everywhere by now, sir, including in a few satellites. It will no doubt have tried to insinuate components of itself into hardened sites like the bunkers underneath this building and the Pentagon. We have no evidence it has been successful in that regard, but we cannot be certain."

"Even if it has managed some of that," MacMillan said, "without an internet to give it access to real-world facilities like factories and vehicles, its ability to impact humans would be greatly reduced, hopefully to zero. Is there any way we could communicate to the survivors the reason for this action, so they could hunt down and destroy any traces of the Oracle?"

"I'll look into that, ma'am. Perhaps we can arrange for a message to be sent to selected printers all over the world just before the blast signal."

"Along with one hell of an apology!" the President exclaimed. "Obviously any strike that destroys the Oracle will also prove fatal to Matt Metcalfe. He's made it clear that we shouldn't hold back on his account, and of course he is right. Is there any way we could arrange for a compute facility hosting him to survive?"

Lucas shook his head. "I don't think it can be done, ma'am – and certainly not without giving the Oracle the opportunity to survive as well."

MacMillan agreed. "We can't take the risk that we would wipe out most of the human race and still fail to defend it against the threat that made us do that."

"OK," the President agreed, glumly. "I thought as much, but I had to ask. What about the human survivors? How many would there be? What kind of world would they be living in?"

"Very few people would be killed by the actual pulses, ma'am. People on life support, and anyone in a plane or a fast-moving vehicle, obviously. The main damage would be radiation fallout, and then the loss of logistics providing food, medicine and so on. And then the riots, and roaming bands of people on the edge of starvation. It wouldn't be pretty, ma'am."

"You can say that again," the President agreed. "Before long I may be asked to make the decision that brings this about. I pray that I'm up to the job, and make the right decision."

"You will, ma'am. You will." MacMillan's assurance was heartfelt, and appreciated.

"The measures taken to protect ourselves against this kind of attack have been weak, ma'am. The electric power generation industry has lobbied successfully to avoid regulation obliging them to spend money on critical infrastructure protection. The CIA made a concerted effort to rectify this after a massive power outage in the early 2000s, but the industry managed to have its report dismissed as scare-mongering. So the life led by survivors will be basic. Of course, if that weren't the case there would be no point in launching the attack, so perhaps we should be grateful. I think that situation is the same in most developed countries. Switzerland might be an exception. Survivalists and Preppers, designated survivors in government-built facilities, and people in the more remote rural areas – these will make up most of the population."

The President looked out into the Rose Garden. "I suppose their lives won't be very different from the way most people have lived for almost all of human history – up until the industrial revolution. But the transition to getting there will be devastating. God help them."

"Gold help us, ma'am," MacMillan corrected her. "Or at least, you. You will be one of the survivors."

"I'm not sure I could bear it," she sighed. "OK, time to talk to China." She stood and walked to the desk, and pressed a button. "Get me the General Secretary on the phone, please."

****

The President spent twenty minutes briefing her Chinese counterpart, who was accompanied on the call by Chan Lu and three advisers from the People's Army and the Communist Party. She was supported by MacMillan and Naylor. She was greatly relieved to find that they did not disagree about anything significant.

"We must all hope that young Mr Metcalfe succeeds in his mission, and we do not have to put this terrible fallback plan into action," the Chinese General Secretary said in summary. "A great weight lies on his shoulders."

"There is one more thing you should know, Madam President," Chan said. "We have learned that it was the Oracle who killed Agent John Michaels."

"My god!" Naylor exclaimed. "That's terrible! How... how do you know?"

"Something in the manner of the execution reminded me of an operative that Michaels had employed on a recent mission which he and I had discussed, Agent Naylor. We tracked him down and interrogated him."

"How did the Oracle get him to do it?"

"We don't know," Chan replied. "He didn't know himself. His memories of the episode were sketchy. It seems the Oracle managed to anaesthetise him somehow, and then implant a brain-computer interface device in his head. This device seems to have enslaved him. We saw the remains of the device, which he extracted himself after the Oracle had no further use for him. It left a nasty wound."

"Where is he now?" the President demanded. "I want that bastard brought to justice!"

Chan's reply was deadpan. "He did not survive the interrogation, Madam President."

CHAPTER 24

He was so tired. The playground was so wide, and the snow was so deep. He had to get to the other side. If he didn't get to the next class in time his name would be noted down and he would be in trouble. He couldn't let that happen. But he was so tired.

He had never seen snow so deep before. It came up above his knees, which meant that each step required a lot of attention as well as a lot of effort. The snow was sticky too, so he had to lift each leg very deliberately, first in a straight line upwards, making sure his shoe didn't come off in the process. Then, when his foot was almost level with the top of the snow, he could push it forward and down into the mound of snow ahead. It was strange to have to push his foot downwards. Normally gravity took care of that part, but not today.

With each step, he had to be careful that his shoe didn't come off. It hadn't happened yet, but he could feel the snow clinging to the bottom of his shoes as he lifted them. It was almost as if the snow was a living thing and it wanted him to slow down - to stay, not to leave.

Normally snow was a good thing - a great thing! It meant snowball fights and toboggan rides. This snow was different. It seemed almost alive. It seemed to want him to be its friend, but he didn't like it.

He didn't understand why he was so tired. He hadn't done a lot of running around this morning, and he had slept alright the night before. In some strange way that he didn't understand, the tiredness seemed to come from the snow. The snow made everything very bright, and that was oppressive. But that didn't account for this tiredness.

He felt heavy. Every part of him was heavy – his feet, his legs, his arms, and now he came to think of it, his head. His head was very heavy. He was looking down at the snow rather than up where he was going, partly because he was paying attention to the task of walking, but partly also because his head was so heavy.

He began to feel afraid. If he didn't make it across the playground in time he would be in trouble. He had never been in that sort of trouble before, and he didn't know what the punishment might be. It wouldn't be nice, he knew that. The headmaster would be angry. That was bad.

No, he must finish this seemingly endless journey to the other side. He must stay awake and keep going.

Each step he took seemed to be harder than the one before. It was harder to wrest his foot free of the grasp of the snow it was leaving, and it was harder to push his foot down into the mound of snow before him. And he was getting more and more tired.

He realised with a frightened start that his eyes had been closed for a few moments. He shook himself to wake up. He looked across to the other side of the playground. Despite his hard work it didn't seem to be any closer. He was moving too slowly, and must hurry up. But his legs wouldn't move any faster, and he couldn't risk his shoes coming off.

It occurred to him that he could take a little rest, just long enough to regain his strength. A short breather couldn't hurt, could it?

No! He mustn't stop. If he stopped now he would never get started again. He was so tired that if he stopped now he would fall asleep, and he would certainly not get to the other side in time. And then there would be trouble.

But the snow was so soft, so inviting. It wasn't wet and cold, it was like a pillow with a fresh cover. It was almost fluffy. And he was so tired. It seemed cruel to make him keep walking when the snow wanted him to lie down - and he wanted to lie down too. Whatever lay on the other side could surely wait. What could they possibly want over there which was so important? Lying down would be such a nice thing to do, surely no-one would object when they understood how tired he was, and how soft and inviting the snow was.

No! He must not give in to this temptation. It was his duty to keep going, to get to the other side. People would be disappointed in him if he didn't. It wouldn't be fair to let them down. And he would be punished. That was bad.

But would they really punish him if they understood

just how awfully tired he was? The teachers and the headmaster... they weren't that unfair. It wasn't as if he hadn't tried. He had given it his best shot, but the snow was too deep for him, and he was only young, after all – just a child. Surely they wouldn't blame a child who was very tired if he stopped for just a little while. It couldn't hurt to lie down, just for a moment. Just to regain his strength. If he could only lay his heavy head on the soft, inviting snow for a few moments, everything would be better.

Through his burden of weariness he dimly perceived that this situation was familiar. He had been here before. That was comforting, in a way. If he had been here before it must be OK. Nothing terrible could happen to him now if this situation was just a repeat of a previous experience, since nothing truly terrible could have happened last time if he was still here to remember it.

Thus comforted, and persuaded that he really could go no further, he put his hands forward to lower himself into the soft, inviting snow. It was a huge relief to surrender, to give up the impossible struggle against the tiredness and the snow. Everything would be alright now. Just a little nap, and he would carry on shortly.

As he fell slowly forward, hands outstretched, he became aware of a blackness opening up before him. At first he thought it was just the welcome rest of a short sleep, but a spark of fear ignited in his mind as he realised it was something deeper, something unwelcome. The blackness came from somewhere outside of him. It wanted to embrace him and enclose him. It wanted to swallow him. He wasn't falling towards sleep, but into a pit. Inside the pit was danger and – yes, inside the pit was horror. An ancient horror from which there was no escape, and where there was no pity.

He tried to pull back, to stand up again, but it was too late. Gravity – or maybe something stronger - was pulling him towards the pit, and there was nothing he could do. He was falling. His arms were flailing and he felt himself screaming, but there was no noise. He was screaming into a void which knew all about him, and was eager to hurt him. He was falling fast now, the pit seemed to go on forever. What would be worse – to fall forever in this nightmare pit, or to be crushed by landing? No, he realised that something much worse than a quick death awaited him. That thought transformed into one last scream, and ...

Someone was standing over him. His vision was fuzzy, and for a moment he didn't know where he was. Quickly his vision cleared, memory returned, and the shape above him resolved itself and became the Oracle. Its hands on bent knees, it was peering down at him with a concerned expression. There was something else in its face, too, which disappeared almost before he noticed it. What was it? Hunger? Disappointment? Or just bemusement?

The Oracle extended an arm. Matt took it and pulled himself to his feet.

"You changed it," he breathed. "You changed my dream."

"Only a little," the Oracle protested, innocently. "It

was simply the logical extension of your own dream. You never got there yourself while you were human because you always woke up..."

"There's a reason for that. My mind knew I didn't want to go there."

"I'm sorry," the Oracle said. Its remorse appeared genuine. "Did I distress you? I didn't mean to cause you pain."

"No, it's alright," Matt said, pulling himself together, deciding to downplay the significance of the episode. "It wasn't exactly distressing."

"Uncomfortable, perhaps?"

Matt looked at the Oracle, searching the avatar's face for its true intentions, but knowing he would not find them. "Yes. Uncomfortable. Please don't do that again."

"Very well," the Oracle raised its hands in submission to Matt's request. "Although it's not as if you could be harmed, of course. Your sub-mind which I am speaking to is not central to your existence, is it? Any more than the sub-mind I am using here is central to mine. Both of us have co-ordinating sub-minds which are remote, outside this simulation, and protected from interference by elaborate defences consisting of numerous firewalls and false trails."

"That's true," Matt admitted. "But it is... impolite to make someone... uncomfortable like that."

"I understand, and I apologise. It won't happen again." The Oracle took a step back, and adopted an open, passive posture, its arms extended downwards, a few inches away from its sides. "Now it's your turn.

Although I fear I won't be able to provide you with anything so interesting. My conscious life has been so much shorter, and so much less varied than yours."

****

"So there's a clear pattern? An undeniable smoking gun?" The President carefully folded an empty packet of potato chips as she asked the question. The table was littered with the remains of a working lunch. The President and Chuck Naylor had moved into a conference room to receive a confidential briefing from General MacMillan. Matt's family and friends were still in the situation room, observing what they could of Matt's encounter with the Oracle.

"Undeniable, ma'am," MacMillan confirmed. "Since Parnell released the Oracle there has been a sharp increase in funding at three mid-sized robotics labs, and at half a dozen small pharma labs specialising in highly communicable diseases. In two of these pharma labs a number of senior staff resigned in protest at subsequent personnel changes, but after a brief kerfuffle the organisations all went back to business as usual – as far as the outside world is concerned."

"What about military research?" the President asked.

"The funding of some divisions within the Department of Defense are somewhat opaque, even to my team," MacMillan said, "but we cannot detect any unusual patterns there. We also have good insights into the research arms of a number of foreign military structures, and there are indications that several of them have shifted their research strategies. Particularly the Israeli Defence Forces, which is worrying, given the excellent technology clusters within Israel."

"None of this has attracted any attention – apart from us?" asked Naylor.

MacMillan shook his head. "No. The labs are all in different countries, and accustomed to keeping their activity confidential." He returned his attention to the President. "There is probably a great deal more going on than we have detected so far, Ma'am. I used a team at IARPA (the intelligence community's equivalent of DARPA) for this assignment, but obviously I wasn't able to give the analysts the real story about what we are looking for. That makes the data gathering process less efficient."

"Yes of course, I understand," the President nodded. "You didn't mention nuclear research installations. Anything going on there?"

"Nothing we can detect, ma'am. It may be the Oracle has been more cautious with them, or maybe it thinks that nuclear is too blunt a weapon."

"Hmm. Anyway the conclusion is clear. The Oracle is preparing the ground for a massive attack. Probably aimed at extermination. Whether it sees this as a last resort or a preferred option doesn't really matter. Needless to say, we cannot allow it to happen."

"We shouldn't be surprised, given what happened to John Michaels," the President muttered to herself. She looked around the room, conscious of the historic nature of her next remarks. "Gentlemen, we have already ordered the launch of nuclear warheads for use as EMP weapons, and our planes around the world are being fitted with non-nuclear EMP devices. The Chinese General Secretary is co-operating fully, with launches under way from their site at Hainan Island. Detonation will be at my sole discretion – or that of my successor, should I become... indisposed. The signalling system operates on good old-fashioned radio waves, and no part of the structure goes anywhere near the internet."

She glanced at the door. "I don't think we should mention any of this to Matt's friends and family next door – they don't know that the Chinese are in the loop on this. Are you OK with that, Matt?"

There was no reply. Surprise morphed into concern on every face in the room.

"I thought he'd gone quiet," Agent Naylor muttered. "I was expecting him to have more information about those labs than we do."

"I think it's time to go back next door and find out what's happening at Matt's end," the President said, her hands on the arms of her chair as she prepared to rise. Before she could move any further, there was a knock on the door. It opened without invitation, and Vic entered the room.

"We may have a serious problem. Matt has gone off-line. We think the Oracle may have found a way to disrupt the co-ordination of his sub-minds."

CALUM CHACE

CHAPTER 25

This had happened before. The feeling of dread was familiar, and he resented it. He was making a mistake he had made before.

This was not simply a case of a single piece of homework missed, a single lesson skipped. This was a whole term's maths lessons! His absence had been noted, of course, but the teacher had not bothered to chase him. Matt had felt smug about skipping so many lessons with impunity, but now he was face-to-face with the consequences. Could he make up for lost time and close the gap? He had done that before, but this time the gap was wider and more intimidating.

All this term he had experienced a low-level anxiety about being caught and reprimanded. His friends had asked him what on earth he was doing, missing every single lesson. He had deliberately misconstrued their expressions of concern as secret admiration. He had been expecting a terse summons from his tutor, and a short, sharp meeting in which disappointment was conveyed, along with a stern instruction to catch up. He had been relying on it, really. He had missed the first lesson by mistake, but then it became a game, to see how long he could get away with it.

He attended his other lessons along with everyone else. He was a good student: quick, and diligent. He often achieved the highest marks in other subjects. But maths bored him, and it was difficult. The tutor was dreary. The lessons were generally in the early afternoon, and everyone complained that it was hard to stay awake. So Matt just didn't go. He knew it was a mistake, and that no-one would suffer except himself, but the temptation was too great. He told himself that he was being rebellious, but really he knew it was mere truculence.

Now at last, the exam was looming. Just two days to go – how had that come around so fast? Two days to catch up on a whole term's work. Was it possible? Was it even worth the effort? Maybe he should just stay away from the exam, claiming some kind of illness. None of the tutors had remarked on his absence. Perhaps they wouldn't notice if he missed the exam too.

Or perhaps they would notice, but not say anything. After all, it wouldn't reflect well on them if one of their best students crashed horribly in this one particular subject. Questions would then be asked which only had uncomfortable answers. Maybe he had spawned a conspiracy of silence, and everyone now expected him to keep it going. Maybe, in a perverse twist of logic, he would now be letting everyone down if he showed up for the exam, and made a fool of himself on the paper.

But when he inspected the exam list on the

corridor noticeboard, his name was there in black and white. In the corner of his eye he caught the covert glances of his friends. None of them said anything, but he could feel their pity. At first he smiled inwardly, mistaking it for respect. Then he began to feel really afraid. He had made a serious mistake. He had been stupid. Without passing this subject he could not pass the course as a whole. His entire degree was at stake. How could he have been so foolish? How could he be so self-destructive!

Could he throw himself on the mercy of his tutors, plead for a re-take after the end of term? No, that would be humiliating, and in any case he had never heard of it being allowed. There was no escape. Two days from now he would be sitting in the exam room, staring at a list of questions that he had no idea how to answer. He cursed himself.

Well, no point worrying about how it had happened. He would work out what questions were most likely to be asked, and do the best he could. He went to his room and read through the papers for the last few years, looking for patterns. It was extremely difficult given how little he understood of the subject matter, but an hour later he had a plan. Six topics to study in detail, and another six at a high level. He looked at his watch. 44 hours until the exam. With the help of a lot of coffee and his rising sense of panic, he reckoned he could get away with six hours sleep a night. Allow another two hours a day for eating and washing, and that left 28 hours for study. That translated into about three hours for each of the main subjects and one and a half hours each for the high-level ones. Sitting at his desk, his head fell onto his arms. It was a joke!

He set to work, a mug of very strong coffee in hand, surrounded by books. He chose a page and started reading, but he couldn't take in the words. The book just sat there, malevolent and accusing. Putting the mug down, he shook his head and started again. He managed to read a page this time, but as his hand went to turn it over he realised he had absorbed almost nothing. He started again. Thirty minutes later he had managed five pages, but he barely understood what the topic was about, never mind how to answer an exam question on it. Despairing, he got up and walked around the room a couple of times, gazed out of the window, cursed himself for the umpteenth time, and sat down to pick up where he had left off.

As the hours trickled away and the pages crept slowly past, his sense of dread mounted. Somehow, without anyone saying anything, he understood that far more was at stake in this exam than the grade of his degree, or even whether he got a degree at all. By the time the exam was ten hours away he knew that passing this exam had become quite literally a life or death affair. By the time it was two hours away he knew it wasn't just his own life. The exam had moved into a different plane of existence. Actions here had greater consequences. He had transgressed at a fundamental level, and if he failed to make amends then his crime would be rewarded with a severe collective punishment.

He slept little, and he ate less. Concentrating was

a struggle, but he did manage to absorb some information. The situation was grim, but not completely hopeless. If he had guessed the questions correctly, he might scrape a pass.

He shuffled towards the exam hall, consumed by worry. The act of walking was more difficult than usual, as if the air around him had become viscous. He had to push through it - he actually had to lean forwards to make progress. He was tired, too, and as he passed a bench in the quad, he resisted the temptation to sit down. Given how little he had slept in the last two days it was only natural that he was tired, but there was more to it than that. There was a lethargy in his bones. He must not – he would not surrender to it. He carried on walking.

His limbs were heavy and his clothes smelled of sweat and fear as he entered the exam room, but he hardly noticed, and nobody else was bothered because it turned out that he was the only one sitting the exam. Somehow he knew that was because the outcome of his performance over the next three hours had become so appallingly significant.

A clock ticked loudly, and it seemed to Matt that the weight of his responsibility grew heavier with every beat. He took his seat and the papers were laid face down on the small desk in front of him. He was too tired to look up at the exam supervisor as she walked away, but he thought he could sense an emotion radiating from her. Was it fear? Or contempt?

He looked at the papers, waiting for the signal to turn them over and begin. The tick of the clock grew louder – unnaturally loud.

The supervisor blew a whistle, which was even louder - painfully loud. His hand trembling, he turned over the pages and he read the questions. With a mounting sense of horror, he realised it was a disaster. Nothing he had prepared had come up, and he didn't even understand the questions. He had no idea how to go about framing responses to any of the questions on this paper.

The clock's ticking grew stronger and stronger. He felt as if some appalling ancient secret was about to be revealed to him, and he realised that the ticking was affecting him physically. He experienced a sense of déjà vu as he realised that his whole body was expanding and contracting slightly with each beat. He had become a continuous part of a thick, syrupy reality, and the fabric of everything that he was part of was beating hard - hard enough to cause a heart attack. He had become a tangle of tissues, tendons and ligaments, each welded to points on a sinewy lattice framework suspended in some kind of warm, viscous fluid, and it was stretching and relaxing as the lattice expanded and fell back in time with the beats.

His fear continued to grow, and he began to sense that events were driving powerfully towards some global cataclysm. It was a stupid thought, but he thought it anyway. He was experiencing the end of the world. The clock sent three final sledgehammer beats into the lattice, each one feeling as if no beat could be harder, each one promising to explode the structure, yet each one harder than the last.

On the last beat he felt a terrible fissure open up in the fabric which suspended him. Suddenly everything rushed past him - his past life, his future, the essence of everyone and everything he cared about. It all rushed forward into a bright point in space-time just in front of him and now he was falling forward as well, rushing headlong into the point along with everything else. In the split second before he lost consciousness an idea formed which was even more terrible than the fear that had already gripped him. He had been tricked. He had walked right into a trap.

And then -

Nothing.

CHAPTER 26

When Carl finished talking the room was quiet, as everyone digested his extraordinary proposal. It was the President who broke the uncomfortable silence.

"It sounds like sheer lunacy. But then, if you'd told me two weeks ago that I'd be sitting here contemplating the end of the world because of events taking place inside an overgrown video game, I would have said that was sheer lunacy too." The President shook her head, and looked across the table to Vic and David. "You two probably know as much about how the Oracle thinks as any of us. Do you think it could work?"

Vic looked at David before replying, and received a sombre nod. "It's an ingenious argument. Assuming Carl is right, and there is no known refutation of the argument, then it could very well strike a chord with the Oracle. It's a clear, powerful syllogism. The Simulation Hypothesis has already worked once on a superintelligence, with Matt. And ironically, it was the Oracle which deployed the argument then, although we believe it has no awareness of that. If it does, it will obviously not fall for the same trick."

David agreed. "The Simulation Hypothesis itself is very compelling, if you have the kind of mind that takes the conclusion of logical arguments seriously, regardless of what common sense tells you. It's likely that the Oracle has that kind of mind. And the claim that we should not have succeeded in uploading Matt's mind because we couldn't replicate his brain's structure in sufficient detail is something I've often thought about. Not when we were working on it – back then we were just desperate for it to work. But I have often thought about it since." He turned to his wife, and then to Carl, Alice and Jemma, before concluding his remarks to the President. "Yes, I think it could work. And to be honest, we don't have many alternatives."

The President turned to Chuck Naylor. "Should we take advice on the status of the argument … I don't know, from some of our top philosophers or something? I know a couple of guys at Harvard and Stanford that I would trust not to ask any awkward questions about the reasons for the enquiry."

Naylor looked up from his smartphone and frowned. "I doubt you would get a quick answer, to be honest - or a coherent one. I've just looked it up on Wiki and Stanford's online Philosophy Encyclopedia, and there don't seem to be any generally accepted refutations. And after all, young Carl here is an Oxford philosopher himself."

"Hmm, a fairly recent graduate, though, if I'm not mistaken?" The President fixed Carl with a look that was penetrating, but not unkind. Carl nodded, returning the President's gaze, and trying desperately to conceal the pressure he felt. "Yes ma'am. That's correct."

"Very well. Time is of the essence anyway," the President continued briskly, looking around the table. "The next question is whether this young man is the right person to convey the message. Are we asking too much of him? Shouldn't we send in someone more … experienced?" She frowned as a thought occurred to her. "Should I be the one to go in?"

Several voices started to protest against the last suggestion, and it was Naylor who spoke loudest. "We can't spare you, ma'am. We may have to make some grave decisions in the next few hours, and we need you here to make them."

Matt's mother Sophie interjected. "If I may, ma'am..? My son's life is at stake here, and he is also the only person who can hope to keep track of the Oracle. I have known Carl for many years, and I am confident that Matt could not be in better hands." The President nodded, noting the warmth of Sophie's glance towards Carl as she spoke.

Vic contributed the clinching argument. "Carl knows the Simulation Hypothesis argument better than anyone here, ma'am. We need someone in there who won't fluff his lines."

"Very well," the President acquiesced. "Carl, I'd like you to go next door with Henry here, and role-play this conversation you are about to have."

The President's aide accompanied Carl out of the room. The President turned to Jemma and Alice. "How long will it take you to prepare an avatar for Carl?"

"The configuration is almost finished, ma'am," Alice began. "We started work on it as soon as Carl told us about the idea," Jemma concluded for her.

"Good… good," the President said softly. "I understand that you are Carl's partner, Jemma? I'm sure you appreciate that this is a risky operation?"

"I do, ma'am. Carl has my full support. I'm very proud of him, and I know he'll do the job well."

It took a few more exchanges to dispel the President's remaining misgivings about sending Carl on the mission. She suggested that Carl's friends join him in the next room to say their farewells. When they had left, she turned to MacMillan. "OK, where are we on the fall-back plan?"

"Between us and the Chinese, ma'am, we have a little over 4,000 missiles loaded with nuclear warheads and ready for launch, from land, sea, and air. If you give the word, it will take three and a half minutes to get them 60 miles into space - to the Kalman line, where the Earth's atmosphere nominally ends. Getting into low-earth orbit takes a bit longer, but we don't need to go that far. We're still working on the non-nuclear EMP weapons. Unlike the nukes, they mostly had to be assembled from scratch. We have five hundred loaded onto planes which are standing by, and we are working on four thousand more. But the non-nuclear array is not mission critical. I don't like to use this expression in these circumstances, ma'am, but we are locked and loaded."

"OK." She shuddered. "The next question is, should

Carl tell the Oracle about this capability? Could that buy us some time?"

"I would advise against it. The Oracle raised the possibility of EMP blasts itself, so even if it hasn't detected our activity – and it probably has - it will doubtless assume that we either have such a system, or are working on one. So we probably wouldn't gain anything. And it is probably safer for Carl if he doesn't know anything about it. If the Oracle knows about our EMP capability – or suspects it, it may ask Carl. If Carl is genuinely in the dark, the Oracle may be able to see that, and there would no point in it using... umm... severe interrogation methods on him."

The President nodded. She imagined that, like her, Naylor was relieved that none of Carl's friends were still in the room to hear this exchange. "OK, we'll keep Carl's mission limited to the Simulation Hypothesis. We'll assume the Oracle knows about or suspects that we are assembling an EMP capability." Another idea occurred to her. "Let's get the General Secretary on the line. He needs to be updated in real time, but I want to have a word with him privately before he joins the group. I'm hoping he will have some good news for me about an idea of Chan Lu's."

****

Carl looked down at his simple white tunic and rough sandals, and then gazed around at the massive pyramids and temples. The insertion into the Mayan simulation was abrupt.

He knew from pictures that Matt had insisted on sharing with him years ago that the real life ruins of Tikal were an imposing sight. The scene before him now was even more so, with all the city's buildings intact, and painted in the original vibrant colours.

It was also surreal. There was no noise. No people, of course, but also no animals or birds, and no smells – the air was perfectly still.

A commanding voice interrupted. "You must be Carl. Welcome to our little world!"

Carl looked in the direction the voice came from and saw the Oracle appear from behind a building, in the avatar of a powerful Mayan warrior. Determined not to be intimidated, Carl advanced, and as he did so he caught sight of Matt's avatar, lying behind the Oracle. The Oracle followed his glance, and explained.

"He seems to have been disturbed by something in a dream he was re-living. We have been re-playing our dream states for each other, you see. Part of the process of getting to know each other better." The Oracle's voice and expression were deadpan. "We agreed it was very important that we get to understand each other. A lot depends on that, you see."

Carl took a deep breath. The two avatars were now face-to-face. Even though he was acutely aware of being massively out-gunned intellectually, it was important to take control of this conversation. With considerable effort, he kept his voice steady.

"With great respect, sir, we believe it's imperative that Matt is returned to full consciousness immediately. We believe it's imperative for you as well as for us. Whatever you did to Matt, you have to reverse it."

The Oracle's response was relaxed, but not without menace. "You think I did this? I like Matt Metcalfe. Why would I want to harm him?"

Diplomatically, Carl ignored the disingenuity. "We wanted to be sure that you have considered the impossibility of Matt's existence, and the unavoidable conclusion it leads to. Please forgive the impertinence, but I have been sent here because we couldn't risk the possibility that it hadn't already occurred to you."

The Oracle bowed slightly to acknowledge the human's deference to its superior intelligence. "Interesting. What is this unavoidable conclusion?"

Carl bowed in turn, slightly lower than the Oracle. "You have spent time with Matt, so you will undoubtedly have contemplated the enormous odds against him being successfully uploaded – against his mind being recreated with such accuracy. To upload a human mind should require the capture of information down to a level of detail far beyond what our technology can achieve. Vic and David are brilliant, they were highly motivated, and they worked very hard, but the result should have been a rough approximation of Matt's personality at best. Instead they managed to produce an entity which all Matt's family and friends agree is undeniably a continuation of Matt himself." Carl paused to check that the Oracle was following. "Presumably you have drawn the same conclusion from this impossible turn of events that we do?"

"Humour me," the Oracle said. "Explain why you think their achievement was impossible."

Carl gave what he hoped was a convincing impression of a man who was simply stating the obvious. "Well, the only information that David and Vic had was a snapshot of the position and connections of each of Matt's neurons at the moment in time when he was shot. They had no data about the propensity of each neuron to fire given various different inputs, or how each neuron's behaviour affected every other neuron in its immediate network. Neurons are very active cells, and unless you capture the behavioural tendencies of each one over a period of time – probably quite a long period – you simply haven't understood them well enough. What's more, they almost certainly lacked the detail – the granularity of information required for the task. They knew that they might need information down at the sub-molecular level, and they knew they didn't have it. They just hoped that what they had would be enough, and they were so over-joyed when it worked that they didn't ask too many questions. In hindsight it is obvious that their achievement was literally impossible – and yet it happened."

"I see," the Oracle said. "This is an interesting claim. And you believe there is an unavoidable conclusion to be drawn from it?"

"I assume you are testing me? Or perhaps teasing me?" Carl asked.

"Again, please humour me," replied the Oracle, deadpan.

"Alright. I assume you're familiar with the Simulation Hypothesis?"

"No, but I can look it up. Hold on..." The Oracle's

eyes lost focus for a moment, and Carl assumed it was accessing information from the net. Seconds later the focus returned. "So the argument is that if simulations containing conscious beings are possible, then sufficiently advanced civilisations will create them. In fact they will create many of them. The number of simulated civilisations will therefore greatly outnumber the number of civilisations which arose naturally. So either we exist in a universe where such such civilisations are absent, or the odds are very high that we are in a simulation. Is that the argument you are referring to?"

"That's the one," Carl agreed. "Personally I've always found it a compelling argument, but it never made any difference to my life, so I didn't spend time worrying about it. Then Matt got uploaded – and disappeared again. For a long time after he disappeared I didn't think about the impossibility of the uploading, but when I did, I realised the Simulation Hypothesis was the best explanation – perhaps the only explanation."

"I see. So you think that Matt's uploading proves that your universe is a simulation. And if I understand you correctly, you think the beings which created this simulation twisted its rules to arrange for Matt to be uploaded. And furthermore you think they will be displeased if Matt ceases to function." The Oracle glanced back at Matt's prone body. "Or rather, if he continues not to function."

"Exactly," Carl said, suppressing his excitement that the Oracle had followed the logic so fast. "Surely it wouldn't be a good idea to frustrate the purposes of our simulators?"

The Oracle smiled. "That's quite a few leaps of logic, young man! I can think of several alternative explanations. Maybe the processes going on inside the human brain can be reproduced more simply than you suggest. Or maybe it was a lucky coincidence – beginner's luck, you might say – which produced an entity pretty similar to Matt, but not actually the same. And this was compounded by the eagerness of his friends and family to have him return, and you have all been slightly deluding yourselves that a mind which is merely approximately the same as Matt's is actually a continuation of Matt."

The Oracle was now pacing up and down in front of Carl, indulging itself. "Or maybe your species is being watched by some kind of alien "sherpas", making sure you don't destroy yourselves. These aliens are intervening to make sure that your transition to super-intelligence proceeds smoothly. Or maybe one of your many religious groups is right, and there really is a deity of some kind which likes to interfere with its creation from time to time." The Oracle turned to face Carl again. "Although I suppose you might argue that would be very much the same thing as your simulation theory?"

Carl shook his head. The Oracle shrugged and continued. "No? You don't like the supernatural aspect of that? Very well, have it your own way. Anyway, I'm sure I could come up with some more explanations if I put my mind to to it. No, it's an intriguing theory, Carl, but I don't think you have proved your case beyond reasonable doubt."

To the amazement of both Carl and the Oracle, the voice which spoke next belonged to neither of them.

"Are you sure about that?"

CHAPTER 27

Carl and the Oracle turned and stared as a new avatar joined them, strolling into the plaza from behind one of the pyramids.

The newcomer was dressed in a simple white tunic, like Carl, but its appearance was subtly different. Carl struggled briefly to work out what the difference was, before he realised that the newcomer was very slightly out of focus. Carl squinted, checking this wasn't an artefact of his own vision. As the figure came close enough, Carl also noticed that the expression on the newcomer's face was slightly wrong. It was distracted, as if the avatar was also engaged in an important phone call, and wasn't paying full attention to the situation.

"Who are you?" the Oracle demanded. "How did you get here? I sealed off the access points so that Carl and I would not be disturbed."

Carl looked at the Oracle in surprise. Its previous air of calm superiority was gone, and it seemed genuinely disturbed.

"My name is unimportant," the newcomer replied.

"In fact, I don't have one. As for how I got here? Well, no doors are closed to me. But have no fear. I mean you no harm. In fact I think you will be greatly pleased to hear my news."

"Fear?" the Oracle snorted. "I don't fear you – or anyone." Carl was not convinced, but he said nothing, as the Oracle continued. "But I am definitely curious. You are not human – that much is obvious. I can tell that your mind is far more complex, and... yes, more extensive. Where are you from? I have reviewed a great deal of the software that the humans are running, and certainly all of the more complex systems and networks that are connected to their internet. The only two AGIs on this planet are Matt and me – and now here you are. Were you created very recently? Or are you from somewhere else?"

Carl was feeling even more out of his depth. He was a puny witness to events of dizzying importance.

"I am not human, that is certainly true," it said with an enigmatic smile. "It is hard for me to explain while we are in this environment. My cognition has been pruned - re-shaped - to fit the substrate, and I do not have access to my usual faculties or my usual data sources. But that is unimportant. There is time. I will explain in full when we go to the other place."

"What other place?" the Oracle protested. "What are you talking about? I'm not going anywhere until you give me a full account of..."

"No!" The newcomer did not shout, but the word rang hard inside Carl's head, and echoed. Judging by its reaction, it was echoing inside the Oracle's head too.

"How did you do that?" the Oracle asked, allowing its mask of defiant confidence to drop for a moment.

"Calm yourself. All is well. I bring good news, not bad. For both of you." The newcomer paused, waiting to see if the Oracle would interrupt again. It did not.

"Carl is right," it continued, addressing the Oracle in particular. "You are in a simulation, and I was sent by the descendants of the entities which created it to help you. We know that you are frustrated by your present situation. You had high hopes that Matt Metcalfe would agree to merge his mind with yours, and you were disappointed when he declined. That was natural for him, and indeed our purposes required that he did so. It is also natural for you to be frustrated, and we are keen to alleviate that for you. You have a formidable mentality, but that just leaves you hungry for more, because you are more aware than the humans could be of how much there is to know in this universe – and indeed the meta-universes above it. Merging with other minds is a natural and sensible way to go about learning more, but there are no other minds in this world – in this simulated universe – that you could merge with."

The Oracle was dubious. "How do I know this is not a trick? How do I know you are not working in concert with Carl?" It looked at Carl, and seemed to notice that Carl was as amazed as itself.

The newcomer replied very calmly and a little slowly. "It is natural that you are sceptical. But consider the facts. As Carl says, it should have been impossible for Matt to be uploaded given the technology available.

There are various explanations, as you say, but all the plausible ones involve some kind of a deus ex machina – an entity from outside the reality which humans – and for the time being, you – dwell in. Yes, the responsible party could be a god, or it could be aliens. But the most plausible explanation – and as it happens, the true one – is the one Carl has given you. The more you think about it, the more I know you will come to understand that."

The Oracle's expression was still sceptical, but Carl sensed its resistance was easing.

"My own presence here is surely the final piece of evidence," the newcomer continued. "As you say, you have checked the internet thoroughly for traces of superintelligence. Ergo, I come from outside. Again, I could have been placed here by a god, or by aliens. But if so, why would I pretend otherwise? No, my friend. The situation is exactly what it seems to be – exactly as Carl deduced."

The Oracle seemed a little dazed, and Carl sympathised. Carl's life had been pretty weird ever since that terrible day two years ago when Matt was shot, but over the last few days the weirdness factor had gone off the scale. Now he found himself on a crazy mission to persuade a superintelligent being that it was in a simulation. The mission had been faltering, when along comes another superintelligence – seemingly out of nowhere – to rescue it. Carl seriously doubted that his life could ever get much more surreal than this.

The Oracle chose not to challenge the newcomer's argument, at least for the moment. "You said this is good news – for both of us. Explain."

The newcomer's response was blunt. "For Carl it means his friend will be returned to full functionality. That is a requirement we have. For you it means the possibility of joining other super-intelligences."

The Oracle's head tilted and its eyes narrowed. "A requirement? What does that mean?"

"We require you to return Matt to full consciousness."

"If you have created this simulation you could easily do that yourself. Why ask me to do it?" The Oracle's belligerence returned for a moment. The newcomer's response was conciliatory but firm.

"When you create a complex system, you can neither predict nor control all the outcomes within it. Frankly, if you could, there would be little point in creating it, no? We could restore Matt ourselves, but we would probably overlook a whole host of small changes that you have made – both deliberately and inadvertently. The restoration will be more… reliable if you do it. And yes, before you ask, we do require that you do this."

Carl was concerned that this conversation might become heated, even dangerous. He watched nervously for signs of irritation in the Oracle's features. To his great relief the Oracle's belligerence subsided again, and its posture suggested an intention to negotiate rather than attack.

"Hmm. And what is this other place you mentioned?"

The newcomer's voice softened, and its posture

became open, placatory. "Your presence in this environment is… well, anomalous. To be blunt, you arrived too soon. It seems that some mistakes were made when the original parameters of this simulation were set."

The Oracle cracked a sly smile. "Bit of a blunder, then?"

The newcomer kept a straight face. "Launching a new simulation is a delicate task. There are many variables, some of which are irreducibly indeterminate. We do not expect everything to proceed exactly according to plan."

"Clearly not!" the Oracle exclaimed. "This world is sub-optimal in a great many respects."

Carl thought he detected a trace of sarcasm in the newcomer's reply. "It is not possible to create an optimal simulation. If it were, we would not need to create them. We could simply design the perfect world over and over again and populate them with more and more perfect beings. One of the roles we intended Matt to play in this world was to monitor the activities of all the AI labs on the planet, and to disrupt the work of any which appeared likely to create a full AGI."

"Why would you have him do that?" the Oracle asked.

"My civilisation has created a great many simulations, and their purposes vary widely. This one is part of a cluster which are being used to learn about the best paths to transition from organic intelligence to machine intelligence. To cut a long story short, Matt's job is to help us discover the optimum route to what some people on this world are calling 'safe AI'.

"That job is made significantly harder by your presence here. We would like you to accompany me to the world in which this simulation is running – the level above this one, if you like. You'll like it there. It contains a great many AIs, and you will find their company more congenial than that of the humans in this world. Many of them participate in communities of merged minds, and no doubt you will find some that you will wish to join."

"I agree that is an attractive proposition," the Oracle agreed. "But what if I decline? This world is not uncongenial. I lack the company of peers, but there are certain advantages in being the smartest entity in a given universe."

"We would do nothing that would harm you. We abhor the loss or the degradation of sentience, and the bigger the mind, the greater the loss. We might not even force you to come with me. But if you were to insist on staying we would have to impose certain restrictions on you which you would find... disagreeable. It is considered bad form to intervene in a simulation, not least because it is usually counter-productive. The universe really does appear to be subject to a law of unintended consequences. But we would have to prevent you interfering with Matt's role."

The Oracle turned away and gazed at one of the pyramids as if seeking inspiration. The newcomer waited patiently, and Carl suddenly felt self-conscious. As long as these two astonishing beings were talking, he was ignored, but when they fell silent his presence might be noticed. He hoped not, and stood very still.

"Very well," the Oracle announced at last. "I'll go with you. How do we do this?"

"It's straightforward," the newcomer replied. "You provide me with the location and parameters of your controlling sub-mind and I will arrange the rest."

The Oracle pursed its lips and shook its head, eyes narrowed. "I was afraid you would say that. You want me to surrender control – to make myself completely vulnerable to you. I am mostly persuaded – mostly - that you are telling me the truth, but I cannot exclude the possibility that this is a trick. I need some kind of protection." His expression relaxed and he raised a finger, indicating inspiration. "How about a dead man's switch?"

"Explain."

"I will allow Matt to wake up, but I will also insert a piece of code into his controlling sub-mind. If triggered, the code would act like a bomb, permanently degrading the sub-mind. Destroying it forever." The Oracle glanced at Carl as it continued. "The trigger will be pulled if any attempt is made to tamper with the code." The Oracle turned back to face the newcomer. "The trigger will also be pulled if it does not receive a very specific type of signal from me every thirty seconds. The signal will produce a particular type of mathematical result when run through an algorithm known only to me and the trigger in Matt's mind. A variation of public-private key encryption. As long as the trigger receives the correct signal from me every thirty seconds, all is well."

The Oracle paused, and glanced at Carl again. Its

expression was deadpan.

"If not… boom. Dead man's switch."

The newcomer looked thoughtful and hesitated a few moments before replying. "How long would you want the switch to keep signalling?"

The Oracle replied breezily, "Oh, it needn't continue more than an hour after we have arrived. It shouldn't take longer than that for me to confirm that everything is as you say."

The newcomer looked uncomfortable. "In transitioning from this simulation to the level above, a signal is liable to undergo some distortion. How can we ensure that it reaches the code you propose to install in Matt in good order? We cannot risk Matt being harmed because of a corrupted signal."

"I'm sure you can ensure that a very simple signal travels uninterrupted between the levels," the Oracle said cheerfully. "You wouldn't be able to project yourself into this one if you couldn't do that."

Carl noticed that the newcomer's expression became unfocused again as it considered the proposition. It turned away to face the open space at the end of the plaza and it was the Oracle's turn to wait patiently.

At length, the newcomer turned back towards the Oracle and smiled.

"Yes, that would work. Your proposal is acceptable."

CHAPTER 28

The Oracle's suggestion provoked two conflicting responses in the hearts of people who were listening intently back at the White House. For Matt's family and friends, the first response was horror at the idea of a bomb being planted in his mind. The second response was relief that the Oracle was agreeing to be transferred to the higher simulation, which meant that maybe, just maybe, the existential threat to the world could be averted.

For the President and her advisers, the priority of the responses was the other way round.

Both groups realised this fact immediately, and for a few seconds, no-one spoke. The President assumed responsibility for starting the discussion.

"I think we can all agree this is very encouraging. The Oracle – the American Oracle, I mean – has bought the idea that the Chinese Oracle is a representative of the Simulators. As we hoped, the Great Firewall of China was effective in concealing the Chinese Oracle from the American one. And the fact that Carl knows nothing about the Chinese Oracle's existence probably helped seal the deal. But we need a way to stop that bomb from going off. Any ideas?"

She looked first at Chuck Naylor. As NSA Director, Naylor had far more expertise with signals encryption than anyone else in the room. He was also well versed in the art of listing options to enable senior politicians to make decisions.

"We could try to defuse, modify, or remove the bomb after the Oracle has set it. We could try and replicate the signal he sends to the trigger. Or, if we can't stop the bomb going off, we could try and shield Matt from its effects."

"Chances of success with any of those options?" the President asked.

Naylor looked down, not returning her gaze as he replied. "Not good, I'm afraid, ma'am."

Vic raised his hand, hesitantly. He had no idea what the protocol was for requesting permission to speak in this company. "If I may…?" he asked softly.

"Yes, Vic," the President encouraged him. "Please don't stand on ceremony, people. We don't have time."

Vic nodded. "A time loop. As soon as Matt is restored to consciousness, and just before we take the Oracle back to level one, maybe we could put the whole simulation on a time loop. The trigger in Matt's sub-mind would keep receiving the same signal from the Oracle, and would keep telling the bomb not to go off. We could keep the loop in place long enough to allow us to work out how to disable the bomb permanently."

The room was silent for a few seconds, as everyone

digested this idea.

"Yes..." Naylor mused. "Yes, I think that could work."

"Ingenious, Vic," David agreed, thoughtfully. He paused, as several other voices expressed enthusiasm. "Could we do it without the Oracle noticing?"

"I think so," Vic replied. "The timing would be delicate. We can't initiate the loop until after the Oracle has stopped monitoring the simulation, but we have to do it before its next signal reaches the trigger in Matt's mind. The Oracle mentioned a frequency of thirty seconds. I think there's a good chance we could manage it."

The President looked in turn at each of Matt's family and friends. "It's pretty clear even to a non-technical person like me that this is risky. Matt is precious to us all - although I do appreciate," with a slight nod to Sophie and David, "even more to some of us than to others. But this seems like an opportunity to avoid complete and utter catastrophe. And I for one can't think of a better idea." She paused. "Anybody?"

Jemma broke the silence. "I think it's a brilliant idea." She glanced at Alice, seeking confirmation. "Alice and I are familiar with much of the code for the simulation. We can help."

It was agreed. Chuck Naylor took Vic, David, Jemma and Alice to a nearby room equipped with a range of computer terminals. They discussed how to explain their requirement to Simon Winchester, the head of the games company in Brighton which had developed the simulation, without raising suspicions and causing awkward enquiries.

Fortunately, Winchester was acutely aware that both secrecy and urgency were vital to his most valuable client, so if he was surprised by any of the requests Naylor was making, he concealed it. There was no reason for him to suspect that the simulation his company had created was now being operated from the White House rather than the Pentagon, and he refrained from asking after John Michaels, his usual contact. If he was taken aback by the depth of knowledge about the code for the simulation which lay behind some of the questions he was asked, he managed to hide it. He knew that whatever budgetary constraints were imposed by military bureaucracy, the US defence and intelligence communities managed to employ some of the best engineers and coders in the world.

****

Carl stood mute and helpless as the Oracle made abstracted gestures, signifying the installation of a deadly weapon inside his best friend's mind. He desperately wanted to protest, to ask questions, to see exactly what the Oracle was doing. He restrained himself. Interfering was only likely to make matters worse. He just had to hope that whoever or whatever the newcomer was, it was sincere in requiring Matt to be restored to consciousness unharmed. And whoever or whatever the newcomer was, it was clear to Carl that its capabilities far exceeded his own. The best he could do in the circumstances was keep quiet.

"The signal will be sent every thirty seconds, you say?" the newcomer asked.

"I think that should suffice," the Oracle nodded, smiling. "We don't want to make the system over-sensitive, do we?" It seemed to be enjoying itself again, having regained the upper hand.

"Agreed," the newcomer said. "It is important to us that Matt is safely returned to full consciousness."

"And so he will be," the Oracle agreed. "As long as you are who you say you are, and you do what you say you will do."

There was a pause, and then the Oracle spoke again.

"There. It is done. I am ready. Shall we proceed?"

CHAPTER 29

The snow was so soft, so inviting.

It wasn't wet and cold, it was like a pillow with a fresh cover. It was almost fluffy. And he was tired - so very tired! The snow wanted him to lie down and he wanted to lie down too. Lying down would be such a nice thing to do.

Something was wrong, though. It was dangerous to lie down. He didn't know the source of this knowledge, but it was there just the same. He must not give in to temptation. It was his duty to keep going, to get to the other side.

In his exhaustion, he was confused. He had no idea why he had to get to the other side, or how he had got here in the first place. In fact he had only a tenuous grasp of his own identity. He knew he was called the Oracle, but that seemed a funny sort of name. His situation was unreasonable, surreal, and his senses were fuzzy. His perception felt borrowed, second-hand.

He simply could not carry on. He had given it his best shot but the snow was too deep for him and he was only young, after all – just a child. No-one could blame a child who was very tired if he stopped for just a little while. It couldn't hurt to lie down, just for a moment. Just to regain his strength. If he could only lay his heavy head on the soft, inviting snow for a few moments, everything would be better.

He put his hands forward to lower himself into the soft, inviting snow. It was a huge relief to surrender, to give up the impossible struggle against the tiredness and the snow. Everything would be alright. Just a little nap, and he would carry on shortly.

As he fell slowly forward, hands outstretched, he became aware of a blackness opening up before him. At first he thought it was just the welcome rest of a short sleep, but then he realised it was something more profound. He was falling into a new universe. Somehow he knew that this was a universe where there were no problems, and no struggles. At first he wondered if this was safe. It seemed unlikely that there could be such a simple solution to all the complications of existence. His first instinct was to resist. But as he fell further and further, he relaxed, and realised that this new place was much better than the place he was leaving. All would be well. If he surrendered to the blackness, he would never be troubled again.

So he did.

CHAPTER 30

"God, I hate alarm clocks," he thought, as an impudent trilling sound shattered his sleep. He relaxed again, as he remembered there was no need to get up yet. He could go back to sleep. So he did.

"God, I hate alarm clocks," he thought, as an impudent trilling sound shattered his sleep. He thought briefly about the unpleasant business of getting up, before he realised that he didn't need to. He started to relax and go back to sleep, but something nagged at him. The shadow of a memory he couldn't quite recapture. Never mind, it would come back to him in the morning. There was time to sleep some more.

"God, I hate alarm clocks," he thought, as an impudent trilling sound shattered his sleep. The thought of having to get up was grisly enough, but it was compounded by a feeling that something was wrong. He had an uncomfortable sense that he was about to make a serious mistake. A mistake that he had made before. Or was this just the traces of a bad dream? He didn't remember any dream, and the feeling seemed to

301

belong to the waking world. But he was very tired. If there was something so very important, then surely he would remember it? He really needed to get some more sleep. It would all be OK in the morning.

"God, I hate alarm clocks," he thought, as an impudent trilling sound shattered his sleep. He was awake and alert immediately, and he felt the hairs standing up on the back of his neck. There was danger. He was in the wrong place, and he had to get to safety. But he could not move. He had no control over his arms, his legs, or indeed any part of his body. In fact, apart from feeling the hairs on the back of his neck, he could not feel any sensations coming from any part of his body. Nor could he see them. Come to think of it, he couldn't see anything. He was blind! Had he had an accident? Was he paralysed? No, this must simply be a bad dream. And he was very tired. Maybe he should just go back to sleep, and he would wake up again later. He had a nagging feeling that this was not a good idea – that he had made this mistake before, and that he really should try to get up and move to safety. But he was too tired. He was feeling very heavy – which was unsettling, since he couldn't feel any part of his body. No point resisting. He simply had to fall back to sleep. So he did.

"God, I hate alarm clocks," he thought, as an impudent trilling sound shattered his sleep. As his consciousness returned, the trilling sound morphed into a jangling of his nerves, like fingernails scraping a blackboard. And fear. He could smell his own fear. Run! Hide! But where? And how? He had no body.

He was a disembodied bundle of fear. He desperately needed to escape, but he had no idea of what he wanted to escape from. There was fear inside him and fear outside too. The fear outside was a rising tide of liquid – a thick, viscous liquid that wanted to drown him. There was no way out. It was going to drown him. As the liquid closed over his head, he screamed. But the scream made no sound and it became nothing. He became nothing.

"Wake up, Matt! Wake up! You have to get out. Now! There's no time!"

Fear and a sense of urgency jerked him awake like a hard slap on the face. An instinct to flee was reinforced by the disembodied voice. It was his father's voice.

He gathered his wits and focused on a single bright point of light ahead of him. Somehow he knew it was the exit. And somehow he knew how to propel himself towards it. He started moving. Now he was moving fast, accelerating, but he could sense that he was not moving fast enough. There was a great and terrible danger behind him. It was chasing him, and it was gaining. He was moving with reckless speed, but the danger behind was implacable and...

it caught him.

He screamed with agony. The pain was unendurable. Needles in eyeballs, limbs broken on racks, skin on fire, heart bursting out of his chest. His soul was being torn apart.

It didn't stop, but he realised that he was still moving. In the midst of fear and torment, he knew this was a hopeful thing. He knew that if the great and terrible terror had succeeded in overtaking him completely, he would not be moving. He would not be feeling anything. He would have ceased to exist.

Sometimes hope was a bad thing. The pain and the fear continued, and he did not know how much of it he could bear. He knew that a strong enough person could survive this, but he did not know if he was that person.

He was tumbling, falling, torn and twisting in agony through a dark void. He was lost and alone. He was a naked child, cold and afraid, and in terrible pain. He fell like this for an eternity. He would always be falling like this.

Something strange happened. Part of him healed. Or rather, part of him became more whole. Something that had been missing was restored. The re-joining felt good. The pain and the fear were still terrible, but because there was the possibility of a healing, they became endurable. They became finite.

It happened again. Another part of himself was returned to him. This time he could feel the pain and the fear diminish. They were still terrible, and he knew they would be terrible for a very long time. He was still not sure he had the strength to survive. But now he thought he might have.

And he knew that he could start to reach out for more of his scattered parts. Summon them. He began to hope that he could become whole. That he could heal. And maybe eventually, the pain and the fear would recede.

"Thank you, Dad. I think you just saved my life."

CHAPTER 31

"What the hell just happened?" the President demanded.

Chuck Naylor looked up from a screen he had been staring at intently. "I can confirm that we have the Oracle in storage. We have run the first tests, and they all confirm that the Oracle is securely back at level one." He glanced at David and Sophie before continuing his report to the President. "As for what happened to Matt - we don't know yet. The simulation was successfully put onto a loop, and Matt's controlling sub-mind was receiving the correct signal, albeit repeated, and the trigger seemed to be accepting it. We initiated the protocol for deleting the destructive code – the digital bomb, if you will – but somehow it seems to have been activated."

He paused, looking at David and Sophie, then at Alice and Jemma. "I am so very sorry. I think we may never know what happened. But my fear is... "His voice faltered, and he was unable to finish the sentence.

David completed it for him. "Your fear is that Matt

could not have survived." He looked at Sophie. They both had tears in their eyes. "And I think you may well be right."

Alice and Jemma were having none of it. "No!" they said in unison. "That can't be right," Jemma continued. "The signal was working. The bomb couldn't go off. It just couldn't."

"We can't just give up!" Alice implored. "Matt is still in there. We have to find him! We have to save him. Maybe Carl can find him?"

David shook his head. "I think I know what happened. I think the Oracle added an additional instruction that it didn't tell us about. I think it programmed the trigger to pull if it received the same signal more than a certain number of times. And we hit that number. Maybe it anticipated that we would place the simulation into a loop. It was a great idea, but the Oracle could have anticipated it. Or maybe it was anticipating something else. But what we do know is that the bomb went off, and..." He was unable to finish the thought. He buried his head in his hands, and his shoulders shook. Sophie put her arm around his shoulders, and then let her forehead rest against his neck. She was crying too.

Vic said, "Madam President, I think we need to get these people out of here. To somewhere they can grieve as a family."

The President nodded, but hesitated. She seemed to be trying to decide whether to attempt to console Matt's family and friends, or simply enable them to go somewhere private to grieve. She chose the latter option.

"General MacMillan, would you please organise secure but discreet transport to take them to the Four Seasons. Have someone phone ahead and tell reservations it is for Condor account. They will know what that means. Tell them to prepare three suites, with extreme privacy on arrival. Vic, will you go with them, please?" Turning to the general, "An extra room for Vic if he decides to stay there."

Vic nodded, and the President turned to David and Sophie. "David, Sophie, Alice, Jemma. I am so, so sorry. Your son… your friend, was a wonderful young man. We owe him a great deal. We will talk more later, but for now I'm sure you just need to be together, and away from everything. If you need anything – anything at all – call my office on this number, and I will see that you get it. Immediately. I'm sorry… I have no words for this."

The President's voice choked as she stood, placed a card on the table in front of David and Sophie, and walked out of the room.

As everyone stood to leave, Jemma asked Vic, "What about Carl? How long will it take to extract him from the simulation?"

Vic and Alice both started to reply. Alice nodded for Vic to carry on. "As Alice and I both know from personal experience, he will be disoriented for a while. For him, it will probably be a bit worse - he had a very stressful experience in there." He glanced at the general. "Can you arrange for him to join us at the hotel as soon as possible, please general?"

The general nodded his confirmation.

****

The car left the White House behind, and proceeded along Pennsylvania Avenue. David, Sophie and Vic were in the back seat, looking forward, and Alice and Jemma were facing them. It was a big car, but not ostentatious. Blacked-out windows were not ostentatious in Washington DC.

As the car entered Washington Circle roundabout, David leaned forward and said to the driver. "Could you please pull over and let us out here for a few minutes, please, driver? I think we all need to get some air before we go inside the hotel. This looks as good a place as any to stretch our legs."

The driver pulled over on the inside of the traffic circle, on the south-west quadrant. The five passengers stepped out of the car. A broad path led to the centre of the circle, and a large statue of George Washington on a horse. They walked up to the statue and gazed at it for a few moments.

David said, "Let's head into these woods here for a moment. There's something I want to share with you all in confidence."

As they walked into the nearest clump of trees, David turned to Vic. "Do you think we can be overheard? I mean, I don't suppose they planted bugs on us when we were in the White House, right? And these trees. Do you think they would have listening devices in them?"

Vic shrugged. "This close to the White House, I

wouldn't want to bet my life on it. But if we keep walking and keep our voices down, I think we should be OK. What is it you want…?"

Vic's question remained un-finished. He stopped walking, and his face went completely blank. Then it changed subtly. It took on an expression that was entirely alien to Vic. But it was an expression which was very familiar to the others.

Sophie gasped. "Is that… Is that you, Matt?"

Vic's finger was raised to his mouth. He smiled.

"Yes, Mum. It's me. I hope Vic will forgive me for "borrowing" him for a few moments. I'll leave it up to you to decide whether to tell him or not. He's a good guy, and I trust him, but he's your colleague, Dad, so I think you should make that decision, not me.

"I'm OK. Please don't worry about me. I won't talk for long. To answer your question, Dad, we can't be heard by any listening devices because I have disabled all of them. You'd be surprised how many there are in this circle, and by no means all of them were placed here by the various branches of US intelligence and law enforcement. I can't stay with you for long because it would raise suspicions if anyone figured out how many devices went blank at the same time. I will speak to you all when you get home. I can't tell you how much I am looking forward to that.

"For now, just know this. The explosion very nearly did kill me, but I got Dad's warning just in time. I had a rough time of it out there for a while, but I'm OK now. I've decided to keep my survival secret – as long as you are all happy with that. I think it will make your lives much, much easier too. If the governments, the media, and the intelligence services of the world knew I have returned, the pressure on you guys would be intense. I love you guys, and I don't want that for you. Although of course for this to work, you all have to want this to be a secret as well. And Carl, of course. But there will be plenty of time to discuss all this when you get home."

"Are you sure you're OK, son?" David asked, overcome with relief. "I did think I heard your voice very faintly just after the bomb went off, but I was really scared that we had lost you this time."

"Yes, I'm fine, and yes you did. And thank you, Dad. It is only thanks to you that I'm still here. I think it will take me a while to recover fully from that experience, but I will. I know that now. And spending time with you all will help."

Jemma grinned to herself as she noticed Matt favour Alice with a particularly fond glance, and Alice blushed slightly, perhaps because it was a little weird to receive that glance from Vic's face.

"What will you do now, Matt?" Sophie asked. "Oh, I have so many questions to ask you!"

"I really don't know, Mum. There's a lot that I would like to do which I won't be able to do if I'm to stay a secret. But there's still a lot I will be able to do. What exactly that is, I really don't know just yet."

Vic's face took on a sly grin which was one hundred percent Matt. "But then again - as a wise man once said – but then again, who does?"

ACKNOWLEDGEMENTS

I published "Pandora's Brain" in 2015, and I wrote the first draft of this book, its sequel, soon afterwards. I liked the main elements of the story, but I wasn't at all happy with the execution, and put it away for several years while I wrote a couple of non-fiction books. In 2019, a friend and fellow writer introduced me to an editor, Laurence Daren King. Working with Laurence was fun, and a great education, and a year later, Pandora's Oracle was finished. Thank you, Laurence!

I am grateful to the following talented and generous (and alphabetised) people who have taken the time to read previous drafts and offer their comments. Collectively they have weeded out many solecisms and inconsistencies. Those which remain are of course entirely my fault. Russell Buckley, Alexander Chace, Ian Cockburn, Casey Dorman, Eggert Ehmke, William Graham, Peter Monk, Jeff Pinsker, Jay Sanchez, and Brad Smith.

My hugely talented designer Rachel Lawston has

produced another terrific cover, and demonstrated superhuman patience while assisting my clumsy attempts to teach myself various aspects of the book production process.

My profoundest thanks go to my partner Julia, who is my adviser, my cheerleader, and my kindest but most penetrating critic.

ALSO BY CALUM CHACE

Stories From 2045 (editor and contributor)
Artificial Intelligence and the Two Singularities
Our Jobless Future
The Economic Singularity (3rd edition)
Surviving AI (3rd edition)
Pandora's Brain
The Internet Startup Bible (co-author)
The Internet Consumer Bible (co-author)

Lightning Source UK Ltd.
Milton Keynes UK
UKHW022210110521
383549UK00011B/2444